Sarah Goodwin completed the BA and MA in Creative Writing at Bath Spa University. *The Island* is her sixth novel to be published with Avon, following several years as a self-published author. She lives in Cornwall with her family and a very spoiled dog.

THE
ISLAND

SARAH GOODWIN

avon.

Published by AVON
A division of HarperCollins*Publishers*
1 London Bridge Street
London SE1 9GF

www.harpercollins.co.uk

HarperCollins*Publishers*
Macken House
39/40 Mayor Street Upper
Dublin 1
D01 C9W8
Ireland

A Paperback Original 2024
1
First published in Great Britain by HarperCollins*Publishers* 2024

A catalogue copy of this book is available from the British Library.

ISBN: 978-0-00-867108-2

Typeset in Sabon LT Pro by HarperCollins*Publishers* India

Printed and bound in the UK using 100%
Renewable Electricity at CPI Group (UK) Ltd

This novel is dedicated to my first year living in Cornwall, and to all its beautiful beaches, which deserve better from our government, than having sewage dumped on them.

Content Warning

THE ISLAND, although fictional, tackles some events and issues that some may find distressing. If you'd like to find out more, please read the author's note at the back of the book but be warned it does contain spoilers.

Prologue

I can feel the pounding music in my chest, racing along with my frantic pulse. My eardrums rebel against it and send sharp throbs of pain through my skull. Even my teeth are vibrating as the headline act takes to the stage.

All at once everyone is screaming, leaping up and down. They're completely focused on the act going on at some point behind and above me as I struggle away from the stage.

"Ari! Carla!" I yell, but it's no use. I can barely hear myself.

I breathe in dust from the ground beneath a hundred thousand shuffling feet and cough. I don't dare stop moving though. I'm tensed for a hand on my shoulder, a sharp sting in my back, it could come at any time. I can hardly move in the crushing crowd. Can't get away.

"Carla!" I try again, clawing my way past a wall of sweaty dancers, all as plastered as I am in yellow-brown dust. "Ari!"

Someone blows a whistle and it sounds like a scream.

I'm surrounded by faces – all baked red and brown and sweaty, slathered in glitter and flaking face paint. None of them are familiar. None of them look concerned, just annoyed as I grab at them, elbow them in my rush to get past. I feel like an ant clambering over a whole nest of its fellow insects. An ant which knows a bird is hovering above, its sharp beak about to strike.

Something sharp does get me then. I feel the cold metal against my skin and scream, preparing for the pain, the blood. I feel hands pushing at me and I turn to find that it was just someone's sunglasses. The sharp hinge has raked against me, there are tiny beads of blood welling all along the scratch.

"What the fuck is her problem?" I hear someone yell.

"Bad trip," a voice says over my head as I blunder into a man's chest, sunburned and covered in blurry tattoos.

"Must be that shit they were warning everyone about…"

"Please," I'm clinging on to this stranger's arm. "You have to help me."

"Go to the medical tent," a girl practically bellows in my ear, shoving me away. "Get lost!"

I stagger away, exhaustion and heatstroke competing to see which can take me down first. My skin is frying under the sun and I'm breathing in the hot air of the crowd, laced with the smell of weed, stale sweat, too much body spray and overflowing toilets. Over it all is the tell-tale stink of rotten rubbish – the festival's official smell since day one. That should have told me everything I needed to know. As hot as it is though, inside I feel ice cold. I wish this was a bad trip. At least then none of it would be real.

I've been turned around by all the shoving and elbowing. I can't tell which direction I came from anymore. Even the main stage, my one landmark in all the heaving bodies, has sunk into the tide of people. I'm too far away from it to see and the speakers all around us are confusing me – the music is coming from everywhere all at once.

"Ari! Carla!" I scream again. "Help!"

I spin on the spot, trying to spot Ari's sunflower crown or Carla's pink space buns, but there are so many other girls who look exactly like them. We're all just part of the crowd now.

There's no one else who looks like him, though.

My heart seems to stop, my chest echoing with the sound of the music, as I turn and spot him, heading straight towards me. I scream and try to claw my way through the crowd behind me. Around us, the first song of the headline act comes to a close. A voice comes bursting from the loudspeakers.

"Lethe Festival! Get ready for the ride of your life!"

Cheers burst out around me and before I can try and make myself heard, my foot tangles with someone else's and I go down, hands outstretched to stop my fall. Before I've even registered the pain of landing, a foot crushes my fingers. My scream is absorbed into the opening of the next song.

"This one's for all the lovely ladies of Lethe! Make some noise!"

Chapter 1

"Jody, I'm baaaack."

Carla's voice eclipsed the slam of the front door and made it up four flights of stairs to disturb me from my half-napping state. She was always loud enough for me to hear from the top floor of our odd little house share, but seemed even more so today. Maybe it was because I'd been alone with my thoughts since she and Ari left that morning. I'd become so used to the deafening silence that even the sound of someone else would have surprised me. Whether or not they were yelling.

The sounds of Carla moving around echoed up through the empty hallways, uncarpeted and chilly as they were. I heard her dump her jacket and umbrella in the hall, then come pounding up the four lots of stairs between the hall and my room on the top floor. Two flights of thinly carpeted stone, one painted concrete and finally, the wooden ones – which were basically a ladder – up to my bedroom under the eaves. Her head and shoulders appeared in the hatchway and she peered up at me, where I was curled up on my bed.

"Cuppa?" she panted, her long blonde hair still thick with rain. "They had doughnuts at the office but everyone's on a diet so some of them came home with me. The doughnuts obviously. Not Marjorie from accounting."

I managed a smile, though it felt foreign on my face. "Sure. Be down in a sec."

Really all I wanted to do was stay put in the silence, but it was hard to ignore my housemates when they were home, even when I stayed in my room. Both Carla and Ari had so much energy that it was impossible to escape it – music, chatter and the thud of feet from the kitchen to their bedrooms and back made the house come alive below me.

Carla stayed there for a second too long, looking firstly at me and then at the dirty clothes overflowing my wash basket, the empty plates on my desk chair and, finally, at the packages she brought up for me yesterday, which I still hadn't opened. I knew already that they were all course materials and textbooks. Things I didn't have the mental energy to so much as look at right now.

"Jody...have you been in bed all day again?" she asked, so gently it made me want to cry.

"Just since *Doctors* was on," I said. It came out defensive, even to my own ears.

Carla looked even more troubled by my answer. "You'd let me know if there was anything I could do, right?" she asked. "If there was anything...really wrong?"

"Yep," I smiled back, knowing that I would literally rather throw myself in the Thames than have my housemates do any more for me than they already had.

Ditto telling them the full story of how I came to be haunting their attic like the ghost of a Victorian spinster.

"Alright, I'll go make some tea – you, pop some proper clothes on. You'll feel better," Carla instructed me as she disappeared back downstairs.

I wasn't in my pyjamas, not exactly. But she did have a point. I'd had the same jumper and leggings on for three days now. I also hadn't had a shower. It wasn't that I didn't want to be clean, it was just the thought of getting all my stuff together and going down to the bathroom, having to get into the shower and go through the whole routine, dry off, come back up and put more clothes on. It was too much. I could barely bring myself to go downstairs to grab some food twice a day.

Dressed in a cleanish t-shirt and jeans with a hoodie thrown on over the top, I descended to the first floor, where the kitchen was. The ground floor being just the entrance hall and a storage space for the mouldy washing machine, mammoth fridge freezer, several car boot sales worth of junk and the landlord's project motorbike. Ludlow House was affordable even on my tiny bursary because it was tall, narrow, practically derelict and shared between the three of us. I only found out about it because I still had Carla and Ari on Facebook.

When I'd first gone to university, they'd oversubscribed the halls, so I ended up getting pushed into private accommodation off campus. Student services found me a room in a house with some third-year girls – Ari and Carla. When they left university and I moved into second year housing with strangers, we stayed in contact, not just in term time but over the summer, sharing memes and birthday wishes. They'd invited me out for coffee a few times and to parties since we were all still in or around London, but I hadn't gone even once. I'd gotten with Nick right after they'd graduated and he didn't like me going into the city alone. We were still living in Surrey at the time. He said he'd happily take me anywhere, but something had always come up, or he'd made a fuss about being busy and stressed, so I stopped asking.

Carla had been the first one of us in residence at Ludlow House, and when her housemates moved on to other things she brought in Ari, who'd been asking around for somewhere to live during her PhD. Then I moved in three months ago, with what I could pack in an hour, whilst Nick was at the gym.

As if I'd summoned her, Ari came up from the entryway, also wet through. It had been raining all day. The perfect June in my opinion, especially given my current mood.

Ari's long dark hair was shoved into her hood and she was carrying a bag of books that had left red rings on her arms where the handle had cut into her. I took the bag whilst she stripped off her coat.

"Did you leave anything in the library?" I asked.

"Just the Kant. I'm not taking that module." She offered me a smile that tried and failed to hide her assessment of my greasy hair and wrinkled clothes. I couldn't help but contrast myself with her perfect winged liner and flawless skin.

"How are you?" Ari asked, eyes practically brimming with concern.

"Fine," I lied. "Carla's making tea."

Ari followed me down the ladder and into the kitchen, where steaming mugs were already clustered between Carla's bags and the mountain of junk mail and actual post she must've picked up on her way in. A slightly battered box of Krispy Kreme doughnuts was balanced on top of three different coloured local directories. The rest of the kitchen was just as messy as it had been that morning. I'd meant to tidy it whilst they were out. I'd meant to do a lot of things.

"Anything vegan?" Ari asked, hopefully, ignoring the crusty washing-up and the crumb covered counter tops, which I was grateful for.

"The box? Maybe?" Carla said, doubtfully. Then she grinned and extracted a packet from her handbag. "Got you a strawberry iced ring from Krispy Kreme on the way home."

"You are a saint," Ari said, already tearing into the cake. "I've had two supervisions today, neither of which gave me much direction for my thesis."

"Beats my all-staff meeting and a full three hours crawling around the filing room, getting into all the low drawers because no one I work with wants to file anything below N in case they can't get back up on their feet again," Carla said. "Though I think my day was worse on the knees – those shitty carpets have shredded my tights." She showed off her laddered fifteen deniers with a wince. "That's the last pair in the pack gone! Another seven quid down the drain. I should get an allowance, or knee pads at the very least."

"Take it to your union," Ari suggested, smirking behind her doughnut.

"I'd have to start one first. National Collective of

Hosiery Deprived Administrators, maybe. Not as bad as the time I wore my new white shirt and they made me change the toner. I came home looking like a bomb had gone off in my face. By the way did you pick up any more milk? I just noticed we're mostly out of almond and normal."

"Got almond. Cow is on you I'm afraid," Ari said.

I let their domestic chatter wash over me. It was reassuring, homely. Just like being back in our shared house at university, as if the intervening two years hadn't happened. Back then we'd sort of drift in and out of each other's orbits, making pasta bake or begging to borrow printer credits. They'd nag me into going on nights out and I'd proofread their essays. One of the many things I was grateful to them for was that easy companionship, even now, when I'd been so bad at keeping in touch.

They'd been so great about everything since I'd moved in. So supportive of me even through all my moods and odd hours, roaming the house because I couldn't sleep. They'd also done their best to make me feel welcome.

I'd been scared of my new-old-housemates at first. They weren't the scatty students I remembered. These were women who had their shit together – Carla with her city job – out the door at six on the dot with an expensive travel mug in one hand, her sleek little suitcase always bumping up and down stairs from fully catered away weekends in the Cotswolds to discuss mainframes over finger sandwiches. Carla said she usually only took notes for two hours and then went to the hotel gym or spa. Then there was Ari studying for her philosophy

PhD, carrying dense, important books around in wittily captioned tote bags, heading off to study sessions in the royal parks and chic little coffee houses. Nimble and energetic even in Doc Martens. I envied her effortless cool and the intelligence that saw her devouring classic novels whilst I struggled to make it through a magazine article without my mind wandering.

Their legions of colleagues and friends and study buddies were always coming to the house too, to hang out and gossip or drink wine and destress. People I only knew by voice because I hid in my room when strangers were around. I wasn't scared of them, not really, I just didn't have the capacity to be social with new people. Most of the time.

Despite my anxiety over how much more professional and grown up they were, both Ari and Carla had been so kind. Almost too nice, I thought sometimes, and then felt bad for thinking it. In the three months since I had moved in, Carla had helped me get hold of some furniture and clothes on the cheap, since most of my stuff was still at Nick's. Ari showed me the places near us to get free Wi-Fi, the best but most affordable coffee and how to make most efficient use of the nearby laundrette, because the machine downstairs was permanently stuck on the wool setting and also stunk of mildew.

"These are for you," Carla said, sliding a clear envelope packed with post over to me. "Someone's popular."

Her forced jolliness was well meant but it only made me feel worse. I smiled back and pulled the envelope towards me. I had set up a diversion on my post from Nick's flat and it all came to me in a big pile like this every now and then. I had changed my address with the university but things still slipped through, bureaucracy being what it was. Most of the envelope's contents was junk, catalogues and newsletters I'd forgotten to cancel. But there were two letters in there. My heart sank. One of them had my university's logo on it. The other had the address written in my mother's handwriting. I hadn't told her my new address in case Nick found a way to contact her, because I knew no matter what I said she'd tell him anyway. Because she knew best, and she was just trying to help. Neither letter seemed likely to cheer me up. Though for very different reasons.

I ripped open the one from Mum first. It was a card from one of her 'correspondence sets' with wild foxes on it. Inside she'd written the latest on her neighbour's bunion (worse) and the state of the roads (improving). Then came a lecture about me not writing enough or phoning enough. She was worried about me. Was I eating properly? I never did learn the value of 'good home cooking'. It carried on like that until presumably she noticed she was running out of space in the card. She'd signed off by asking how school was going and when was I bringing Nick down to meet her? The last line asked me (again) to phone her. The idea of hearing her voice, of having to explain without telling her the full story, made me feel like there was a weight pressing down on my chest. The weight of her expectations and my own humiliation.

I slowly opened the letter from the university, as if what was inside might sink its teeth into my fingers if I surprised it. My eyes skipped over the niceties and landed on a bolded paragraph halfway down the page.

Your attendance has become a cause of concern in the latter part of this term. Please contact your head of department with any issues relating to prolonged absences in future. Please note that, if your overall attendance falls below the threshold outlined below, following the summer break, your bursary for the next academic year may be affected.

"What's the matter?" Ari asked.

I realised I was shaking, the paper shivering in my hand. I slapped it down on the table and reached for the steadying influence of my cup of tea. Half of it sloshed over the table, drenching the letter, but Ari still managed to see the paragraph that had nearly reduced me to tears.

"Oh, hon," Carla said, reading upside-down from her side of the mountain of post. "You need to get in touch with them, explain about…" her eyes met Ari's and she bit her lip, clearly unsure how to finish that sentence. They didn't know the half of it. To them, I was just taking the break-up with Nick really, really badly.

Ari took over from Carla. "No one can blame you for needing some time away. For not being able to focus after having to move and everything. I'm sure the university would understand if you just arranged to talk to your tutors. I could go with you, if you want?"

They were clearly trying to be kind but that's what made it worse. I felt as if my skin was on too tight, like it might split open and all the awfulness inside me would spill out. I was emotional roadkill, getting more rotten by the day.

"Maybe you should try and get away somewhere,

12

you know, for summer break?" Carla said, hovering nearby with a bottle of water. "You could visit your mum?"

I shook my head. The last thing I wanted was to have to look Mum in the eye and tell her I was failing off of my course after she's worked so hard to support me during my training in veterinary medicine. I was meant to be qualifying as a proper vet, making her proud and securing my future. Which, a bitter little part of me whispered, was almost impossible anyway, even without messing up as royally as I had. Ever since Dad died when I was six, Mum had been obsessed with what would happen to me 'after she was gone'. By now I was meant to have a big circle of friends, a boyfriend and a career in the making. Instead of that I was hiding away in my tiny attic room day after day, watching shit TV and rotting in my pyjamas.

"Or we could go somewhere, the three of us," Carla said. "What do you think, a girls' trip? Like that time we all went to Southend for the week – like all of us and the girls from Oakhill hall. Only we could go somewhere better... Spain maybe?"

I thought of that Southend trip and my stomach turned over. We had very different memories of how that all went down. I decided, as I had then, that I wasn't going to bring it up. Especially not after all this time.

"I can't afford it," I said, still looking at the letter. "I'd barely be able to afford the fare down to Dorset to see Mum, what with trains being the way they are, never mind booking a hotel abroad, flights, food, drinks, going out..."

Neither of them seemed to have an answer to that. None of us were exactly rolling in it. Ari was a foreign student and had to save money for getting to and from her family in Norway and Carla was on the second rung from bottom on the corporate ladder (the one below her was just…Angie, the post-room attendant). They were better off than me, but not by much. A surprise holiday for their depressed roommate was definitely not something they could afford.

"Well, you never know," Ari said, sounding slightly less positive than before. "I might be the next person to win Lethe tickets – I entered a draw on Twitter and about twenty sponsored giveaways on Instagram. Then we'd have somewhere to go for free. A luxury festival no less."

"Sure, and I'll get invited to the next Royal Wedding," Carla said, nudging me to include me in the joke. "Besides, even if you did win tickets for the festival – we'd still need to afford flights to Greece."

Whilst the two of them shared a fantasy of winning the tickets of a lifetime, I sat and looked down at the college letter. In only a few months I'd managed to completely fuck up my entire life plan. I'd wanted to be a vet, like my dad, since before I could remember. Mum hadn't been fond of the idea – she'd wanted something that paid more – but I'd persisted, in Dad's memory and eventually she'd given in. Her final words on the subject were 'at least you'll always have work', and I could see her thinking of her own years spent out of the labour market whilst she was raising me. Things had been hard once Dad died, and she'd barely scraped by on her receptionist's wages.

I'd been working towards this all my life almost, firstly by watching my dad, learning from him. Then after he died, I'd fostered animals in my teens, done work experience and wildlife rescue volunteering, worked at a cattery in the summer holidays. My GCSEs, A Levels and degree had all been aimed at getting me here. I'd put nearly every single one of my twenty-one years on the planet into this dream. Now I was probably going to lose my bursary and end up having to drop out of the course. All because I'd been stupid enough to get involved with Nick a year and a half ago. It had seemed perfect – I didn't have to go home, and Mum was happy because I'd 'landed' someone.

What would I do once I lost my place at uni? Go home to Mum with my tail between my legs? Marry one of her friend's boring sons and pop out a few kids to 'take care of me' when I got old? Surround myself with WI friends to bring me cakes when my husband died? I shuddered just to think about it. It was everything she'd ever wanted for me since Dad's death left her with nothing and nobody but me. There'd be no escape.

"I think I'm going to go back to bed," I said, causing a tense silence to descend on the kitchen.

"If you're sure," Carla said. "Let me know if you fancy that doughnut later, OK?"

I nodded, forced a small smile for Ari and then left the room, heading for the stairs. The kitchen door swung closed behind me and if I hadn't been moving so slowly, I probably would have been gone by the time Carla spoke again.

"Do you think we ought to call someone, her mum maybe?" she murmured to Ari.

I paused on the carpeted stairs, tears stinging my eyes.

"I don't know...if she doesn't get better soon I suppose we have to. Though I'm not sure it'll help – you know how she gets about her mum. But...she won't tell us what's wrong and it seems like it's getting worse, not better."

"It's definitely that guy. She never talked about him much when she moved in, but now...she reacts like you've slapped her if you even say his name. It's like she's scared of him. More scared than ever. Do you think something's happened?"

I heard the chime of mugs being gathered up, then Ari heaved a sigh. I braced myself, wishing I had the strength to walk away and stop listening to them.

"I don't know but...she needs to be able to tell us what's wrong. We can't do that for her. I know it sounds harsh but...we can't help her, until she helps herself."

"What if she can't?" Carla asked.

I can't, I thought. *I'm trying so hard but I can't.*

There was a long silence. "Then she'll be stuck like this. I'm just worried that something will happen that'll push her over the edge. I don't want us to be responsible if something bad happens, you know? I want to know we did everything we could."

I pressed my lips together to smother the sounds of my sobs and crept upstairs. Alone under the eaves, I looked at my pile of textbooks, the unopened packages and unwashed clothes, and crawled back under my duvet.

I wasn't sure when exactly I fell asleep, just that when I bolted awake again it was pitch black and there was a scream echoing in my ears. My heart was pounding and I was half convinced it was a nightmare.

Then, Ari screamed again.

Chapter 2

My foot slipped two rungs from the bottom of the ladder-steps to my bedroom. I landed on my arse with a jolt that shook my bones and made me cry out in surprised pain. Still, I didn't waste time lying there. I clambered to my feet and hurried down the hallway just as Carla's light snapped on and her door opened. The yellow glow spilled into the hall and she flinched in surprise when she saw me stagger to a halt.

"What's going on?" she slurred, rubbing at her eyes, a purple satin sleep mask dangling around her neck and an earplug in her hand, its pair still jammed in her other ear.

"I don't know. Ari screamed and then…"

Both of us turned as the other bedroom door burst open. Ari was in her pyjamas, hair piled on top of her head in her usual 'sleep bun' and she had her glasses on. She looked alert and excited, not terrified as I'd expected her to be given that she was screaming bloody murder in the middle of the night.

"I got them! I fucking got them!" she leaped down the corridor in three bounds and shoved her phone under Carla's and my noses.

It took a second for either of us to make sense of the screen as she bounced in place, but then Carla whooped and threw an arm around Ari, jumping with her. I hadn't been able to read the screen before it was jostled away, so I just watched them, dumbfounded. What the hell was this about?

"We're going to Lethe!" Ari explained gleefully, grabbing my shoulder to encourage me to join them. "I won the latest draw! We got tickets!"

"That's...great!" I said, trying to force some enthusiasm into my voice but accidentally waiting too long so it came out sounding stilted and awkward. Not that Ari seemed to notice the difference. "I mean, you guys are going to have so much fun."

"WE, are going to have so much fun," Ari corrected. "I've got three tickets, Jody – we're all going! Sun, sea, sand and festival tickets no one can buy. We are so fucking lucky! Can you believe it!?"

My initial reaction was blind panic. Immediately I was filled with thoughts of how to get out of this without offending either of them. I'd never been what my mother would call a 'joiner' something she'd been on at me about since I was six. The constant refrain of 'you need people around you Jody, you don't want to end up alone' haunting me as I looked at birthday party invites with unicorns on them. What with everything that happened to me in the past two years, I was even less comfortable around people. The idea of strangers in the house made me hide away in my room. Never mind going to a festival full of them, a thousand miles from home. I didn't want to go to Greece. I didn't even want to go to the corner shop.

19

"I can't afford the flights," I tried, despite knowing that I could probably borrow some money from Mum, or live off toast for a month after we got back. Would Mum lend me the money? Probably not. She wasn't in dire straits anymore but she was still quite panicky about money. Besides I'd have to answer all sorts of questions if I wanted so much as a tenner from her, which was why I hadn't asked for her help when I realised I had to leave Nick. Well, that and I knew she'd only tell me to stay. That any man was better than no man at all. My own unkind thoughts made me wince uncomfortably.

"I have air miles," Ari said, batting my feeble excuse away. "From going back and forth to visit home. It's enough for a couple of absolute bottom tier economy seats, and for the third one we can split it three ways. That way we all pay the same and it won't be much."

"Except you, because you've used your miles," Carla pointed out. "Are you sure that's OK?"

"Well, I only pay for my cabs and hotel when I go home. Dad pays for the flights so…technically, they're free," Ari shrugged, a sly smile on her face. "Besides how can we pass up a chance to be the first people to go to an entirely new festival? We'd be mad not to. This is like…going to the first Glastonbury, but it's in sunny, sunny Greece!"

They both looked at me expectantly, excitement still on their faces but slightly dimmed now. I realised I was bringing down the mood, ruining their moment. I managed a smile and accepted a group hug, but inside, I was quivering with stress. A festival – all those people, the noise, the discomfort, the lack of privacy – almost the complete opposite of the safe little bolthole I'd managed to create in my room on the top floor.

A bolthole that isn't working, a tiny part of me piped up. *You're not getting any better and it's starting to get worse. Ever since you saw him again.*

I pushed the thought away, along with the memory of running into Nick again. The start of my downward spiral. I'd not been fine exactly, but I'd been managing. Until I wasn't. Until I saw him again a few weeks ago and he reminded me of just how small the world was, and how much of it he inhabited. How much he controlled. My wrist throbbed with the phantom grip of his fingers, grinding the bone.

Maybe this was what I needed? I thought. A chance to expand my world again. To go further than he could reach. If I was in Greece I wouldn't be at risk of 'accidentally' bumping into him again for a while at least. Maybe in that time I could gather enough strength for if, when, it happened again. Maybe I could find a way to open up enough to tell Ari and Carla what I was so scared of.

"How long's the festival again?" I asked.

"It's Friday to Monday," Ari trilled. "So four days, including two full days of music, partying, sunshine." She raised her eyebrows meaningfully, hair still messed up from the earlier rain. "I cannot overstate, the sun. Do you remember the sun, Jody?"

I knew she was talking about the shit weather we'd been having, but I felt the dig, just a little. When had I last gone outside?

Carla eagerly interjected. "I saw on TikTok that they're having an oxygen bar, spiral dancing and these

21

like, dome things where they're screening silent films and sensory stuff – all different experiences. Someone commented about there being sunrise yoga and one of those rain rooms too. You know with the panoramic screens and all the water coming down?"

I shook my head, completely nonplussed. "Never heard of it."

"Oh my God, you have to see," Carla pulled up a video on her phone. "Here."

It actually did look sort of relaxing – a massive pool with a screen running the entire way around it, showing a stormy sea. Speakers hidden somewhere were playing ocean sounds and rolling thunder as 'rain' poured from the ceiling, drenching the models in the pool as they flicked their hair and held their arms out, ecstatic.

"I thought this was all about escaping the rain," I said, amused.

"It's always nice to have the option though, isn't it? As long as it is optional," Carla grinned. "Bake all day in the sun and then cool down in a relaxing rain shower."

"Make sure you email your manager so they pick it up first thing," Ari chimed in, gesturing to Carla's phone. "We need to get that time off booked. I think I'm good on my end. I don't have any supervisions left this year. What about you Jody? You're basically done too, right?"

"Yeah, almost," I nodded. I knew I had labs and lectures next week, but I wasn't sure if I could face it. I was already in trouble, one or two more absences wouldn't make much difference. "I can definitely go... thanks, for inviting me. Sorry if I was weird before. It's just been a bit of a...difficult time."

"No worries," Ari assured me, looking genuinely touched. "We're going to party so hard, by the time we come home you'll be one hundred per cent over him. A new woman."

I forced a smile and rushed back to my room as soon as Carla said she needed to get back to sleep because she had to work tomorrow. I knew from experience that she got a little sluggish without her usual nine hours. Hence the sleep mask, ear plugs and whatever other paraphernalia she had in her room. There was one week when our faulty smoke alarm used to go off at random in our uni house, all through the night. I thought she was going to rip it down with her bare hands. I was worried how she'd handle the stresses and strains of camping and interrupted sleep at a noisy festival.

Upstairs I paced around my tiny room, chewing on my lip as I tried to process what I'd just signed myself up for. A full four days of travel and festival activities in a country I'd never been to. Not that I'd been to most countries, my limit was mostly France and the one time my parents took me to Florida on an ill-fated Disney trip. I'd been too shy to talk to any of the characters and then cried on the way home because I knew we were never going back.

I realised I was worrying at the bruise on my arm absently. A habit I'd developed in the past year, when I always had a bruise somewhere to rub at when I was stressed. I'd been keeping it hidden under long sleeves but now I slid the cuff of my hoody up and looked at it. Four long bruises, now turning from purple to green. I shuddered.

It had happened at the supermarket. I'd been home

alone that night – Carla and Ari were both out, Carla with colleagues and Ari with students from her course – I'd fancied something sweet whilst I watched one of my comfort sitcoms. Lidl was only up the road and even though it was dark outside and quite late, I wasn't worried. The house was on a major road, constantly full of traffic. Even the pedestrian routes were usually bustling with people on their way towards or back from the tube station round the corner. I'd grabbed my bag and gone out into the chilly summer night in shorts and a sweatshirt, keys jingling in my pocket. I'd been living with the girls for just over two months and it was starting to feel like everything that had happened between moving in with Nick and arriving at Ludlow House was a bad dream.

I'd not been in a hurry really, there wasn't anything to rush back home to. The shop wasn't busy and I browsed a bit, throwing things into my basket on a whim – pink grapefruit juice and a croissant for tomorrow morning, a notebook I'd optimistically bought in the hope that I'd magically feel like going back to uni if I got myself a little more organised and a new kind of shampoo. I'd been looking through the chilled desserts when he grabbed my arm.

My mum always said she could tell when Dad was home because he shut the car door and then the boot to the same rhythm every day. Bang, pause, bang. Then the jingle of his keys and the buckle on his satchel as he walked up the path. She'd cried about how much she missed those sounds, found herself waiting for them and remembering all over again that she was alone. I knew it was Nick grabbing my arm, because he was twisting

24

it just the way he always did, small movements, like revving a motorbike.

I jumped in shock and dropped a container of trifle. It exploded over my shoes, spattering red jelly and cream up my legs. My basket got caught between us when he pulled me around to look at him and he pushed it back against me until the rough edges on the metal wire were digging into me through my top.

Nick looked just as he had the day I'd left him; the same tight t-shirt straining over his gym-built muscles, the ruthlessly sculpted undercut and his eyes, blue like a Disney princess' and surrounded by long lashes, were narrowed and cold with dislike. His dad's signet ring on a chain around his neck, winking in the fluorescent light.

"I've been looking for you," he said, all casual like we'd come in together and I'd wandered off.

"Nick...I..."

I winced as he tightened his hold on my arm.

"You owe me, for the last three months' rent," he said. "That's over a grand."

"I don't live there anymore," I said, hearing and hating the crack in my voice.

"Well, all your shit still does. So, £1.5k – or I start selling stuff to pay back what you owe me."

I'd had to leave a lot behind. I didn't have a car for starters and was limited to what I could get into a wheelie suitcase and a small backpack. Most of that was my textbooks, mementoes, important documents and some clothes. The big, valuable stuff was still at Nick's flat. The flat we'd shared for eight months, after getting together nearly two years ago. He had the big

25

TV I'd bought for the living room, my consoles from home – which I'd let him use because I was busy with work anyway, my foldaway treadmill and so much more in the way of clothes, shoes and makeup. I wanted that stuff back. It was mine, but I wanted to get away from Nick more.

"Fine," I'd squeaked. "Keep it, sell it."

Nick hadn't looked pleased about that. I should have known by then that he didn't want to be handed a win. He wanted to drag defeat out of me, inch by inch. The sharp pain that spiralled up my arm reinforced his scowl.

"Or, I could come by your new place, drop it off when you're all alone," he said, a threat curling through his tone like smoke.

My insides were like ice. Did he know where I lived? I'd done the special 'domestic violence' procedure with Royal Mail to keep my new address secure but there were other ways he might have found out. Had he got my address from the uni somehow, or followed me? Ludlow House was so far away from where our old place was. Too far for him to just stumble across it. Was he still reading my emails, even now I'd changed all my passwords?

"Oh!"

The cry of surprise broke the spell Nick had me under. I looked past him and spotted a middle aged woman a few aisle ends away, carrying her own basket. Her eyes travelled between the mess on the floor and Nick, who'd let go of me as soon as she spoke.

"Should I get someone?" she asked and my heart leaped with panic.

"No! I'll…I'll tell someone about the mess," I said, too brightly.

Nick didn't say anything else, he just turned and left. I was shaking as I walked up towards the tills, the mess and my basket forgotten. I saw his car race out of the almost empty carpark and breathed out, my stomach still knotted up. I rushed home that night, alert for any sign of his white Nissan every time I passed stationary traffic. I had the wild fear that he'd drag me into his car given half a chance, take me somewhere to finish our 'chat'.

I'm still not sure if it was a coincidence. Nick lived miles away from me, but there was always the chance he'd come into town and dropped in for something urgently on his way back. Still, I wasn't taking any chances. I'd stopped going out by myself, stopped going out after dark full-stop. I didn't want to give him another chance to corner me or worse, follow me home.

I shuddered myself back to the present, safe in my room, and sat down on the bed with the duvet around my shoulders. That's if he hadn't already followed me back to the house. He could even know the address. I'd spent the first week after moving in fixated on the possibility that I'd left the address lying around somewhere at his flat – scribbled on a post-it or left open in the web browser history on my desktop computer. I'd managed to convince myself that I hadn't, but there was always the possibility. What if he'd gone back through my Facebook friends and found a clue somewhere in Carla and Ari's history?

I sighed and flopped back onto the mattress. I needed to get away for a bit, get some distance. Maybe if I vanished for a bit Nick would get bored, give up on me and find someone new to fixate on. Not that I liked that idea. But maybe whoever he picked next would be stronger than me, able to stop him. To stand up to him.

When I'd had trouble at school Mum had always said to ignore bullies, that they'd go away. If you didn't react, didn't give them what they wanted, you'd be safe.

It had never worked back then either.

Chapter 3

I spent the two and a half weeks leading up to our departure for Greece in the house. I was officially on a break from uni and no more inclined to leave than I had been before we found out about the Lethe tickets. I did, however, try to get back on top of things, in whatever small ways I could. I wasn't able to fool myself that I was actually improving. Not in any real way. But it was a sideways move from 'not coping and lying in bed' to 'still not coping but trying to exhaust myself with busy work'.

The day after Ari won the tickets, I dragged the hoover upstairs and pushed it around. I changed my bedding and conducted a dirty mug and plate amnesty. I opened my packages and put away the text books I'd ordered, dusted my desk with a stray sock and checked my emails. I cleaned the mildew off my window and took an old toothbrush to the grout in the shared shower. I felt like I was going slightly manic after being stuck on autopilot for so long, but I couldn't seem to stop. Every time I passed Ari or Carla I was clutching a bag of rubbish or a bottle of cleaning fluid, my hair in a messy bun and my tie-dye joggers freshly splashed with bleach.

"You were like this about landlord inspections at uni," Carla joked one day, watching me go past. "It's making me feel like I need to take down all my posters and hide my bong."

I smiled at the joke but I couldn't relax. I felt wired and exhausted all at once, but my burst of energy at least seemed to convince the others that I was 'doing better'.

By the time I was packing my suitcase for the trip my room was clean and organised again. It was great to feel more in control of my surroundings, even if I now couldn't sit still for longer than twenty minutes. But it didn't last, as I knew it wouldn't. My intense periods of productivity were always accompanied by overwhelming anxiety and followed by a crash.

The closer the day of our flights came the more wound up I felt. By the day before we were due to leave I'd cleaned the whole house, packed my bag and still couldn't sit still. I didn't even feel slightly in control anymore. I felt like I was running at twice the speed of everyone around me and it was horrible, but I didn't know how to make it stop.

I got maybe two hours of sleep the night before waking up at two in the morning to head to Heathrow, my heart already racing so hard it made me feel sick. It was then that I was forced to confront the reason for all my busy work – I was dreading this and my anxiety was fizzing through my blood like a lethal dose of caffeine.

Even though it was a good chance to get away from Nick, to try and de-stress, I still didn't want to go away. Or I did want to go somewhere but that didn't mean I wanted to go to the festival. Even if it was the opportunity of a lifetime as the only way to get tickets was to win them. Ari and Carla had been reeling off lists of celebrities who were meant to be going, as well as the ones who hadn't been able to get tickets. I wasn't sure how much of it was just internet hype but it was working on them anyway. It just made me more anxious.

I just wanted to leave London, and Lethe was the best of some bad options. I knew I was lucky to even have the chance to get away, but that didn't make it any easier to actually go through with it.

"Are you OK?" Ari asked, whilst we waited in the hallway for Carla. "You look a bit...pale."

"Just a bit nervous," I said, trying to make light of things.

Ari nodded, chewing her lip. "No pressure, OK? You don't have to have a go at everything, you can just chill out. We're cool with whatever."

I nodded, a lump in my throat. She was being so nice to me and I wasn't yet used to people letting me move at my own pace. I'd always been pushed towards things – parties, choir, the netball club – 'oh go on you'll have fun' was basically my mum's motto whilst I was growing up. Always prodding me towards making friends and bringing them over to tea. Mum had always wanted me to fit in, to be included. She wanted me to be surrounded by a whole gaggle of friends but I was happy being forgotten about. The more she pushed me towards people, the harder I dug in my heels, until I outgrew the few friends I had and didn't make any more. Mum had despaired of me.

Nick had been sort of the same – cajoling me, dragging me out to places. Only with him it had been less 'you'll have fun' and more like 'come on, don't be boring' or 'don't show me up'. The pair of them – the carrot and the stick. The wheedling and the threats.

"Found it!" Carla came stumbling down the stairs with her case in tow, crashing against the scarred wallpaper. In one hand she was waving a power bank patterned with rainbow sprinkles, several cords whipping around in her wake.

The night before, Carla had dyed her hair princess pink and it was scooped up in a ponytail for the journey. Carla and Ari had spent the past two days painting their nails, putting outfits together and doing enough hair and face masks to completely resurface themselves. I was starting to feel a bit underprepared, style-wise. Both Carla and Ari had also been ordering 'camping essentials' for the trip, though most of the parcels had come from Boohoo and Missguided. My own bag was packed with mostly shorts and t-shirts as well as a selection of actual camping equipment.

The three of us were sharing a tent we'd found second-hand online and had divided the supplies up between us so our luggage was mostly the same weight. Which meant we were all equally weighed down as we left the house and trundled our cases up the uneven street, the deafening scraping of the plastic wheels making me wince. I had asked if we should get proper backpacking bags, but between the lure of new clothes and 'hideous nylon things that we'd have to check in' the clothes had won out. We'd just be dumping them in our tent anyway.

Getting all our stuff to the tube station was tiring but not too bad. Though we had to lift Carla's case over the barrier because it was too wide to go through the turnstile and the wheelchair accessible gate was broken and taped shut. After that came an 'out of order' lift, a lot of stairs and by the time we reached the platform below I was sweating through my t-shirt and wishing I'd thought to use real deodorant instead of the natural one I wasn't sure was working. Something else to worry about. We boarded a mostly empty carriage and flopped into seats on either side of the train, our bags cluttering the aisle.

"Lethe, here we come," Carla said, dancing excitedly in her seat. I'd expected her to be a complete grump given the lack of sleep but she'd confided on the way to the station that she'd taken some caffeine pills to keep her going until the flight. I vaguely remembered her doing the same thing whilst we were at uni – the consequences had been a dissertation nobody could understand, not even her.

"Save some energy for when we get there," Ari said, wryly. I glanced over and saw her scrolling through her downloaded podcasts and lazily tapping a queue together for the plane.

"Did you say Lethe – like the festival?" a curious voice asked.

All three of us looked up at a group of six girls at the other end of the carriage. I could tell immediately that they were either going to Lethe or, less likely, to another festival; they were wearing the same mix of practical footwear and sparkly clothes that Carla and Ari had put together and two of them had pastel streaks in their hair. The girl closest to us, the one who'd spoken, had a flower crown threaded onto the strap of her bag.

"Yeah," Ari said, smiling. "We were able to get tickets."

"Me too! Well, Chel won four and I got two. I'm Darcy by the way."

"Ari. This is Carla and Jody."

"Hi," I said, then added a wave which immediately felt awkward. Darcy didn't seem to notice, but I felt myself blush anyway. If this was how I was going to feel for the next few days I wanted to get off at the next stop and go home.

"What flight are you guys on?" Chel asked.

"Like…five forty-something?" Carla said, checking the time on her phone.

"Oh, cool," Chel said. "We're going on a later flight but we were too excited to wait. Plus you know there's going to be so many other people with metal tent pegs or whatever in their carry-on and security's going to be so delayed," she pulled a face. "See you when we get there though maybe?"

"See you," Ari echoed. She went to put her phone away and sighed. "Shit, I forgot my lockbox."

"You're going to have to develop a little trust in the festival-going community," Carla said. "We're going to be living amongst it in a nylon bag with no lock, no door even."

"Which is how my iPhone got stolen at Reading two years ago," Ari pointed out.

"Well, you know, be trusting but don't leave shit lying around," Carla said, trying and failing to hide a grin. "Also, to be fair, they'd probably just nick the whole box, wouldn't they?"

"We're getting the bus from the airport, right?" I asked, trying to chase my nerves away with logistics. "Do we know where from? Is there a special station or is it outside…"

"It's a bus provided by Lethe, so it's probably not got an official stop, but I'm sure we'll be able to find whatever temporary one they've set up," Ari assured me. "If in doubt we'll just follow anyone else who looks like they're going that way."

I nodded and tried to make myself relax. It worked for a bit, until we got to the airport and had to do all the security stuff. I always felt guilty as soon as bag searches were involved. Even having my pencil case checked before exams at school had broken me out in a cold sweat. I'd always been worried I might accidentally break a rule without realising, even after studying them over and over again.

We ended up being funnelled into separate queues to go through security. I was glad when we were done with it and I met up with Carla and Ari on the other side.

"Shall we grab a quick drink, while there's time?" Carla asked. I turned in time to catch her giving Ari a significant look, her head tilted in my direction.

"It's barely five in the morning," Ari pointed out.

"It's always after five p.m. in an airport," Carla said, waving her away. "We'll find something. Besides, it'll help me get a nap in on the plane. Or I'm going to be a total bitch later."

Ari was proven right though. Every bar looked like it was closed or being prepared to open in an hour or so. Carla got moody, as she usually did when she felt embarrassed about something. In the end, Ari attempted to keep the peace by getting us hot chocolates from Starbucks and a couple of heavily marked up whisky miniatures.

The three of us tucked ourselves away on a padded bench behind a giant planter full of spiky tropical vegetation. Around us the sterile airport was quiet and mostly deserted, too cold and open to be comfortable.

"Mmmm, such a good idea," Carla said, after sipping for a while. "Should we grab anything else from duty free on the way through? Vodka, rum, something we all like?" she asked, casting a wistful eye towards the shops.

"We get a free bottle of vodka with the tickets I won," Ari said, having finished her drink she was reapplying her dark lipstick. "I've been burned by venue security too many times to try to bring drinks in. Besides, duty free is basically a scam at this point."

"Is that to share?" I asked.

"Each," Ari said. "Something to do with a sponsor I think, part of the luxury package – not having to smuggle shit in. Not sure. We pick them up at the gates though, after the bag search. So, I suppose it'll be nice not having to smuggle anything in."

"Maybe that's why they've done it that way," I said, relieved that I wouldn't have to chance being caught with contraband. Just the thought made me go hot with embarrassment.

"Probably. We will need snacks though," Ari said, as a small boy rode by on a scooter/suitcase combo that his parent had probably thought seemed a great idea before letting him loose with it.

"Nothing Marmite flavour or Marmite adjacent," Carla immediately forbade us. "I'm not having our tent reeking of that stuff. Makes me feel sick just thinking about it."

The mother of scooter boy rushed past in clompy espadrilles. I watched as she separated him from the suitcase and carried both him and it back towards Starbucks.

Ari and Carla started to debate the merits of seaweed thins verses Sesame Snaps and I tuned them out for a bit before excusing myself to the shops nearby. I needed a little break from socialising for a while and I wouldn't get much of a chance of one once we boarded the plane.

I ambled around for a bit before ending up at the makeup. Most of mine was still at Nick's place. It just hadn't been essential. I had found myself missing it though, especially when I was packing for the festival. Ari had her go-to liner and red lipstick, Carla had all her fun glitters and unusual colours, but I only had a few basic bits – mostly concealer and foundation products. The few times I'd tried to do my makeup since leaving Nick I'd ended up looking half finished, like part of my face was missing.

I started picking up lipsticks and swiping my hand with colour, not really intending to buy, just browsing. It had been ages since I'd worn anything colourful. Nick had never liked 'unnatural makeup'. Again, it surprised me how similar he was to my mother in that regard. He'd wanted me to look perfect, but natural, even if it meant layering on my foundation until I felt like I was hiding some kind of terrible illness. I'd once dared to have a bare-faced chill day and he'd told me I looked 'weird' or 'old' at least ten times. So I'd never done that again. It was easier to just give in than to try and stand up for what I wanted and be steamrollered.

But Nick wasn't here and I could at least have a look around, maybe even try some samples out. It had been ages since I'd bought anything fun for myself, or even window shopped.

"Finding everything OK?" asked the woman from the counter, a cherub-cheeked blonde in a slightly creased uniform shirt.

"Just looking," I said, trying for a smile, but it felt tense even to me.

"Off anywhere nice?" she asked. The shop was otherwise empty and I supposed she was bored.

"A festival. My first."

"Wow," she grinned. "Hope you have a good time. We've got some glitters and stuff in, if you want a look. Half price."

She gestured to a display and I spotted a familiar pink and purple palette. I'd had that one – bought it during fresher's week. One of the first bits of makeup I'd ever owned. I could still remember the feeling of seeing it online, and just having to go into town to try it out, to buy it. My first trip into town by myself after I got to uni. I'd found the right bus, had a coffee by the river, bought my palette. A whole afternoon just for me and what I wanted to do. No Mum telling me not to waste my money on 'that muck' and before there was a Nick to go through my things and throw them away.

Seeing it there felt like a sign. This was like my first step away from the horror of Nick. A chance to reinvent myself or at least, reclaim what it was he'd taken from me. Both figuratively and literally.

I picked up the palette and added a few other items to round out a full face. Then I approached the counter.

"These please," I said, with a small smile to the woman at the counter. She slid my new pink lipstick, glitter gloss, eyeliner and the eyeshadow palette into a bag.

Yes, it was an added extravagance on top of the cost of going to the festival, but it turned that ball of nerves inside me into a little flutter of excitement for a moment. I was going to play with makeup again, just because I wanted to – glitter lip gloss and bright eye shadow, the works. It was my face, not Nick's. I was done listening to his voice in my head.

Still, as I made my way back to Carla and Ari on their concourse bench, I scanned the crowd around me. Just in case.

Chapter 4

The flight went pretty quickly. Carla took a power nap and Ari was lost in her podcasts, so I read for a while. I felt a lot calmer now that we were actually on the plane and not out in the world, where anyone could be around. The flight attendants had done the tea and coffee round and we were all in our own seats, our own spaces. I could breathe again.

I leaned back in my seat and closed my eyes for a while, dozing. I let myself forget that we would eventually land and have to go through the rigmarole of getting out of the airport and to the festival. Then I'd actually be at the festival and stuck there for days. For the duration of the flight I convinced myself that there was no 'after' there was just me catching a nap in a comfy chair.

It didn't last. My anxiety returned almost at full force once we deplaned and joined the crowd heading out into the world. The only thing that made it bearable was knowing that Nick was over a thousand miles away. It would be days before I had to worry about him again. For now I just had to worry about everything else – the new people, the fact I couldn't dance and didn't really know what people did at concerts and the idea of spending the night in a tiny tent without plumbing or a lockable door.

The 'official version' of our break-up story was that he'd cheated on me. It was the first thing that popped into my head after I found Carla's house share post on Facebook and reconnected with her. It also matched up with the suddenness of the move and the fact that I showed up with very little in the way of possessions. I didn't want to have to answer too many probing questions.

Carla presumably also told Ari about it. Since then they haven't asked me any questions about Nick – though I did once see Carla stalking him on Facebook. She must have found him via my profile, which I hadn't updated in ages, because Nick always quizzed me about the people liking my posts. I assumed she was just curious to see what he looked like, when she saw me looking she called him 'a gym-bro with a fivehead'. It had simultaneously shocked and amused me. Before he showed up again the idea of joking about Nick had felt rebellious, almost freeing. Seeing him again just reminded me how dangerous disrespecting him was. The one time I'd joked about an ugly jumper he'd been given as a present, he'd gone straight to my wardrobe and taken out the new grey coat Mum had sent me for Christmas and said it made me look like a tramp. Then he'd shoved me out of the way and thrown it off the flat's balcony into the road. I washed it, but the filthy marks on it wouldn't come out. It was ruined.

41

"Where's the bus then?" Carla yawned, popping a pair of sunglasses on top of her head in preparation for the Grecian sunshine as we walked through the airport, having bought snacks on the way out.

"Not...sure..." Ari said, from behind me. I turned and saw her frowning at a group of girls nearby – mid-twenties and dressed much as we were. More Lethe attendees. Like us they were milling in a circle, crowded around two girls with their phones out, tapping away. About twenty feet back from them, another gaggle had formed, the same thing going on. I felt my stomach turn over. No one seemed to know what to do now that we'd landed.

"We'll check outside," Ari said, striding past me with purpose. I was glad she was taking charge, and scuttled after her, Carla following after me with a tired sigh.

Outside the temperature was already in the high twenties and climbing. The ground sizzled and a heat haze shimmered in the pale dust. The sunlight was blisteringly white and I immediately rescued my own sunglasses from the bottom of my bag. The cheap plastic creaked as I put them on. I wished I'd thought to buy some sun cream whilst we were in the airport. It wouldn't take me long to start to burn.

"There! That sign says 'Lethe'," Ari said suddenly – a note of clear relief in her voice as she pointed at a signpost on a concrete island just across the road from the doors we'd come through. We crossed over and I heard the clatter of wheelie bags as we were followed by a Noah's ark style line of girls in crochet crop tops and flip-flops, two by two.

The sign did say 'Lethe Festival' though it had run a bit in the rain at some point. It wasn't laminated or even in a plastic pouch. Someone had printed it out on an inkjet and taped it up with holographic sticky tape. *Lethe Festival Bus Service – Every Half-Hour* and then a list of dates starting from today and running until the end of the festival. It was translated into several languages, including French, German and Spanish.

"It's quarter to," Carla said as she put her phone back in her pocket. "Fifteen-minute wait then. Great. I'm already sweating."

"TMI," Ari said. "Hope you're wearing a lot of deodorant or you're sleeping outside the tent tonight."

I tried to lift my arms and unstick my damp t-shirt unobtrusively. Travel always made me feel grubby and this was no exception.

We stretched out after being packed into our cramped airline seats and Carla took the opportunity to vape, sending up a cloud of cotton-candy vapour. Festivalgoers in groups and on their own, came out of the terminal and peered around before coming over to us with relief on their faces. We were officially 'the people who knew what was going on'. Or at least, we looked like we were. I didn't think I'd relax until we were actually on the bus.

At five past, Ari sighed and started trying to get her mobile data to work now that we were out of range of the airport Wi-Fi. Around us, casual conversations were drying up. The layered 'where are you from?' and 'when did you win your tickets?' questions tapering off into stressed silence as people checked and re-checked the time.

At quarter past, people became more talkative again, this time in mutinous murmurs and huffy complaints. A few were searching online for answers and angrily relaying the lack of information available.

"They haven't updated the Twitter feed since Friday," one girl sighed. "No updates on Facebook either."

"I mean, the bus is part of the experience," I heard one of the only guys in the queue say to his friend. "It's what makes it bespoke or whatever, right? What a piss take."

By the time a second bus had failed to materialise half an hour later, people were clumping together into groups and discussing their options. Still more festivalgoers had arrived in the meantime and the veteran members of the queue were filling them in on the outrageous situation with relish.

"I can get a five-seat Uber here if anyone wants to share with us three?" a girl in a maxi dress said, flicking her hair off of her already sunburned face.

"I've got space for another two in a taxi!" another girl called, waving her phone.

Looking around, most of the group around us was made up of women and girls. There were only two guys that I could see. Weird. Maybe it was something about the flight being early, I thought wryly, perhaps all the men coming to Lethe were sleeping in. Good for them.

"What should we do?" I yawned to Ari, who was frowning intently at her phone, chewing her thumb. Carla had become so restless after the second bus failed to appear, she'd gone into Departures to grab some drinks.

"Let's...go get Carla and then we can work

something out," Ari said, sounding the least certain she'd been since we left the airport. I felt my stomach drop. I really needed someone to take charge and Ari was pretty much the only option. Compared to Carla and I she was the most alert.

We retreated from the 'bus stop' and headed over to Departures, dragging our cases and Carla's over the now quite busy road. Carla met us as we reached the automatic doors, three cans of Coke balanced in the crook of her arm. She saw our expressions and sighed.

"Still nothing?"

"Nope," Ari said. "Look, I think we should get a local taxi – it'll be safer than a rideshare right, without all those bullshit service fees for extra bags and stuff? Who has euros?"

After working out how much cash we had on us, Ari pulled up a map and checked how far away the festival was. About a forty minute drive. That was going to be pricey. I glanced at the map as she zoomed in – the Lethe Festival site was on a little island, connected to the mainland by a bridge.

"I think I saw a taxi rank type situation over there when we came out," Carla said, gesturing in the opposite direction of the signpost where a few newcomers were now waiting. "Shall we try and get there before that lot wises up? I am so not down to hang around here for another hour."

There were a lot of people waiting around by the taxi pull in, not just festivalgoers but people who looked like they were just on holiday or travelling for work. Normal people just trying to go about their normal lives, standing out from the scrum of flower-crowned new arrivals like cockatiels from starlings. Most of the other travellers were looking at the heaps of impractical luggage, tents and duty-free bags of booze with amusement or annoyance. I started to feel out of place and stupid, seeing myself through their eyes. I was relieved when it was our turn, finally, and we managed to grab a taxi as it came in.

"Can you take us here, please?" Ari asked, showing the map location to the driver from her spot in the front seat.

He nodded in a bored way, indicated and pulled out into the flow of traffic as if we had all the time in the world. I watched the red numbers on the meter and tried to calculate how much this was going to come to. We should have gotten more cash out at the airport, I realised. There probably wouldn't be anywhere to do so at the festival. But it was too late now. We'd have to manage. Maybe they'd take card payments?

My thoughts were locked in an anxious holding pattern for most of the drive. Even the bright blue water on one side and the sunshine bouncing off of the white walls of hundreds of villas and apartment buildings fighting for space with the ruins of ancient Greece on the other couldn't switch them off. Overhead white gulls stood out against the brilliant blue sky, mirroring the white boats on the serene water. Still, I couldn't relax.

The car was very tatty inside, the upholstery old and sagging. I started to wonder if this was one of those dodgy cabs you hear about on the news, when someone goes missing in a foreign country.

I glanced over at Carla to see if she was worried, but she was leaning against the door with her elbow on the edge of the window, looking at the scenery. I peered over Ari's shoulder and saw that she was typing out a long text. I saw the words 'fucking bus' a few times, as well as some peace symbol emojis, so she was probably messaging her friends about the festival. She didn't even have her Maps app open to see if we were going the right way. I got my phone out and tried to use mine, but despite setting myself up for roaming data, it wasn't working. Maybe I'd done it wrong? Frustrated, I put my phone away. I didn't want to say anything in case the driver heard and either got offended or turned nasty. Maybe both.

Just as I was trying to work out what to do if he locked all the doors, we hit the bridge. It was a relief to pass a printed banner reading 'Lethe Festival 2024' in big purple letters. We were going the right way. I was just being paranoid.

The bridge was packed with traffic, a lot of it taxis and cars with rideshare stickers on them. The bridge itself was ugly grey concrete and pretty boring to look at. Eventually we reached the far side and sat, idling, waiting to pass through a rusty chain-link fence onto the island proper. As we cruised by I saw part of a sun-bleached plastic sign zip tied to the fence, five letters printed on it in black – XYTA – was that the name of the island? Or part of it at least? Maybe just a postcode? I automatically took my phone out to Google it, then remembered that my data wasn't working.

"Hey, Ari," I leaned forwards. "Will there be Wi-Fi at the festival?"

"Hmmm? Oh, I think so. It said something about the grounds having free hotspots set-up."

"Do you have data now? Can I Google something?" I asked.

"Mine's not working," Ari said, showing me her phone screen and bringing up the browser so I could see. "Carla?"

"Mine's not either. Maybe it's a network thing? Are we almost there?" Carla asked, sitting up straight, one headphone still in. She was starting to look paler now, clearly feeling the lack of sleep, as we all were.

"Sort of, if the traffic would clear...no, wait, I can see the entrance!" Ari cried.

We peered out of the windows, anxiously shifting in our seats until we pulled up on a concrete forecourt in front of the security checkpoint. Which was in actuality just a few tables sheltered from the blazing sun by a large purple gazebo. The taxi driver didn't help with our bags, and left without giving us change for the fifty euro we passed him in notes. At that point even I didn't care – I was just glad to be out of the cab and finally at the festival itself. I was done with the stress of travelling, the stress of arrival would be a nice change of pace.

As I tuned out the sound of the cars still arriving and manoeuvring for space, I caught the pulse of music coming from beyond the purple bannered security checkpoint. I couldn't hear the words to the song, just the rise and fall of a voice and a bassline that travelled through me from the feet upwards. I'd made it, after worrying so much and almost talking myself out of it a hundred times, I'd made it. My reward? A different kind of dread – the dread of ruining everyone else's good time because I didn't belong here. Still, Mum always said 'a change is as good as a rest'. Then again she'd mostly meant that in the way parents do when they want you to do something 'productive' instead of something fun.

"Tickets ready, please!" A stern voice called from the front of the line.

We joined the left-hand queue and Carla immediately got into conversation with the girl ahead of us. Ari was fiddling with her phone, trying to get the Wi-Fi working or looking for the screen shots of our tickets, I supposed.

Looking up and down the queue I noticed that the line was mostly girls. It also skewed a bit younger, which I supposed was always going to be the case as the contests that determined who got tickets were all on social media. To wildly stereotype, most of the people entering would have been younger women, like Ari. Still it felt weird that not a single person over thirty-five seemed to have won tickets. At least not in our line at that particular moment.

"Tickets," a very tanned man asked when we reached the front, waving at Ari's phone.

Ari showed her phone screen and waited for the QR codes to be scanned. The guy added three clicks to a handheld counter and plucked three purple tote bags from a box at his feet, all branded with the Lethe Festival logo. Each one was weighed down with a litre bottle, the free drinks Ari had mentioned. The ticket checker then opened our bags and had a brief rummage through. Finding nothing, he zipped them back up and checked our handbags.

I noticed a line of large black bins lined up behind

the checkpoint, two of them were full already, heaped with contraband – alcohol, flares, and nitrous oxide canisters. As I watched, one of the marshals piled three-litre bottles of rum into one of the containers, which was already partially filled with cans, bottles and plastic pouches of booze. Ari was right, if we'd have hit duty free, we'd have wasted our money.

With holographic bracelets on our wrists, we passed through the checkpoint and through the gates in the metal security fence. Ahead of us, an already well-trodden path led through the dusty grass. A train of festivalgoers with bright bags and pop-tents proceeded us into the campground.

The music was louder now, accompanied by the sound of a crowd of people determined to have the best time of their lives, whooping and chanting along. The air carried the smell of the sea, fried food, weed (despite the best efforts of the security checkpoint) and the weird, rotten tang of bins. Surely they couldn't be so gross already? I wrinkled my nose.

Carla slung an arm over my shoulder. "We're here babes! Lethe! Not sure if I want a nap or a drink – but we're here!"

I smiled and tried to ignore the fluttering of nerves that still filled my stomach. A feeling that only grew stronger with every strange face and uncertainty that presented itself. Together, the three of us trundled after the stream of other attendees, into the heart of Lethe.

Chapter 5

The first thing I noticed – as we reached the campground – was the music. It was so much louder here, but it was also a physical feeling. A pounding that reverberated through my body and shook my heart. I pressed a hand to the centre of my chest to try and still the fluttering echo of the beat. Like a second, manic pulse. For a second it felt like I was having a panic attack.

The second thing I noticed was the dust, yellow and billowing. It was everywhere, stirred up from the hard ground which had cracked open in places. Clearly there had been no rain for a good long while. What little grass was there hung on in straggly brown clumps, like a sweaty comb over. Beside me I heard Carla angrily puffing to try and keep it out of her mouth. I could feel it sticking to my skin, and when I looked down I saw that our cases and shoes were already thick with it.

"Ugh, it better not be like this all the way across the island," Carla muttered. "Can you imagine trying to wear lip gloss in this? I'm glad I didn't put on my SPF yet."

"I won't be glad when you're a red angry mess later," Ari said under her breath.

"Where are we meant to set up our tent?" I asked, already desperate for a sit down and a drink. The early start combined with the heat and the walking was making me feel lightheaded. I was craving a cold drink and realised I was unlikely to get one any time soon – there were so many people around I just knew the lines at the bars would be out of control.

"Not sure…I can't see anyone directing people…" Ari looked around the dusty field. "Just sort of looks like people are setting up anywhere."

"Well, then let's get a good spot. Not too near the toilets or too far from the action," Carla said.

Ari and Carla argued over the merits of several spots before picking a place that looked to me like every other spot in the field – dry, dusty and uneven. It was also just off the direct path from the festival entrance to the gate separating the campgrounds from the festival proper. We unpacked the tent components and set about trying to put it up – having not had the space to practise with it at home. It was a recent purchase from Facebook Marketplace and had clearly been to a festival or two before. There was glitter in the seams of the groundsheet and it smelled of stale beer and vanilla body spray.

"You're sure we have all the bits?" Ari demanded, glaring at Carla after the second time the frame collapsed in on itself.

"No?" Carla replied, scornfully. "What am I, Bear Grylls all of a sudden? What the 'ell do I know about tents? This is why I wanted a pop-up."

"What about the instructions?" Ari turned to me. I was holding the crumpled bits of paper that had come with the thing. "They can't be right."

I winced, feeling like she was angry with me specifically and not just the situation. Though I told myself it was just tiredness and stress. We were all feeling it.

"That's all it says to do...but there are a few bits ripped off." I said, gesturing to the incomplete pages as they fluttered in the dust-filled air.

Ari snatched the papers and sighed. "Fantastic – they've made roaches from the instructions. I knew that guy was an idiot when we picked this thing up." She aimed a kick at the crumpled canopy, got her foot caught and tried to kick herself free, stumbling on one leg.

Carla giggled, clearly enjoying Ari's embarrassment.

Ari glared at her, then her mouth wavered and she snorted a little laugh. I felt my shoulders shake and a tiny laugh slipped out. One by one we spiralled into full on laughter. For a while we were all useless, laughing around our pile of collapsed poles and beer spattered nylon sheets. Then Ari extracted herself from the tent and gestured for calm.

"Right, right, OK," Ari said, tightening her ponytail. "Let's get this thing up so we can start drinking."

We got it on our fourth try. Just about. Once we realised one of the clips was bent and substituted two kirby grips and an elastic band it sort of worked. Together we looked over our home for the next three days.

"Just try not to turn over too much in the night," I suggested. "Those pegs are barely in the ground."

"I can't believe we forgot a mallet," Ari sighed.

"It wouldn't have made a difference, the ground's like brick anyway," Carla pointed out. "That's gonna be fun to lie on. But Jody's right – just try not to move around too much and it'll probably stay up."

"I don't do that anyway," Ari said.

"You do, Jody," Carla said. "I can hear your bed through the floor – you spin like a rotisserie chicken for about forty minutes every night."

I felt myself flush, thinking of all the nights that I'd been too anxious to sleep, just turning over and over on my creaky futon as I wished I could go back and change near enough the past two years of my life. Thinking about what Nick was doing, hoping he wasn't thinking about me. Reliving that awful night that had finally tipped me over the edge and made me desperate enough to run from him.

Carla smiled, reached over and patted my hand. "Hopefully you'll get a better night's sleep after a day of dancing, drinking and doing permanent damage to our eardrums."

"Speaking of which," Ari, turned around and retrieved the three Cokes Carla had bought at the airport. She passed them around then screwed the top off of one of the bottles of vodka we'd been given at the gate. I gulped down a few mouthfuls of fizz and let Ari top up my drink. "Here's to the first of many more grown-up girls' trips to come."

We toasted and swigged at our drinks.

Carla grimaced and I coughed, my face flaming. The alcohol burned down my throat and nearly made me retch. I wasn't a big drinker, but I'd never had anything like it before.

"Fuck me, that's like...lighter fluid," Ari grabbed the bottle and took a closer look at it. The label on it was just the festival logo and the word 'Vodka' printed straight from an inkjet and taped to the bottle.

"Guess we know why it was free now," Carla snorted. "Are you alright, Jody? You've gone a bit red."

"Fine," I managed, blinking back tears. I felt like I'd just gargled sugary paint stripper. "Shall we, maybe find a bar – get some other drinks? Drinkable ones."

"Good call," Ari said, and dumped her Coke can out on the ground. The fizz was immediately sucked into the parched earth, creating a tiny patch of semi-soft dirt. I poured mine away beside it.

Carla looked down, then shrugged. "Whatever, I'm not wasting mine."

"On your own head be it," Ari said. "I'm not holding your hair back. Come on, let's explore a bit."

More and more people were showing up now, the campgrounds rapidly filling up with colourful tents and clusters of festivalgoers introducing themselves to their new neighbours. The noise of so many conversations made me feel like we were navigating through a beehive. The low buzz came from everywhere, a second bassline which made the air feel heavy. Even in the open air I was reminded of the tube – the crowds and noise, the chaos and the heat, not to mention the stink. My heart started to beat very quickly and I had to force myself to breathe and calm down.

There wasn't anyone beside our spot, yet, but there probably would be by the time we got back, I realised. I hoped they were nice. I wasn't sure I wanted to meet them really – the idea of talking to a stranger felt impossible just then. God I wanted a drink so badly now. I shouldn't have thrown mine away, no matter how vile it tasted. It would have done the job of loosening me up a little.

"You'd think they'd have given us a map or something," Carla said as we wandered through the campground in the direction of the music. "Or put up signposts at least. Total amateur hour or what?"

"Hmmm," Ari agreed. "Maybe they have and we just haven't seen…oh my God, look at those tents. Very posh. Wish that was us."

I followed her gaze and spotted the creamy canvas of several yurts. A group of men in jeans and vests were wrestling with them, either putting them up or taking them down, it was hard to tell. As the loose canvas flapped in the dusty breeze I spotted brightly coloured gauzy curtains inside. The kind of thing I'd desperately wanted for my bedroom when I was fifteen, but which Mum had called 'tacky'.

"Do you think they're having events in there?" Carla asked, dubiously. "Not much room."

"Maybe it's some kind of premium accommodation?" I said. "Like glamping."

"Could be," Ari said. "There might have been extra stuff you could pay for, I didn't see anything though. Maybe it's like, special tickets or something? Though you'd expect it to be up by now – festival's already started. I suppose the traffic on the bridge is holding things up. They might have only just been delivered."

We'd been walking that way and were close enough now to see that the men were clearly trying to put the tents up, not take them down. Trying being the operative

56

word. As we drew level with the construction crew a sharp crack came from under the canvas. I jumped, then looked around in time to see a man emerge holding a splintered piece of wooden pole. He threw it down and started shouting at one of the other men, in what I assumed was Greek. I noticed several other shattered bits of wood. The frame was clearly not holding up too well under all the heavy canvas and drapery.

"Thank God we brought our own," Carla said, as we reached the gate into the festival proper. "Whoever was expecting to stay in those is going to be pissed."

"Everyone expecting to actually drink their free drinks is going to be sort of pissed off too," Ari muttered.

"Oh my God, they're just drinks," Carla sighed. "Don't let it ruin the festival. Look, I will buy you a cocktail, how about that?"

"I'm not going to let it 'ruin the festival'," Ari said, rolling her eyes. "I'm just saying, if you're going to hand out drinks and make people think twice about bringing their own booze, it ought to be drinkable."

"I'm drinking it," Carla pointed out.

"You would." Ari nudged her jokingly. "She's got lower standards than us, right Jody?"

I smiled, but I was distracted by the sights that greeted us as we reached the actual event space. There were so many people for one – so many faces and voices and everyone moving together like a giant magic eye picture. I felt a bit sick at the sight of them all – so many people and I felt like all of them were looking at me, judging me. They probably weren't, Mum always said people cared more about themselves than anyone else, but it didn't feel that way to me. My sense of being watched had always been cranked up way too high and just then it was going haywire. I'd known this was going to be a big event but there seemed to be no space between any of them. We were packed in and I immediately wanted to run back to the tent where I at least had a piece of space to call my own. Maybe if I shut myself in there with my book it would still count as 'enjoying myself'?

Between the people and the clouds of dust they'd stirred up, I could see white domes made up of hexagonal canvas panels – reminding me of the Eden Project, but scaled down. Outside each one was a sort of patio made of black rubber mats, with folding bistro chairs and tables in different colours set up in little groups. Every table was occupied and people were sitting on the mats too, or leaning against the solid domes. It looked like they were all types of bar – from cocktails to shots, beer tents and even those ridiculous slushies I sometimes saw people with at the cinema, though these were probably swimming in vodka.

"One of these has got to have some space," Carla said, as we passed several girls with plastic cups of cocktails, tripping out of a packed dome.

We made it to the end of the busiest areas and the domes further back seemed to be other kinds of amenities. I glanced into the doorway of one and for a moment I thought it was empty, then a light flickered on. It was from a projector on a table, with another one on top pointing the other way. The small portable ones teachers brought out at school to show you YouTube videos about gravity or the life of Henry VIII. Only this projector just showed a video of a coastal view which repeated every few seconds. The same seagull swooping across the canvas screen over and over again.

"Is that the sea thing you showed me on TikTok?" I asked, catching Carla's attention with a nudge, disappointment carving out a space in my chest. It was nowhere near what she'd shown me on her phone back at the house.

"Is it…? No, it can't be," she sidled up to the tent and looked in, tugging me after her by my bag strap. "This is so not what I was picturing."

It was definitely less of a spectacle than the one she'd shown me on her phone. There was no deep pool with simulated rain falling on it in the dark, no walls made of LCD screens showing a proper, panoramic view of a storm at sea. Inside this dome, there were the two projectors, both showing the same sea view but with blank darkness between the projections. There was no rain falling, and when I looked up I couldn't see anything that looked like it would produce any. The floor was bare dirt, with four inflatable pools squeezed into the dome, each one sprinkled with shreds of dead grass. A hose, in one, was filling it, unattended. Someone had left a cup of cold coffee with a cigarette butt in it sitting next to the projectors.

I looked at Carla and then at Ari. There were two pink spots on Ari's cheeks and she looked both annoyed and mortified. She'd brought us here, so clearly she was feeling responsible for this monstrosity. Carla appeared to be feeling much the same. She had been so excited about the pool and her disappointment was obvious. I was less disappointed, having been a bit wary of the concept anyway, but it still sucked to see that we'd been let down again – for the third time since arriving. First the bus, then the drinks and now this.

"I wasn't that keen on it," I said, trying to diffuse some of the unpleasant tension. "I mean. Festivals are about music, right? Not the gimmicky stuff they put on alongside."

"Right," Carla said, clearly also trying to make Ari feel better about it. "I mean, we've got the actual ocean like ten feet away – who needs a video of it?"

Ari gave us both a look that said 'I know what you're doing, but thanks'. Then she sighed. "Let's turn around, grab some cocktails and head to the beach then."

Chapter 6

After queuing for too long for it to be really worthwhile, we ordered three of the same cocktail, plus some pre-mixed cans and pushed our way back out of the bar dome. I necked half my drink in one, trying to settle my nerves. It was strong, which was all I cared about. I could feel the warmth of the alcohol in my stomach, spreading outwards through my veins.

"Thank God," Ari said, as we wandered on through the masses of festivalgoers, sipping. "It's actually nice."

"Mmmm, what do you think, Jody? Bit like a jammy dodger right? If it was in liquid form and could knock you off your feet," Carla said, nudging me.

I hadn't really tasted it to be honest, but it was working, thankfully. The twisting in my stomach no longer felt sharp and I was a tiny bit fuzzy around the edges. Just enough so that as we passed the amusements set up near the beach, they seemed more fun than frightening. Overhead strings of multi-coloured flags, shiny disks and round, purple lanterns caught the dusty breeze. Music throbbed through the air, coming from the stage area and we were surrounded by laughter and

61

raised voices as everyone tried to get drinks and shake off the journey.

We passed by more domed pods containing arcade machines, an oxygen bar and a surf machine. I was surprised and not a little concerned to see that one dome contained a circle of padded chairs, each one with an IV-drip stand beside it. A poster on the wall advertised 'hangover beating IV hydration and vitamin blasts'. Yellow dust had blown in, layering over the shiny leather of the chairs.

"Oh wow," Carla peeped in around me. "Do you think that actually works?"

I gaped at her, horrified. "You can't seriously be considering it. Look, it's filthy in there."

Carla blew a raspberry. "No one is going to need it 'til the second day – they'll probably clean it up by then. Besides, when will I ever get the chance to try it again?"

"Never, hopefully," I muttered. I meant it too, the only time I wanted to be hooked up to something like that was if I was in a horrible accident or literally dying. The idea of having an IV just for the hell of it was wild. Maybe because I'd actually administered them before, albeit to animals.

"Come on guys," Ari complained. "I want to get to the beach before it's absolutely mobbed."

As we started to walk again she nudged in between us. "But I agree with Jody. If you let someone hook you up to an IV here, you'll get all forms of hepatitis and die – and I don't want to pay your third of the rent this month so, no dying for you."

Carla groaned. "Right...especially now that..."

Ari coughed hard and took a deep slurp of her drink, apparently I wasn't the only one getting dust caught in my throat. It was impossible to avoid breathing it in.

"Spoilsports," Carla muttered, then poked her tongue out at me.

Ari was right to be worried as it turned out – the beach was rammed already. The metal fence ended in an arch of purple windmills, the kind you'd put on top of a sandcastle, all whirring away in the wind. It made a big statement, but the crowds beyond it had more impact. I realised, as we picked our way through sunbathing groups, that it wasn't even that nice of a beach. I'd been expecting white sand, blue water and blinding sunshine. The stuff of Instagram holiday pictures. Well, the sun was definitely out and it was sweltering hot, as for the rest…well.

The beach wasn't sand at all, mostly chalky pebbles and course grit, like something off of a building site. I spotted one chunk of concrete and then started seeing them everywhere – wedges of weathered grey concrete, some pierced with rusting rebar. Even a few bricks with the mortar worn down and clinging on. It was like a building site. Or a bombsite.

The sea, where it met the pebbles, was a wide band of yellow foam, clotted with rubbish and seaweed. Beyond that, it was at least blue and clear, so you could see down to the odd take-away container or dark brown blob of what I really hoped was seaweed.

Having grown up in Dorset and spent most summer holidays there, or visiting family in Devon and Cornwall, I'd been on some of the most beautiful beaches in England. I'd appreciated them all, from the rugged to the smoothest golden sand. This, was however, not one I could find the beauty in. It was also not how I had imagined my trip to Greece. It looked more like the one time I'd been to Skegness with the school – in winter when the sand looked like dirt and the strong tides had thrown up rubbish for the wind to toss around.

I glanced at Ari and Carla to see if they were disappointed. Ari looked as grossed out as I felt. Then again she was from Norway and from what she'd shown me of her family pictures, they had amazing beaches. Or at least, she'd only been to the really good ones. Carla however was gamely picking her way over to a slanted slab of concrete. She climbed up onto it and arranged herself so she'd get the sun on her legs. Ari and I settled on the lower end of the slab.

"Isn't it lovely and warm?" Carla said, with her head tilted back. "God, I haven't been to the beach since... Southend, when we were in third year. And that was hardly a scorcher of a week, was it? I think I actually caught a chill."

That explained it then. Though I found my mood dipping at the mention of that trip. The first time I'd known either of them to lie to me.

I remembered Carla telling me about trips she'd taken to Amsterdam, Berlin and Prague in the two years since university, but she'd never mentioned anything that wasn't a city break. As a London girl all her life I guessed she was more suited to having everything within easy reach.

Whilst Carla sunbathed above us like a mermaid on a chunk of crumbling cement, Ari took out a bottle of sun cream and began to reapply. She'd always made her opinions on skincare very clear, especially when it came to sun protection. It had been her ever-present refrain even in our university days as she waved a bottle of factor fifty at us, yelling "You'll thank me when you're forty!" as she did so. She didn't just wear sun cream in summer, she wore SPF daily – something about even indoor lights and screens causing damage to the skin. I was never going to be able to keep that kind of routine up, but it did seem to be working for her. Her face didn't even have a faint trace of what might one day become a wrinkle. Carla, like me, had baby frown lines and freckles. Though on her they looked adorable. I just looked five years older than I really was, according to Nick at least. Who had never missed an opportunity to remind me that my 'peak years' were fast running out and that soon I'd be twenty-five and hitting 'the wall'. Even then, he'd complained about me 'wasting money' on anti-aging creams, and said they cluttered up the bathroom. More than once he'd thrown away whole jars of Olay because they were in the way of his hair trimmer or deodorants.

"The dust's just going to stick to you, and the sand," Carla pointed out, once she noticed what Ari was doing.

"What sand?" Ari said. "It's basically road salt."

Carla tisked. "So negative. Lighten up, babe. We're in Greece! Loosen up."

Ari rolled her eyes and dotted sun cream delicately across her cheekbones. "Do you want some of this or are you committed to the leather suitcase look?"

Carla made a grabby hand motion for the bottle and applied the barest hint of sun cream on her arms and face before passing it on to me. I went for full coverage,

65

even though, judging purely from the tight, dry feeling on my shoulders, it was probably already too late for me. It was far from the thick white cream Mum had forced on me as a kid. Even Ari's sun cream was some fancy brand imported from Japan that didn't leave a horrible white cast behind. I was probably never going to feel even half as cool as her.

I dug three of the pre-mixed cans of cocktail out of my bag, where the sweating metal had picked up scraps of fluff and particles of crumbling receipt. With our plastic cups refreshed I raised mine up, already feeling self-conscious before I even began to speak. My suncreamy fingers slid against the plastic.

"Here's to…Lethe, then, I suppose?" I said.

Ari huffed, clearly still nursing bad feeling over our experience so far.

"Oh come on, it's not that bad," Carla said, knocking her cup against mine. "Look, you've got sun, sand…"

"Grit."

"Sea," Carla continued, ignoring Ari's attempt to derail her. "There's music, drinks, good vibes and so many people to have fun with. Even if it's the worst festival you ever go to in your life, at least you got to be here. It's exclusive, remember? That means even if it sucks we can say 'we were there!'. Best of all, we're not stuck at work or hiding from the rain in our damp little house share, watching other people have fun on Instagram."

"…true," Ari allowed, then cleared her throat and raised her cup. "Alright then – to being anywhere but home."

"Anywhere but home," we chorused, and chugged

semi-chilled rum and colas which tasted of aspartame and little else.

With the second drink (third if my first swallow of that petrol masquerading as vodka counted) I felt the warmth in my chest expand. All the clenched up, sharp little worries in me were unravelling. At the very least I was numbing them away. It was the most relaxed I'd felt in weeks. Months. Nearly two years. The sun on my face felt so good and even if the beach was littered with rubbish and the festival was at the centre of a dust cloud, that didn't change anything. I was going to have a good time, no matter what.

"Hey again!"

I looked up at the stranger, a girl about our age in cut-off shorts and a 'Lotus-eaters' t-shirt with the sleeves hacked off.

"Um…hi?" Ari said, sounding just as confused as I felt by this stranger's arrival.

"Micah, hi!" Carla smiled, beckoning her into the heart of our group. "Guys this is Micah, I met her while I was buying drinks at the airport. She lent me change for the vending machine – which I can now pay back," she said, rummaging in her bag.

Micah waved her off with a heavily tattooed hand. "No worries – you two must be Ari and Rosie?"

"Jody," I said, feeling slighted, despite my buzz. That was me, the forgettable one.

"I'm camped up over in the like…southern corner of the campground," Micah continued. She didn't seem to have heard me. "If you guys fancy popping by for a drink one evening or whatever. I've got a link here too, if you're in the mood for something else."

"Oh, cool," Carla said. "How do they get stuff past security? You should have seen the stuff they were confiscating, there was so much of it."

"No idea," Micah shrugged. Her easy smile made me envious. She was so clearly comfortable even though she barely knew us at all. I was anxious around Ari and Carla even having lived with them for a while now. "I mean, it's probably not that hard – not with all the staff, the different businesses coming in and out – plus you know, the sea. Anyone could rock up on a boat, couldn't they?"

"That's a good point actually," Ari said, glancing at the water. "There's no security to stop people just turning up and getting into the festival, is there? Anyone with a boat could just get in for nothing."

"And with anything," Micah said, raising an eyebrow. "Here, let me give you my number in case you feel like hanging out later."

She gestured for Carla's phone and tapped her number into the contacts. Her own phone buzzed with a message and she took it out to save the contact. "Carla, with Ari and Joey."

"Jody," I said, slightly too loud, I realised when all three of them looked at me. "Sorry…it's Jody."

"…cool," Micah said, then widened her eyes slightly at Carla as if to say 'the fuck is her problem?'. I felt my face flush beyond the beginnings of sunburn.

"See you around," Micah exited our little group and headed off across the beach. A moment later I heard her cheerfully greeting someone called Meg. She was just the life and soul of the party. I winced at my own bitterness as if it was a taste on my tongue. I wasn't being fair to her. I was being jealous because she made this all look so easy and I felt like it was the hardest thing in the world to do.

"Right, well, I for one could use something to eat," Ari said, draining the last of her drink. "What do you guys say to finding some chips or something on the way back to the tent?"

"I might stay here for a bit," Carla said, lying out on the concrete. "Work on my tan, recover a bit from the early start. You go on though."

"Alright – Jody what do you feel like doing?" Ari asked.

I felt pulled in two directions. I'd had no plans to leave their sides through this whole four-day nightmare, but I hadn't considered that they might split up. Anxiety churned in my stomach. It was something Mum had drummed into me before I went off to uni. You never walk home alone and you never, ever, let a friend go off on their own. Though no one I'd met at university had seemed to follow that rule. Not even Ari and Carla.

The few times I'd been roped into going out with the girls and their extensive friendship groups, all of them third year students and much cooler than me. I was always the first to head home. I was never good at staying up late when I was tired and footsore and sick of pretending to have a good time. Then everyone else would just stampede towards the next club, leaving me to get the bus by myself. The most Ari or Carla had ever done was say goodbye or ask if I was sure I wanted to go home. Still, nothing bad had ever happened to me. So maybe Mum's insistence was just another of the rules she'd lived by that no one else did – like it being rude to share your problems with people you didn't know well. Something which had locked her away in loneliness after Dad died, and made her determined to surround me with people – no matter how I felt about it.

"I'll...come and get some food," I said, realising that as well as needing the loo, I was also feeling a bit lightheaded from hunger.

"Catch you up later," Carla said, hardly lifting her head up.

Together Ari and I navigated our way across the beach, now completely rammed with people sitting and standing, eating and drinking. The smells of the sea and the sun cream on my skin mingled with that of ripe rubbish which pressed in on me from all sides. I was already dreading the concert that evening, dreaming of the moment I'd be able to get into my sleeping bag and shut out the world. More than something to eat, I was craving the privacy of being in my own head. At least once we were trying to get some sleep I wouldn't have to worry about looking like I was having the best time of my life.

Chapter 7

Ari and I found a stall that wasn't absolutely swarmed with hungry people and got two containers of fries. I got nuggets as well, because I needed something to help keep me from tipping over the edge of buzzed into messy drunk later on. Not because I was particularly hungry. I'd started to feel a bit queasy. It was probably the smell of rubbish, or the early start.

I'd been expecting maybe something a little bit more regional, food-wise – gyros perhaps, or even just kebabs. This stuff was straight out of the late-night takeaways of home, produced so quickly that nothing was crisp or brown, just barely cooked through and bland. It was oddly comforting in a weird way. Something familiar.

"Not a single proper vegan option," Ari groused on the way back to the tent, eating her salted fries. "Not even vegan *mayo*. Festivals are literally packed with veggies and vegans and…new-age type people. Not a single vegan option! We should burn this place to the ground."

I suppressed a laugh at her pantomime of outrage.

"Maybe there're other stalls that have better options? We can look later."

A cloud of purple smoke drifted over us and I waved it out of my face. There were coloured flares going off all over the place. I had no idea if people had brought them in or if they were part of the overall 'experience', but it was making navigating the crowds even more confusing.

"I hope so. I can't last three days on fries. I mean...I could but I'm not gonna. For a start my stomach'll be a mess and I'll be bored out of my mind. Where's the falafel? Where are the smoothie bowls and the bean burritos?" We'd reached the tent and Ari dragged a cheap fleece blanket out of her suitcase and tossed it on the dusty ground to sit on. "I'm making myself hungry."

I sat on the blanket and kept half an ear on Ari's fantasy food rant, the rest of me was taking in the sprawling mass that the campground had become. More and more people had been arriving whilst we were at the beach. We were packed in, only the first to arrive had space between their tents. We'd been lucky to find a patch to set up that wasn't yet hemmed in on all sides, but in the time we'd been gone our neighbours had arrived and pitched their tent less than a meter from ours. The paths between the wobbly rows were barely a foot wide and littered with guy ropes. In just the short time I'd spent looking around I'd seen three people stagger over them, and even as I thought that, I spotted one girl completely face-plant, scattering chips everywhere.

"Ouch," Ari said. We watched her friends scoop her

up, the group weaving drunkenly onwards. "I forgot how fast people get messy at these things."

"Is it going to be like this for the entire four days?" I asked. "Don't they want to remember any of this?" Though to be honest, I would be happy if I could spend the next four days in a semi-drunken fog.

"You do remember it...mostly," Ari shrugged. "It's like...childbirth. You have to forget how horrible it was and cling to the magic or you'd never do it again."

I stared at her in horror, but Ari just laughed. "It's true! Just think of a double rum and coke and a spliff as being the epidural. It gets you through sleeping on the ground, stinking of sweat, hovering over a loo with no seat and eating greasy, awful food that costs twice as much as it should. Being constantly exhausted and thirsty and hanging. Then, once it's over and you're home and you've slept it all off and unmatted the glitter from your hair...you remember the way you felt in the crowd and the moment the beat dropped on your favourite song with thousands of people there screaming. That's the magic part."

I wanted to believe it but I was also worried that I couldn't feel the 'magic' like she could. In a crowd, hemmed in by bodies and sound and being seen – I wasn't sure I could ever feel anything but the desire to escape.

"Speaking of which," Ari said, her philosophical musings apparently done for the evening. "I'm going to get ready to head to the stage. Can't go looking the way I feel – tired and fresh off of a cramped plane."

She zipped herself into the tent and I heard the

rustling of bags being opened. Right, the concert. There had been music all day, pumping through speakers all the way along the security fence. I'd felt its heavy bass line like a second heartbeat since we arrived. But I supposed Ari and Carla would want to see most of the acts live, from in front of the stage. Especially now it was getting dark and there would surely be more of a light show.

The atmosphere was electric and expectant. The campgrounds were full of girls whipping out battery powered curling wands, cases full of makeup and stick on gems. I felt like I was backstage on opening night of a big budget Broadway show – only I was the only one with stage fright. Worse, I didn't even feel like I belonged there, I'd just wandered in off the street and been handed a microphone.

The panic had digested what alcohol in my system hadn't been absorbed by the food. Now the prospect of several hours on my feet, pretending I could 'dance like no one was watching' felt about as enticing as a job interview for something I not only didn't want to do, but which I was unqualified for.

It took Ari a long time to get ready and I sipped my way through another can of pre-mixed cocktail as the air turned gold with sunset and the crowds milled past me. I was starting to suspect that Ari was browsing on her phone or taking a nap. Just taking some space for herself after the long journey, which was fair enough. Though I wished she'd just told me that's what she wanted.

Finally Ari emerged from the tent in a waft of hairspray. She'd put her hair up in a big beehive of a messy bun, leaving plenty of dark strands to frame her face. She'd also changed out of her travelling clothes and into a t-shirt – that she'd cut the sleeves off – and jean shorts, both black. Like the fishnets underneath. Her tattoos, usually at least partially hidden under leggings at home, were on full display – a whole nest of black snakes wriggling down her left leg. She sat down on the blanket and set to untangling a fist-sized knot of silver chains and leather straps.

"Knew I should have wrapped this around something," she muttered, tugging at the tangles.

"I'll do it," I said, holding my hand out. It would give me something to do with my hands. Sometimes I wished I still smoked, just so I had a reason to fidget with something when I felt like this, all jumpy and out of sorts.

"Really? Thanks." Ari passed the…whatever it was, over and I started worrying at the tangled chains. "Are you going to change or go like that? Because I can do your makeup if you want?"

"Oh…yeah, that'd be cool," I said, knowing that even though Ari was great at doing her own winged eyeliner and all-day red lip, I'd probably still manage to look ludicrous. "I actually bought some at the airport."

"I noticed!" Ari grinned, snapping open a magnetic palette and examining her face in it. "Saw the little bag poking out of your pocket. Good for you. There's nothing wrong with rocking a bare face but you deserve to feel special sometimes too."

I squirmed under her attention and carried on with the task at hand. I realised that the thing in my hands

75

was actually two things – a collection of layered silver necklaces and a sort of under arm gun holster without the guns. They came apart suddenly and I held them up for Ari's approval.

"Amazing, thank you." She put both of them on and started to comb out her brows.

"There you are!" Carla said, right behind me. I jumped even though I recognised her voice. "I've been walking around the campsite for twenty minutes. It's a zoo."

Carla sat down on the blanket and eyed our empty take-away containers. "Aww, you didn't get me anything."

"It'd be cold by now anyway," Ari pointed out. "And dusty, probably."

"True." Carla stretched and smiled at me. She was pink with faint sunburn and a handful of new freckles had broken out across her nose. Her pink hair was messy from the sea air and she looked effortlessly cool, just like Ari. She looked like she belonged here.

"Is there time for me to go get something?" Carla wondered aloud, looking around us at everyone else getting ready and drinking, the sun half-set and easing towards night, golden glow fading to blue tinged dusk.

"I've got cereal bars in my bag," I said. "Plus there's the snacks we bought at the airport."

"Hmmm…maybe I'll grab something after the concert," Carla said. "I party better on an empty stomach anyway. Less risk of throwing up over the people in front."

"Just for that, you can stay in front of me," Ari said, glaring at her over her makeup mirror.

"Yeah, yeah...I'm gonna get changed." Carla crawled into the tent and zipped it up. Ari and I exchanged glances as she rustled about, bumping into things. I prayed that the tent wouldn't fall down.

"She's already pissed as fuck," Ari sighed, rolling her eyes in a way that was only half-playful. "I so don't want to end up babysitting her by the end of the night."

"I heard that!" Carla called from inside the tent.

"You were meant to," Ari trilled back, then flashed a smile at me. "C'mon, let me do your makeup. Show me what you bought."

I dug the stuff out of my handbag and Ari picked up the glitter gloss. "This is going to look so cute on you. You've got that like...cherub face? Like I put on glitter and I look like I've been on one for three days with no sleep – but you're going to look like something out of *A Midsummer Night's Dream*."

I didn't really believe her, and yet, once she was finished with my face, I could kind of see it. She'd used some of her own makeup to give me rosy cheeks and a tint of pink to the tip of my nose. My eyelids were dusted in micro-glitter and outlined in violet. With the gloss on I looked a bit like a children's TV presenter at Christmas, but not in a bad way. I felt sort of cute.

"Oh my GOD, what have you done with Jody?" Carla said when she poked her space buns out of the tent. "And who is this ravishing Disney princess?"

I felt myself blush. Ari rolled her eyes and spritzed me with setting spray.

I did end up getting changed in the end. Just into a fresh t-shirt – pale pink, with daisies on it. Carla looked at me for a moment when I exited the tent, then she dived inside and returned with a crown of fake flowers and popped it on my head.

"There, very flower child. Literally. By the way, can I put my phone in your bag? Mine's got no zip and anyone could dip into it."

"Good plan, can you take mine too?" Ari said. "I refuse to lose another phone at a festival."

I accepted their phones and tucked them into my cross body bag. It wasn't a huge bag and the added weight was quite noticeable – what with Carla's phone being a massive slab she could barely wrap her hand around. It was a struggle but I zipped up the inner compartment and the outer zip too. No one was getting their hands on those.

At that moment, the speakers all around us suddenly went off. The air simmered with whoops and cheers, people calling to their friends to hurry up. There were lights flashing over the other side of the festival area – stage lights. Then the music kicked in, louder and more chaotic than the recorded stuff that had been blaring out all day. The sound of an electric guitar was like a fork of lightning.

Carla bounced on her feet. "It's starting! C'mon – let's go!"

My nerves, which I'd managed to forget about during the impromptu makeover, came roaring back. It was like water in the ears, making me feel like I was being dunked underwater without warning. My chest tightened and I felt suddenly like I might throw up. But I hadn't come all this way just to give up now. I couldn't disappoint Carla and Ari, not after they'd tried so hard to make me feel welcome, to make sure I had a good time.

"Ready?" Ari asked, giving my arm a quick squeeze as we followed Carla's bobbing head through the crowd.

"Yup," I lied, offering what I hoped was a convincing smile. "Can't wait."

Chapter 8

It was somehow both better and worse than I'd imagined. Better, because it wasn't like my few experiences of nightclubs, which were always less packed and more brightly lit than in films. Places you could never believe that no one was watching you. Which meant I never felt comfortable in them. Not that I'd been to many in my life. After a few tries in uni I'd sworn off of them. The invites to 'hit the club' had dried up once I was no longer living in my first year spot anyway, my housemates in second year had their own lives and we'd never really gelled as a group. By that time Ari and Carla had cottoned on to how much I hated going out on the town and invited me for coffee instead. Then of course I met Nick and that put paid to that.

In the massive festival crowd, so far back from the stage that it was nearly pitch black except for the phone torches and the occasional overhead flash that reached us, I felt anonymous. I was also too hemmed in for much 'dancing' to be expected and even I couldn't get jumping up and down in place wrong. With several of my worries put to rest I actually started to have a good time. The music was pretty good, at least to my ears, and it was so loud that with my eyes shut I could block out the crowd noise and pretend I was alone if I felt overwhelmed.

Whenever I checked on them, Carla and Ari were right there with me, pogoing up and down to the music. Every so often someone would come past us, sidestepping and weaving through the crowd. Lots of girls with plastic baggies of pills, half-inflated balloons or silver canisters of gas. I'd seen enough of the things rolling around in the street to know what they were – nitrous oxide, laughing gas. I was surprised that they'd made it past security, then I remembered our conversation down on the beach and wondered if a boat had chugged up to the festival like a floating pharmacy.

I was initially a bit worried about the drugs, but no one tried to push anything on me. No one even asked me if I wanted any. It seemed to very much be an 'I'm here if you're interested' sort of arrangement. As I got my breath back between songs I thought of all the assemblies and educational films I'd sat through about 'just saying no'. It seemed all that had been a waste of time. I'd spent most of my teenage years preparing myself to say 'no' and I'd never been asked. It seemed as if the whole thing was more of a buffet situation – there if you fancy it, no worries if not.

It was sort of great actually. Finding out that something I'd been schooled to be so scared of was actually no big deal. I just wished it was as easy to tackle the things that I'd taught myself to be afraid of.

Though it was hard to separate those things from my mother's hang-ups and Nick's rules. Most of the time I wasn't sure where my thoughts began and theirs ended. It was all too jumbled up to separate.

"Do you want half of this?" Carla yelled into my ear during the next song. She was sweaty and glowing in the flashing lights, a tiny white pill held between her thumb and index finger in front of my face.

"No! Thanks!" I yelled back.

That was really all there was to it. Amazing.

"What is it? Where did you get it from?" Ari stopped bouncing to the music and grabbed at Carla's arm, bringing her close enough so they could talk at a more normal volume.

"Some girl and I've got no idea!" Carla shouted, making Ari wince and whack a hand over her own ear.

"God's sake Carla – that could be aspirin for all you know," Ari chided.

Carla just grinned. "Then I won't have a headache later – win win! Do you want some or not?"

Ari glanced at me, then shrugged. "No, I'm good!"

"Are you sure you want to…" was all I got out before Carla popped the pill onto her tongue and swallowed. I really hoped it was aspirin or something equally benign. I had no idea how to handle high people, or what to do if things went south. Especially here.

"Suit yourself!" she crowed, before flashing both of us a megawatt smile and whooping with the crowd. Another song had ended, and anticipation was building for the next. I tried to tamp down my concern about the pill. For all I knew Carla was used to taking random drugs at festivals and clubs. I hadn't gone out with her since I was nineteen and I hadn't spent much time with her on those nights either. I'd mostly stood in a corner, hugging my one drink until I felt like I could justify going home.

After another handful of songs I was starting to feel a bit tired. Everything was catching up to me – the early start, the alcohol, the hours of anxiety – my legs were starting to cramp a bit from the jumping. I paused to stretch them a bit and someone immediately trod on my foot. Inside my canvas combat boot my toes throbbed. Ouch. Limping a bit, I took a few side-steps to keep my balance. When I looked up I realised the people around me had moved too, flowing into the space I'd created like water. Between the shifting people, flashing lights and dense shadows, I couldn't see Ari or Carla anymore. Every time I thought I caught a glimpse of the outline of Carla's hair or the flash of Ari's silver chains it turned out to be a trick of the light, there one moment and gone the next.

As soon as I realised I'd lost them, I started to panic. I couldn't just be out there with no one around me, no one between me and all those overwhelming things. The one loner at the festival. What if I couldn't find them again? I could get lost on the way back to the tent and not find it again. I could feel tears prickling my eyes at the very thought of wandering around the dark campground alone amongst strangers. I wasn't jumping to the music anymore but everyone around me was and I was being jostled about, trapped by the crowd.

When I was eight, two years after Dad died, I'd been sent to a children's therapist because I never talked at school unless someone asked me a question. Even then

I'd only give one or two word answers. It wasn't to do with Dad's passing, I'd always been like that. But Mum had made it her mission to turn me into an outgoing social butterfly, and could finally afford to send me to someone who could 'fix' me since she'd started working again.

The therapist had this poster on her wall. Some Zen thing about surrendering to the flow of the river so you don't get dashed on the rocks. It hadn't made sense to me back then. I'd been quite a literal child and saw no meaning to it except that the picture of the river was nice. Now I understood it – I'd stopped dancing, stopped surrendering and now I was being smashed to bits. I wasn't part of the crowd anymore. I was just in it.

I turned, still looking for the others but also hunting for a clear bit of space – a way to get some distance from the mob. A flash lit up the audience and amongst the smiling, cheering faces, I saw one I recognised. A face that didn't reassure me, but filled me with a sudden, cold terror.

The flashing lights from the stage sparkled off of the ring as it swung on his chain. His hair was freshly buzzed at the sides, the pale skin under the stubble dyed purple and blue by the chaotic lighting. His sweaty t-shirt stuck to the hard lines of his arms, the muscles their own kind of threat – I vividly remembered how they stood out when he heaved a chair across the room.

It was him.

Nick was there, in the crowd.

I felt like everyone around me had used up all the air. A fist clenched tightly around my lungs, around my heart. The sweat on my skin turned cold and as much as I wanted to move, to turn, to run – I couldn't twitch a muscle. Inside I was screaming at myself to go, to get away. But it was like I was a ghost trying to drag someone else along.

Then a pyrotechnic went off, a huge bang that cracked the night air apart like a missile. I flinched and the spell was broken, I was back in my body. I turned and started pressing through the crowd, muttering 'move, please move, thank you' under my breath without listening for an answer. Just repeating it over and over again like it would save me. As if anyone could actually hear me. My head was spinning and I felt sick. The back of my throat tasted like rum and chewed up chips.

I stumbled out of the crowd, to one side of the field – near the security fence at the rear. I caught the metal wire in my fingers and felt my way along it. There had to be a gate somewhere. A way out. I felt like a moth battering against a window, powerless to escape. Any moment now I expected to feel a hand on my arm, fingers on my shoulder or grabbing at my hair. No matter how many times I looked behind me I could never be sure if he was following me or not. There was too much noise and motion and the flashing lights made it impossible to tell if he was right behind me or nowhere to be seen.

I was breathing hard, sucking in lungfuls of dust. I nearly choked on a flying bug, spat it out, and carried on, air sawing in and out of my lungs. Around me I was dimly aware that people were moving, talking, dancing. But none of them mattered. There was only one person in that crowd of thousands that I was thinking of, and I had no idea where he'd gone.

I turned, seeing him in every bulging arm and partially shaved scalp. Every glimmer was the light hitting his dad's ring. Every deep, raised voice was him shouting at me. He was everywhere and nowhere. Like a ghost, haunting me.

With no gate or even a gap in the fence to be found, I went for the next best thing. At the very back of the stage area was a scrubby bit of uneven ground with portaloos on it. This far back from the stage there were also people sitting on the ground or on blankets and jackets to keep the dust off them. It was a bit more relaxed, with more space to move in. Though it was harder to see people's faces away from the light of the stage. I stumbled over broken bottles and crushed cans all over the place. The light from people's phones wasn't enough to see where I was going.

I found a portaloo with its door hanging open and shut myself inside. Standing there, in the dark, I shut my eyes and tried to breathe normally. It didn't help that the inside of the loo stank already, making me feel even sicker than when I'd spotted Nick. My boots squeaked on the wet floor and I felt a wad of something wet and soft squish under my heel. I hoped it was toilet paper. At least inside the little cubicle I couldn't see a thousand different pieces of Nick, swarming in the night.

After a few seconds of fumbling I managed to get out my phone and put the torch on, as the overhead light didn't seem to be working. The slightly warped reflection of an ashen woman speckled with glitter, her mascara smudged over her cheeks, looked back at me.

Slowly, watching myself do it, I calmed my breathing. As the panic dwindled, other thoughts and feelings flooded in. I felt so stupid. Had I really thought I could get away? That I could dress up and become someone else? The sort of girl who never would have put up with Nick for an hour, let alone two years. The type of girl – woman – who could stand up for herself, who always knew what to say and what to do. Who never, ever, ran away with her heart in her mouth, blinded by panicked tears?

Slowly though, my heartrate began to slow. No one was banging on the door or shouting at me. If Nick had seen me in the crowd, he hadn't managed to follow me here. Still, when I took hold of the damp door latch, I couldn't bring myself to release it. I couldn't find the courage to step outside in case he was there. Even if he wasn't – it was dark and there were strangers everywhere. I could hear them whooping and shouting and laughing through the walls of my plastic bolthole. I couldn't face them all, not without Carla and Ari. Every time I thought about opening the door my pulse sped up so quickly that I felt sick.

I couldn't get back to the tent on my own, not like this. I pulled my phone out and scrolled through it before tapping Ari's number as it was first on the list. My heart nearly exploded out of my chest when her phone went off in my bag, buzzing angrily against Carla's. Right, I'd forgotten they'd given them to me to look after. My bag had felt a bit stuffed when I got mine out. We really hadn't thought that through – now I had no way of contacting them.

I stood there for a while longer, my feet aching in my boots. My only options were to try and find Carla and Ari in a crowd that still contained Nick, or to try and get back to the tent by myself. Even without the threat of Nick I knew the odds of finding two people in this crowd were insanely low. Still, I couldn't quite bring myself to step outside and go looking for a way out of the security fence encircling the stage area. Not with everyone else out there anyway. I'd have to wait until it got quieter and then go for it.

I flicked the lid of the loo down with my boot and sat down on it, elbows on my knees so I didn't risk leaning against the walls. The sterile white light from my phone torch illuminated graffiti and patches of melted plastic on the inner walls of the portaloo – names, dates, hearts, swears and nonsense little phrases that probably meant something to one other person in the world. Plus a lot of rude doodles. I read over them, still listening to the crowd outside and the music reverberating through the plastic walls. It helped a bit to have something else to focus on.

Eventually, when I was practically falling asleep, the music ended with a final round of explosive cheers and pyrotechnics. The artillery bombardment was followed by talking, singing both in and out of tune and the rattling of the other portaloos as the crowd dispersed. I knew I ought to leave and try to find my way back to the campground now whilst there were still people to follow, but I still couldn't face it. I sat and waited as the noise quietened down and then, when all but a handful of voices had faded away, I opened the door.

The night air was a refreshing slap to the face after being cooped up in the stuffy portaloo for so long. The sky yawned open above me, free of the light pollution from the stage, the stars shimmered. I stumbled a little, my legs having gone a bit numb whilst I was sitting for so long. The air felt slightly damp as if dew was already forming in it and its chill crept over me.

"Jody! There you are!"

I jumped, but recognised Carla's voice and turned to find her standing a few metres away. She looked dishevelled, one of her buns had come loose and slipped to the side and she was sweaty, her makeup separating. She also looked both irritated and incredulous.

"Where the hell did you get to?" Carla demanded. "We've been looking for you for ages. Ari!" she turned and shouted, getting the attention of everyone else still in the field as well as Ari, who came jogging out of the darkness. "I found her!"

"What the fuck, Jody? Are you ill or something?" Ari asked, sweeping strands of sweaty hair off of her face.

"I'm sorry, I...can we talk about this somewhere else?" I asked, eyes darting about in case Nick had done the same thing as them – hung around to search for me once everyone started to leave.

Carla and Ari exchanged glances. Looks of confusion and concern that made my stomach clench with embarrassment.

"...do you need like, a tampon?" Carla asked eventually, eyeing the portaloos. She dropped her voice even lower. "Imodium?"

"It's nothing like...just, can we leave, please?" I stressed, desperate to get away from the remainder of the crowd and into the tent where no one could spot me.

"...sure, OK, let's get back to the tent," Ari said,

cutting off Carla, who looked like she was about to demand answers on the spot. "I think we could all use a sit down and something to eat. Sober up a bit."

Together, we made our way out of the field and back towards the campground. I was surprised to see that the domes were all still open to anyone who wanted to go in, despite being in complete darkness. There wasn't even a bit of chain across the doorway or a sign saying they were closed. That seemed like asking for trouble, especially with the number of drunk and stoned festivalgoers milling about. There didn't seem to be any staff around either, except the food stall holders. I couldn't remember the last time I'd seen a marshal in a branded t-shirt.

The domes were lit up by fairy lights crisscrossing overhead and the flashes of fireworks from over towards the beach. I could smell a barbeque somewhere and the smell of burning meat made me feel a bit queasy.

We found our tent slightly faster than we had last time and piled inside. Ari wrapped a blanket shawl-style around her shoulders and opened a bag of crisps. Carla kicked off her shoes and dragged her sleeping bag over her lap. I curled up with my arms around myself, still clammy with panicked sweat.

"Alright, so, what the hell happened at the concert?" Carla asked, digging around for snacks in her bag. "You were right next to me and then you disappeared. Did something happen in the crowd, or did you just want a break or…?"

I took a deep breath, already feeling insane before I got the words out. "I um…I saw Nick."

Ari stopped mid-crunch and Carla dropped the

chocolate bar she'd been trying to open. Both of them stared at me as if I'd just told them I'd seen a ghost amongst the festivalgoers.

"Nick as in...your ex, Nick?" Carla said, cautiously. "Here?"

I nodded and felt a chill creep over me that had nothing to do with how late it was. I wet my lips and tried to steady myself with a deep breath.

"I saw him and I panicked. I wasn't thinking clearly, I never can when he's there but...I thought he was going to do something to me. That he'd come here to hurt me," I admitted. "I tried to lose him in the crowd but, I also lost you guys and then I remembered you'd given me your phones so I didn't know how to find you again. I ended up just sort of hiding, waiting for everyone else to leave." I felt pathetic even as I said that last part. "I didn't know what to do."

"The phone thing was a mistake," Ari said. "We realised that once we started trying to find you. Definitely not doing that again, but...hon, do you think you really saw Nick, or was it just someone who looked like him? Wouldn't that be more...likely?"

"I saw him," I maintained. "He's here. He followed me."

"...or," Carla said, gently. "Maybe he's just...also here? I mean there were thousands of tickets to be won and maybe it's just bad luck that you're both here at the same time?"

I thought about it but, it just seemed too unlucky, even by my abysmal track record. That Nick should be here by accident? That would almost be evidence that there was a God and he was out to get me.

"Plus, you know, a lot of guys look like Nick – he's a scruffy white boy with a beard and a creatine habit, they're everywhere," Carla said with a shrug.

"No, I know it was him. It…" my voice trailed off as I realised I wasn't so sure anymore. Or, I was sure, but I was running out of evidence and the will to keep arguing against my friends. In my head I could still see Nick standing there in the crowd, bathed in the light from the concert. But now I had competing versions of that moment, conjured to mind by their doubts. They played alongside my memory, confusing me. Had I just seen someone who looked like Nick and that had spooked me enough to send me running? Was Nick there but not chasing me, just shocked to see me like I was to see him? I wasn't sure which option made me feel worse.

"It did really look like him, if it wasn't actually him," I finished lamely, trying to stop the debate because I just didn't have the energy for it anymore.

Carla reached out and patted my shoulder, then offered me a chocolate bar with her other hand. "Sounds like it really freaked you out, seeing him? You said you thought he was going to hurt you?"

I nodded, taking the chocolate but making no move to unwrap it. I still felt queasy, as if I'd been shaken up like a can of sickly cocktail. At the back of my mind a tiny part of me just wanted to stop the conversation here and crawl into bed. But the rest of me wanted, needed, to just talk. To tell someone, finally.

"It's OK if you don't want to tell us why," Ari said, copying Carla's soft tone. "But if you wanted to, we're both here and we'll help any way we can, OK?"

To my horror I felt myself starting to tear up. I sniffed, tried to fight the burn in my nostrils and the sting in my eyes. Ari and Carla each put an arm around me, squeezing me between them.

"He wasn't just a shitty boyfriend, was he?" Carla said gently. "It's OK…you can tell us."

I shook my head. "No, he wasn't just…" I managed to squeak. "He…he was really awful."

None of us said anything for a while, I was trying to pull myself together, wondering if I could stand to tell them everything. If I could take going over everything and then take knowing that they knew. The two of them were quiet, waiting. They must have been as exhausted as I was but they didn't seem about to give up on me. It felt like they'd wait for the rest of the night if I needed them to. That's what finally did it – the feeling that they'd be there for me, for as long as it took.

"When we met, he was so lovely," I started. "I've never been good at making friends or…but it was like we clicked right away. You guys had graduated, you were moving on, moving away. I wanted to dive right into my second year but I didn't know anyone and I was miserable in that shared house. I never had anything in common with those guys, not really, and they were so hard to talk to. But Nick, he…he did all the work, kept asking me to things or showing up. It was easy, to just let it happen. I'd never had a proper boyfriend before, not even in school when you say you're 'going out' but you never go anywhere really. It felt special. He made me feel special…and then he said he was looking for a housemate and so why didn't I just move in. It seemed like the perfect way for me to have somewhere to live that wasn't that grotty student house, and I'd get to be with him…but right away things were different. He was different.

"He started…telling me off I suppose. Said I was too quiet, too childish, too…everything. Nothing I ever did was right. He said my clothes were embarrassing but he'd change his mind about things so often that I was never sure what would make him happy. I was too slutty, then too frumpy, it changed all the time. He used to shout at me for doing stuff he'd never mentioned before, like leaving a book on the arm of the sofa or making tea in the wrong kind of mug. I bought a new console without asking him – even though it was my money – and he got so angry he threw a chair at the wall.

"He didn't like me talking to anyone else, online or on the phone. He always listened to my calls with Mum and checked my laptop, my phone. I wanted him to be happy with me, to go back to how it was in the beginning, so I kept doing what he wanted and changing things to suit him. I was trying to work out what he wanted and be that, for him. And then…then there was the night I knew I had to leave."

After a short silence, I felt Carla's hand shift on my back, patting gently. "Did he…hurt you?"

I sniffed, nodded once, sharply.

He'd already been hurting me for a while by then, actually. Nothing like you see in films or on TV. He never punched me in the face or broke any bones. He'd just grip me, shake me, or back me into a corner like he *wanted* to hit me. So I knew he could if he wanted to. Nick never dragged me to bed by my hair or knocked out my teeth, but he'd talk and talk and talk at me until I just let him do whatever he wanted. Because the alternative was to hear the awful things he was saying, all whilst he held my wrist like the lead on a dog. The night I'd finally realised I had to get out of there though, that was different. That was the first time someone else had been involved.

I swallowed thickly, not knowing how to put it. "I was at home, doing some coursework and...Nick came back from the gym with a friend. A guy friend."

I felt Carla's hand on my back go completely still. Beside me, Ari inhaled sharply through her nose. They knew. I hadn't even said it yet and they knew. Maybe that was why I was able to get it out.

"He said that it'd be fun and when I told him I wasn't up for...doing that with the two of them, he told me I was being boring and that I was embarrassing him. That he'd promised his friend and I was making him look like a liar. That if I was going to be like this he didn't want us to be a thing anymore. That I'd have to move out." I sucked in a breath and ploughed on. "I was upset and...he twisted my arm a bit, pushed me. I told him I wanted to leave. I had my phone and I wanted to call my mum, because I was thinking about hotels and how I didn't really have a lot of money in my account but maybe she could book me a Travelodge for the night or something. Not that I wanted to call her but I didn't have anyone else at that point. But he took my phone and told me to sit down and when I tried to leave he...um..." a whimper slipped out and I gritted my teeth. "He pulled me back by my hair and kicked my legs so I fell over."

They were both holding on to me like I was about to fall through the ground. I felt solid, real for the first time in a while. It didn't just exist in my head now. It was out there, someone else knew.

"I was freaked out and I think that worried his friend a bit because they started arguing and then the guy left. I still don't know who he was. I never even found out his name. After he ran off I locked myself in the bathroom while Nick was distracted, trying to get him to come back. He tried to get me to come out and I was terrified he was going to break in – even thought about climbing out of the window. But after a while he came and told me that he was going for a walk and that when he got back I'd better have 'calmed down' from my 'tantrum'."

I'd watched him from the bathroom window, not trusting him to have left. Once he was gone I'd come out and seen that he'd thrown a bunch of stuff around – all of it mine. My laptop casing was cracked, though thankfully the screen was fine. He'd smashed my cute mugs, a picture of me and Mum at my graduation ceremony. I'd felt numb, surreal. I tidied up and sat on the sofa and when Nick came back we both pretended like nothing had happened. He said we should go to bed and I went. Like it was all fine.

Only it wasn't fine. I'd lain in bed next to him and it had just…hit me. I was never going to be good enough and Nick was only ever going to want more from me. I knew I ought to leave, but knowing it and doing it were two different things. He'd been pressing me into the dirt for so long that I was too exhausted to fight. I didn't know how to fight. Worse, I was all on my own.

I had no one to turn to except Mum and…even just imagining her reaction made me feel paralysed.

Two days later, I'd been mindlessly scrolling and seen Carla's post about the house share. I looked at it and I wished I had the strength to just message her and make plans and leave. That I was brave and clever enough to do it. But for a year and a half Nick had been reminding me every day that I was stupid and cowardly and messed everything up. So I didn't message Carla then.

I messaged her three days later, when Nick casually announced he'd be bringing his mate over after the gym and that I'd 'better not show him up again'. It turned out that I didn't need to be brave or clever – I just had to be scared enough to run for it.

Carla seemed so happy to hear from me, it almost felt easy. I waited for Nick to go to the gym. I acted like everything was fine and I was the perfect girlfriend until he was gone. Then I packed some stuff and left without so much as leaving a note. I'd had a flood of texts from him when he got home, calls too. From the pleading to the threatening and obscene. I'd been ignoring them all and after a few weeks it had gone quiet. He hadn't shown up at uni like I was worried he would. I'd thought it was over.

"After I moved in with you guys, without telling him where I was going, I thought that would be it. That it was over…but then, recently I went to the supermarket and he was just there. Like I'd never managed to get away. I still don't know how he found me, or if it was just a coincidence. He said he wanted one and a half grand of rent because I just walked off. Said he was going to sell my stuff and he was gripping my arm like…like he was going to drag me out of that supermarket and take me somewhere and I was so scared," I covered my mouth and sobbed, completely losing it as I remembered the look on his face.

Carla and Ari crowded in on me, folding me up in a group hug.

"Oh, Jody," Ari said. "It's OK, it's OK love, he can't get you."

"I saw him," I managed. "I swear I…"

"I know, it probably seems like you see him everywhere," Carla said. "But he's not everywhere. He's just some fucking shit bloke and you're hundreds of miles away from him, OK? And even if he is here, by some fucked up coincidence, he'd have to get through us."

They squeezed me tightly and I let myself cry, properly, for the first time in months. Until finally, I had nothing left to cry out. Carla cleaned my makeup off and the three of us went to sleep – one of them on either side of me, like guard dogs in Primark pyjamas.

Chapter 9

When I woke up it was with a banging headache, partly hangover related and partly caused by crying. In spite of that I felt better, emotionally at least. Not good, or fine or fixed, but better. By a narrow margin, I was somewhat not as devastated as I'd been the night before and that was actually more than I'd hoped for.

Carla and Ari were already awake, making tea on our single burner gas stove outside. One of the only practical things we'd thought to bring. I pulled a hoodie on over my pyjamas and crawled out onto the blanket that had become our outside seating area.

"Morning," Carla said, offering me a cautious smile. "Guess what, we forgot the little things of UHT milk."

"You forgot them," Ari corrected her. "They were on your packing list. Teabags were on mine, which is why we have them," she added, pointedly.

Carla rolled her eyes. "It was a long list."

Ari's eyes narrowed. "That's because it had everything we needed on it. Did you at least remember to pack the instant porridge pots, you know, so we have something to eat?"

"Yes," Carla said, rolling her eyes. Then she paused, looking as caught out as a cat creeping past a security light. "I mean…I packed most of them. Some I might have taken out to fit my curling wand in and then never put back? I'll just buy you guys breakfast if we run out."

"That's going to cost a fortune – you should have seen the cost of the chips we had yesterday," Ari said. "I forgot how expensive festival food is. And the drinks, ugh."

"Daylight robbery," I agreed, and looked up the row towards the gates into the general festival area. There were people all over the place, carrying pale orange takeaway containers, lidded cups and bottles of water. The smell of coffee and frying potato wafted through the air, only slightly tempered by the reek of old cigarette smoke and stale beer that clung to the tent. It reminded me of walking to uni in the morning, past the market and the coffee shops just coming to life.

When I focused on the others again I found them both looking at me. Their expressions of quiet concern almost identical. Though Ari quickly busied herself adding sugar sachets stolen from Costa into my tea and handing it to me. Carla twisted her hands together, nudged Ari's foot and then finally took a breath.

"Jody, listen," she started.

"We don't have to do this now," Ari cut in meaningfully. "Let her have her tea first at least."

"Is this about last night?" I asked, feeling my face go hot. The tin camping mug was burning my fingers and I put it down to tug my hoodie sleeves over my hands as improvised oven gloves.

"Yeah," Carla said. "If…when we get back home, if you want to go to the police we will totally go with you. Won't we, Ari?"

"Of course we will," Ari said. "Anything you need. And you should tell them he's still got your stuff, or have them send someone around with you so you can get it. It's not right for him to get to keep it. Especially if he's going to sell it – he doesn't deserve to get away with that."

My insides were clenched into a tight little ball. I felt like I couldn't breathe, all that panic settling over me again like the clouds of yellow dust drifting through the air around us.

"I told you we should leave it," I heard Ari mutter to Carla.

"No!" My head jerked up and I tried to arrange my face in an expression that wouldn't worry them more. "It's…thank you, for offering I…I just don't want to have anything to do with him and, if I go to the police, if I start trying to get my stuff, it's just going to give him the chance to get at me. He'll get angry and it'll make things worse. It's just not worth it in the end, is it? I'd rather lose all that stuff than have to see him again. What if he…does something?"

"We won't let that happen," Carla assured me. "I meant what I said – he's just a guy and there's three of us. He doesn't stand a chance."

I smiled, trying to placate them, but didn't say anything. I didn't have the heart to tell her that no matter how many of us there were, I'd still be afraid of Nick. It didn't matter if they came with me, along with a dozen police. I couldn't face him. I'd never have the strength to go back to that flat.

I was also afraid that if I ever did find the courage to go to the police and try to get my stuff back or get Nick to stop harassing me, they'd find some way to make it all my fault. It was the same with Mum. I could imagine her voice telling me she'd warned me about London, about moving in with someone so soon, without being married. The idea of being married to Nick made me shudder. At least I wasn't legally tied to him. Even the rental agreement on the flat was in his name only. If it had been even slightly harder to get away from him in the first place, I might not have been able to go through with it.

I still wasn't sure if I had actually seen Nick the night before. In the moment it had seemed so logical – of course he'd followed me to Greece, of course he was right there, trying to get me. But in the light of day it felt farfetched to think he'd followed me to Greece. Nick hadn't followed me from the supermarket to Ludlow House. I still wasn't even sure if he'd meant to run into me in Lidl.

Yet still, I couldn't help the tiny part of me that kept my eyes roving over the people passing our tent. Just in case he happened to be one of them. If Ari or Carla noticed, they didn't let on. There was no way to know if he'd managed to win a festival ticket, like thousands of others. What if one of his friends had won tickets and encouraged Nick to come along? After all, he'd just been dumped as far as they knew.

Whilst I was scanning the crowd for any sign of Nick, I noticed something else. Someone else. A girl was moving from tent to tent, stopping to chat to the clusters of hung-over festivalgoers. She was tall, skinny, with black hair down to her waist. The thing that made her stand out were her clothes – she was wearing a jacket for one, even though it was already really warm, a leather jacket at that, scuffed to hell. Everything else she had on looked like she'd bought it years ago and it was as cheap as it was generic – plastic flip flops, thin maxi dress, a green baseball cap with a peace sign on it. But that jacket looked like it had been expensive, once.

When she reached us she met my eye and gave a friendly smile. Her eyes were hidden behind a pair of purple tinted sunglasses.

"Hey guys," she said, surprising me with an American accent. She'd come a long way for the festival.

"Hey," Carla said. Ari waved, one eye still on the power bank she was trying to plug her phone into, turning the USB connector upside-down and shoving it back in. I smiled at the stranger but didn't say anything. I was more than happy to leave the social stuff to Carla, more so today than ever before.

"I'm just going around asking everyone but, have any of you seen this girl?" She showed her phone around, a photo of a smiling red-head flashing a peace sign at the camera. She was skinny, pale and with slightly fewer freckles than me. Her red hair was on the curly side of wavy. She looked like she was at a festival, judging by the stage in the background, but it wasn't Lethe. The stage was bigger and better than the one we'd seen last night and judging by the smears of mud on the girl's clothes it was somewhere a little less dry and dusty.

"I'm Evie. Her name's Roisin, we came together but I've not seen her since the concert last night," Evie said.

"Oh no," Carla frowned. "And she's not called or texted? Nothing?"

Evie shook her head. "No. I thought she might have hooked up with someone – it's sort of her go-to at these things. But she always texts me and she didn't come back to the tent to get changed this morning or anything. She probably just forgot but, I'm a bit worried. She's never been to Greece before, doesn't speak the language, kind of sheltered, you know how it is."

Carla and Ari shared a look which I told myself was not about me.

"Have you spoken to any of the festival staff?" Ari asked, setting the charger aside with her phone plugged into it.

Evie scoffed. "Tried to, haven't seen a sign of 'em since we came in the gates."

She had a point, I realised. I'd expected to see some kind of staff presence inside the festival. The closest I'd ever come to an environment like this was cutting through a gay pride event in a public park – the same kind of thing, a stage, musical acts, and of course lots of marshals and staff in very visible day-glo jackets. The people making sure everything ran like clockwork and who handled issues on the ground. I hadn't seen anyone like that since we arrived.

"Anyway, if you see her can you tell her to call me, please?" Evie said.

"Sure…can we take your number? In case she's lost her phone or something?" Ari, ever sensible, suggested.

"That's a good idea, I'll send you her picture too – here," Evie took Ari's phone, power bank and all, and added her number to the contacts. "If you text me, I'll let you know when I find her? And if you bump into her just keep her with you and let me know where to pick her up. She can be a bit flaky."

"I hope you find her soon," Carla said. "We'll keep an eye out."

Evie flashed a worried little smile and moved on to the next tent. My phone vibrated in my pocket.

"I just sent you two the number, and Roisin's picture," Ari said. "Just in case you see her and we're not all together."

I opened the text and saved the photo to my gallery. I realised belatedly that from certain angles Roisin and I might look similar. Her hair was redder than mine and she was also much, much prettier than me, with fuller lips and brighter eyes. That felt weird, like finding out I shared a birthday with a tragic event – something that only felt significant because of the pain involved. I shook myself mentally – I was being very dark, considering I had no idea if anything 'tragic' had happened to Roisin.

"Do you think she's OK, wherever she is?" Carla asked. "You hear all kinds of horror stories about festivals, everyone drunk or high, people taking advantage…that's not what's happened here, right?"

"Not sure…there is something a bit off though, isn't there? About the security I mean." Ari was looking around, chewing thoughtfully on her lip. "Normally it's really tight at festivals, keeping out anyone who hasn't paid, and you know, trouble makers. But yesterday at the beach I thought it was strange that there was nothing to stop people just bringing a boat right up to the festival and getting past the security on the gate – I mean, when you think about it, this is kind of a terrible place to hold a festival. Only one road in or out but anyone can just rock up on a boat and get in."

"I suppose," Carla said. "And she was right, wasn't she – Evie. I haven't seen any security guys or festival staff about since we arrived – have you?"

"No," I said, thinking back to last night and my panicked flight across the concert field. I hadn't seen anyone so much as standing by the gates or directing the people to prevent a crush. Not even at the back by the loos, where you might expect to see some loitering, making sure no one was messing about with them.

"It's usually much tighter at these things, security-wise," Ari said. "This is quite lax. No metal detectors, and did you notice how many dealers there were last night at the concert, out in the open? And now, just all over the campground they're not even trying to hide it."

"It was pretty blatant," Carla agreed. "Normally I'd expect a bit of secrecy, but they're passing stuff in the open. It's kind of…cool, though – right? I mean, this is what festivals are meant to be like – the original thing, the summer of love. Not security checks and getting told off by some idiot in a neon tabard for smoking outside of the designated area. It's like…real."

Ari nodded slowly. "You've got a point. I suppose it is more authentic this way, even if it is a bit… unexpected."

"But what if something goes wrong?" I said, a coil of worry squirming in my belly. "A fire or an overdose or someone going missing like this girl – Roisin?"

"We're fine, Jody," Carla assured me. "Just because

the place isn't swarming with health and safety goons doesn't mean we're not actually safe. There's a difference between being prepared for the worst and trying to police everyone and everything that happens here."

I glanced at Ari who only looked semi-convinced. I wasn't at all reassured by Carla's attitude to be honest. I was thinking about how scared I'd been last night, running for my life, afraid that Nick was going to drag me off somewhere for a 'quiet word' and not a single person had tried to help me. I was remembering the metal fence and how I'd not seen any signs pointing to a way out of it. I thought of the chaotically pitched tents and the paths booby-trapped with guy ropes. Despite the constant feeling that I was exposed, surrounded by people watching and judging me, I was starting to realise that we were all sort of on our own. If something did happen, what would we do? Who would we listen to, where would we run?

"Come on, I can't be arsed with porridge," Carla said abruptly, tossing her sealed plastic pot back into the tent. "Can we get some proper food please? Just for today? I didn't even get any dinner yesterday."

Ari eyed the plastic pot of dehydrated oats in front of her. "Fine, but you're buying. They'd better have smoothies. I need vitamins. You coming Jody?"

"I think I'll stay put," I said, feeling like the tent was the one rock I could cling to in the churning ocean of other people. "Finish my tea, maybe have a shower."

"Alright," Ari said, though she shared a look with Carla. "When we come back we'll get ready and go have some fun in the domes, yeah?"

"Sure." I watched them go, sipping on my milk-less

tea. Nick or no Nick, I was starting to feel more than just anxious about being at the festival. It wasn't all just in my head, my neuroses and hang-ups. There really was something about Lethe Festival that was putting me on edge, and whatever it was I wasn't entirely sure I'd seen the worst of it.

Chapter 10

The restless, 'bad feeling' followed me from the tent to the showers. I wanted to freshen up without the added worry of Carla or Ari wanting to go with me. Strangers seeing me shower was one thing, people I knew would be worse. Besides, going by myself would prove that I was over my panic of the previous night. I wanted things to go back to normal. Even as I told myself Nick wasn't around and that I was safe, I could hear him in my head, telling me I needed to 'watch myself'. Could feel his fingers prodding at my thighs and tummy so hard that they left little round purple bruises. At least with strangers I could pretend they weren't there, weren't looking, and reassure myself that I'd never have to see them again anyway.

The showers, I already knew from Carla, were communal. In practice they looked a lot like the ones I'd seen but never used at school – because it had been standard practice to drench yourself in deodorant after P.E. instead of stripping off in front of everyone. In my entire time at school I'd never even seen the shower floor wet. It had always been an extra part of the changing area, and a place to store hockey sticks.

The festival showers were in a sort of shipping container, just spigots on the wall and a partition between each one which only reached about shoulder high. I'd changed into a swimming costume – a black one-piece I'd bought on Ari's recommendation for exactly this purpose. I had a hoodie and shorts on over the top for good measure, with a bottle of two-in-one shampoo and body wash in the front pocket.

There wasn't a queue. It was still early and it seemed as if everyone else had much more to drink last night than I had. Even so, the shower floor was already gross, wet and covered in dead grass and mud where the yellow dust in the air had met the spray from the rusty nozzles. Thankfully like everyone else, I'd chosen to wear flip-flops. Though I noticed as I quickly walked down the centre aisle that not many people were wearing swimming costumes. Despite this, and despite Ari and Carla's reassurances that it wasn't Nick, I still glanced at every face, just in case one of them was him. The jolt of recognition I'd felt in the crowd was still too fresh in my mind. No reassurance, no reasoning, could downplay that. I had seen him and I knew that on an animal level, even if the more logical parts of me had been slightly swayed.

In a cubicle I hesitantly removed my layers. The shower was barely lukewarm but it lathered up my mint shower gel just fine. I didn't linger, but once I was done I felt marginally cleaner and slightly more recovered from last night's drinking and crying. I towelled myself off and put my clothes back on over my swimming costume, which almost immediately started to soak through. It wasn't the most comfortable feeling but at least I was cleaner.

On my way back the campgrounds seemed busier. More and more people were surfacing from their tents, crawling into the daylight as if being born again. Most of them looked bedraggled from last night, sticky with sweat from staying in their nylon sleeping bags in the heat of the day. Everywhere I looked I saw the same weird mixture of sequins, pyjamas, rats' nest hair and made-up faces. Every now and then I heard a whistle or a jeer and spotted a girl scampering by, barefoot in the dust, clutching her heels in one hand, the back of her head invariably tangled to Hell.

"Where the fuck is it?" a man's voice barked, making me jump.

"I don't know!" I heard a woman say back, annoyed but verging on afraid.

My sense of calm was shattered by the anger in the man's voice, tapping into an instinct to freeze. Maybe because he was British and for a second he sounded just like Nick. I came to a halt, maybe a hundred yards from our tent. I was a few feet away from the source of the shouting, a couple, both British, both annoyed and apparently looking for something. He was flinging things out of a two man pop-up tent whilst she stood outside, glaring with a cigarette in her hand. She was chewing her other thumb and shifting from foot to foot.

"You've had it, haven't you?" The man snapped, struggling to his feet. He was red in the face, arms bulging out of a faded t-shirt, another reminder of Nick.

111

Panic darted through me at the thought of him using the fists clenched at his sides.

"No, I haven't. You probably dropped it." The woman glanced around nervously. "I've got to go anyway. My friends'll be waiting for me."

"Not until I find my shit, you don't," he said, as he grabbed her by the arm. "Turn out your pockets."

"What? No!" The woman tried to wriggle away but he had a grip on her that I was very familiar with. There was no getting out of it once you started to panic, Nick had taught me that. "I don't steal from people, Jesus Christ!"

"You sure? Seems like a good racket. You sell me the stuff and then crawl into my tent, nick it right back. The fuck are you looking at?"

I realised, to my horror, that he was talking to me. Probably because I was just standing there, staring at him. The woman turned to look at me as well. I was aware of other people moving around, passing me on the narrow path. Yet no one was stopping or trying to intervene at all. They were all either caught up in their own business or trying hard to ignore what was going on. The few I managed to make panicked eye contact with quickly looked away. They didn't want to involve themselves as I stupidly had by simply freezing in place.

"Well?" the man demanded.

I was caught between wanting to run away with my head down and standing frozen in place. This wasn't something I was built for. To my everlasting shame I was the sort of person who hunched down in their seat on the train when someone else was being harassed. I'd turned around in the street before to avoid a drunk

112

cornering some poor pedestrian. I pretended not to see or hear it when my fellow customers berated baristas and receptionists. I didn't want to get involved, ever. But this time was different. This time I didn't get the choice.

He was in front of me within moments and I staggered backwards, off balance as I tried to put some distance between us. My wet feet were slipping around in the stupid cheap flip flops I had on. My heart was trapped in a fist, being crushed and I wanted to run but couldn't make my legs work properly.

"You one of her friends, eh?" he said, gesturing between me and the woman he'd been fighting with. When I looked at her she was watching me with big eyes, her face frozen between worry and relief that she wasn't alone in this anymore. As if I was going to be any help.

"She either gives me my stuff back or I get my money off of one of you," he said, taking another step towards me, one hand moving towards my arm. "I don't care which."

I thought of Nick grabbing my arm; telling me I needed to lose weight, clean up, wanting to know where dinner was, demanding rent money. I shuddered. The tea I'd had at the tent swirled in my otherwise empty stomach, threatening to rocket up my throat. I could feel my airway closing up, my fingers turning cold as terror set in. I felt quite far away suddenly, watching myself as he came closer, as his fingers curled around my wrist and squeezed. I tried to cry out but my tight, dusty throat just made a croaking noise. Like a dying bird.

The girl ran. Fair, I wished I could do the same but I was stuck.

"Hey!" he twisted around but didn't let go of me. "Stop her!"

No one moved to do so, a couple of people glanced our way. A few even frowned. I wanted to shout for help but my throat was clenched tighter than a fist. I could barely breathe, let alone speak. The man's grip on my arm was grinding my bones together now as he turned back to me – the other woman now safely out of his reach, swallowed up by the morning activities of the rest of the festival.

"I want my sixty euro back, or the pills," he said, tugging hard on my wrist. "Look at me!"

He shook me again and I dragged my eyes from the passers-by back to his red face. A day's worth of stubble clung to him and there was a smear of pinkish lipstick by his jaw. His face was glistening with sweat but his eyes were cold, dead things. More grey than blue but still, they were the same as Nick's when he was angry.

I flinched when his other hand started grabbing for the front pocket on my hoodie. The bottle of shower gel fell out the side and hit me on the foot, crushing my little toe. I hissed in pain but he didn't react, didn't stop.

Then, abruptly, he was gone.

I was nearly knocked off my feet by the force with which the man was pushed away from me. I staggered a bit on my flip-flops and automatically ducked as I tried to make myself as small of a target as possible. After scuttling several steps I turned back, fearful of being grabbed from behind.

The red-faced man was struggling with another guy, who had him by the arms. This man, who had come to my rescue, was the same average height, but obviously stronger. When my attacker was shoved towards his tent, he tripped over his own feet and landed on the nylon canopy, immediately crushing the poles underneath. He rolled around in the decimated tent, kicking at the bags and other rubbish that were caught under the canopy, swearing and flailing as he tried to get up.

"Stay there," the new guy ordered. He had an accent, Russian maybe or eastern European. I wasn't that good of a judge. He looked about my age, maybe a bit older, with curly dark hair and a neat beard. He also looked absolutely furious – which didn't exactly fill me with relief, but then, he wasn't looking at me. He wasn't angry with me. All that fury was reserved for the man whose grip I could still feel on my arm. When I looked down I saw the imprints of fingers turning from white to red as blood flooded back into my skin. It would bruise, I knew from experience. One way or another I was never going to be rid of Nick's mark on me, I thought.

"Who the fuck do you think you are?" the man on the ground was raging, pulling himself to his feet using the battered tent.

My rescuer kicked at his leg and the guy fell back again. I winced as he flopped onto the hard ground. My eyes darted away but I was still unable to really move now that the adrenaline of my rescue had passed and I was afraid again. Of what I didn't know. The man who'd been hurting me or the furious man who'd stopped him?

115

"I said, stay there," the latter said. "And listen."

"You'd better start running now before I…"

"No, you'd better pack up your shit, and get out of here before I decide you're worth the trouble of dragging you to security," the dark-haired man interrupted him. "Threatening people, extorting money—"

"I haven't extorted anything!" He wasn't trying to get up now, just frozen there in the middle of his crushed tent, glaring up at the two of us. "I just want what's mine! She stole from me, sold me some pills then practically threw herself at me last night. Now I can't find the pills because she took 'em to sell 'em again."

"This woman?" the dark haired man gestured at me. "I doubt it."

I felt a stab of embarrassment. I clearly looked too boring to be a drug dealer, or too unattractive to pull even this horrible man. It was like feeling too ugly to be catcalled – I knew it was really screwed up to feel invalidated by it, but I was hurt just the same.

"It was the other one! She ran for it," my attacker snapped.

"That's done with then, right?" the dark-haired guy said. "Either that girl took your shit or she didn't, but this woman hasn't done anything so leave her alone."

I glanced his way and was surprised to find him holding out his hand in my direction. He was wearing a faded grey band t-shirt and jeans, one of his arms had a tattoo down it, of an arrow with multiple black triangles and lines coming off of it. He waved his fingers impatiently, and I realised he was indicating the path ahead. Inviting me to leave.

"You should go," he said, when I still didn't move. "Now."

I opened my mouth and managed a small, dry, squeak. After swallowing to try and dredge up some saliva, I said, "Thank you."

He shrugged. "No problem. Enjoy the festival."

It was as if having permission to leave released the tension in my body. I hurried away and didn't look back until I was back at our tent. When I got there and finally glanced behind me I couldn't see either of them anymore.

Carla and Ari were already back, sitting on the blanket and halfway through their takeaway breakfasts. A third polystyrene container was sitting, closed, in the empty space and I sat down next to it. My legs felt rubbery and it was probably mostly shock, but the sight of food reminded me that I'd also not eaten anything yet.

"Are you alright?" Carla asked. "You were gone a long time – we've been back ages and that was after the queue. You wouldn't believe how many people here didn't bring any food."

"How irresponsible," Ari muttered, smirking to bring me in on the joke at Carla's expense, but I couldn't smile back.

"She's so mean to me," Carla pouted. "Where were you anyway?"

"I, uh…I went for a shower and—"

"Oh, was it gross?" Carla asked, interrupting me and wrinkling her nose. "I kind of wanted to give my hair a refresh but if it's nasty in there I won't bother. I'm getting flashbacks to swimming lessons with the school –

117

you know, there'd always be that one soggy plaster on the floor and you'd get a notice about verrucas a week later." She shuddered and made a theatrical retching noise.

"I'm still eating," Ari complained.

"Verrucaaaaaaaas," Carla said, wriggling her fingers spookily. "Great big fungal, mushroomy verrucaaaaaaaaaaas."

Ari threw a piece of fried mushroom at her and Carla shrieked, batting the oily food away from her clothes.

"It was fine, I suppose," I said, not really listening to them, I still felt weirdly distant. "I took so long because I got sort of...sucked into this argument on the way back. There was a guy going absolutely mad at this girl he'd hooked up with. Said she stole drugs from him." I tried to sound a little blasé about it, the same way Carla occasionally talked about creepy men on the tube at night. But even I wasn't convinced by my performance. My voice was actually shaking.

"Oh my God, what happened?" Ari said, a forkful of fried mushroom halfway to her mouth.

"He saw me looking at them and turned on me. She ran off and he...he grabbed my arm," I swallowed, dug my fingernails into the Styrofoam container. "It was really scary."

"Where is he now? We should get security," Carla said. "If we can find them that is. If not I'll kick his arse for you. We both will, won't we, Ari?"

"Oh we absolutely will. I am full of mushrooms and tofu scramble and I have the strength of five men, easily," Ari agreed, but she still looked worried. "How did you get away?"

"Another guy jumped in to help me. Pushed the first guy over and told him to piss off and leave me alone, basically."

"Oooh," Carla grinned and nudged my knee with her foot. "Was he cute? Your face says he was cute."

I felt my cheeks burning as I thought back. He had been really attractive, I just hadn't had the mental space to process it. But now I felt even more embarrassed to have acted like a mindless idiot in front of him. "He was...actually quite cute, yes."

"Did you get his number?" Carla demanded.

"No. I just ran back here," I said, wincing as I remembered how he'd had to tell me to go multiple times before he got through to me.

Carla looked very disappointed. "Oh."

"She was in flight-or-fight mode, Carla," Ari sighed, clearly exasperated. "I know you've added 'flirt' into that combo but the rest of us haven't."

Carla picked up a piece of toast crust and threw it at her. It landed in Ari's hair and she shook it off with a sigh.

"Well, at least someone was around to help," Ari continued. "I think you were right, Jody. The security situation isn't great."

I nodded, then finally opened my breakfast box and started picking at the mostly cold contents. I was worried about the security thing and the general lack of safety precautions like first-aid stations and fire buckets. It all felt very precarious suddenly. Like we were just waiting for some trigger to turn everything on its head.

Still, the thing at the forefront of my mind just then

was the guy who'd rescued me. I had a little daydream about him rescuing me, defending my honour and then scooping me up off my jelly-legs and reassuring me that no one would ever speak to me like that or grab hold of me again. As fantasies went it was very tame but it also helped to relax me a bit. Even if the reassurance wasn't real, it still worked.

There was no way I could have handed him my number or even asked his name. I'd have died of embarrassment before I managed to get out half a sentence. But there was no harm in thinking about him. It wasn't like I was ever going to see him again.

Chapter 11

After breakfast Carla took forever to get ready. Once she had her hair coiled into space buns and a full face of makeup on, including stick on gems and a metallic temporary tattoo, she started on me. Hair, makeup and an outfit accessorised with borrowed bracelets. It took two t-shirt changes and three attempts at my eyeliner before she was satisfied. But I didn't mind. I was happy to be chilling at the tent actually. At least there I was in one place and could keep an eye on the people passing us by. I wasn't sure who I was more worried about seeing again; Nick or the horrible little man I'd met that morning.

Unfortunately, once we were all dressed and Carla was satisfied with my makeup, she and Ari wanted to go and explore the amusements outside the campground. Since my choices were to stay behind alone or tag along, my anxiety made the decision for me. True, I could have asked one or both of them to stay with me. They'd promised not to abandon me, but I'd have rather walked on broken glass than make myself feel like I was ruining their good time. So I went along. It wasn't just out of guilt that I went with them though. I was also slightly worried that one of them – most likely Carla – would go off the rails or get into trouble and I'd wind up feeling responsible. After all, Carla had already taken drugs from a stranger and once we reached the amusement area, I remembered the way she'd been drawn to those hangover IV set-ups.

"You weren't being serious about having a go on those drip things?" I asked Carla as we navigated the crowds in between the amusement domes.

"Not right now," Carla replied. "I mostly feel alright after last night but, maybe tomorrow if we go hard today. I don't want to lose a day to a hangover."

I wasn't sure if she was poking fun at me or if she really was considering it. I decided not to mention it again. We hadn't been back in each other's lives long enough yet for me to argue about it with her. I didn't want Carla to start thinking of me as more boring or annoying than she already did.

"What do you want to try first?" Ari asked.

"Not the rain room. Big fat pass on that one," Carla muttered. "How about the hookah bar? Wasn't that a thing on their social media? I've never used one before, that could be cool."

"I think I saw that on Instagram. None of us smoke though," Ari pointed out.

"But I used to. You used to. We could give it a go just for today, it wouldn't kill us to just try it," Carla said.

"Jody hasn't smoked though – have you Jody?" Ari said, giving Carla a pointed look which only I caught, ironically.

I felt the back of my neck go hot. "I have actually."

"Jody!" Carla practically shrieked, throwing an arm over my shoulder and squeezing me tightly as she bounced in place. "You dark horse!"

"It was just for a bit, in second year." I didn't add that it was mostly because my second year housemates smoked and I wanted to fit in. I'd picked it up so it was less obvious that I was trailing after them at parties. That and I knew Mum would hate it. Smoking was right up there with huffing glue and anonymous sex on her list of 'things that will destroy your future'. The furthest I'd gone was puffing on a Marlboro on the back doorstep. I hadn't even enjoyed it and I'd quit when I met Nick and he gave me a lecture about my health – at the time I thought that was sweet.

"Come on, let's find it and see who else is around," Carla said. "We might join up with a group or something."

She moved through the crowd like a human cowcatcher, towing Ari and I behind her. We exchanged looks and Ari stuck her tongue out at Carla's back. I giggled, but still my eyes wandered to the faces of those around us. I kept thinking I saw Nick, and I did – in the shape of one man's eyes, or another's hair. I smelled his deodorant in passing and thought I heard his voice raised in the distance. Nick was everywhere, in tiny pieces of everyone. Inescapable.

Carla led us on a looping trail which ended at the hookah dome. Inside, the dirt floor was covered with cheap mandala throws and dotted with beanbags and floor cushions. There were quite a few people in there, with very little space between the groups.

The atmosphere was predictably smoky and oddly scented – not just tobacco but other, more perfumed smoke. It didn't stink of weed, I wasn't sure it was drug related at all. Though I didn't have much experience to draw on.

"There's a free one!" Carla grabbed my arm and steered me towards the far side of the dome. I winced as her fingers jabbed into the beginnings of the bruise left by the guy I'd met that morning. Thankfully she let go when we reached the vacant hookah, which looked far more complicated than a simple cigarette.

"Blue lotus and mugwort," Carla read from a card tied around the neck of the pipe, "sounds witchy…and like something from *Lord of the Rings*."

"They're both herbs meant to open you up spiritually, give you a bit of a high," Ari said, taking a seat beside us on the floor cushions.

"Of course you'd know that," Carla said, rolling her eyes. "I bet you had a witch phase when you were a teenager – I can see you sticking pins in pictures of girls you didn't like and waving incense around."

"Who says I don't still do that?" Ari said, a wicked smile on her face as she wiggled her fingers as if casting a spell.

"Is that why you're so private about your room? Is there a little altar in there with our hair and toenails on it?" Carla asked. "Actually the one time I used your laundry detergent I did twist my ankle on the way home from the laundrette."

I snorted a laugh and immediately felt embarrassed, but Carla only grinned at me.

"You got me – I curse all my household essentials,

don't touch my almond milk or you'll go blind," Ari said as she picked up one of the pipes. "Do they have sanitizer or anything?"

"I don't think so," I said, looking around. How many people had used these hookahs since the festival started yesterday? Just thinking about it made me feel like I needed to brush my teeth and gargle. I hadn't even touched the thing yet and my tongue felt furry.

"Oh come on, don't be such a princess." Carla wiped her pipe off with the hem of her lavender t-shirt. She took a puff on it and wiggled her eyebrows at us as she held it in, then slowly let the blue-grey smoke flow from her mouth, wrinkling her nose thoughtfully.

"It's rank, isn't it?" Ari said, unimpressed.

"Surprisingly no. It's OK actually." Carla watched the smoke drift upwards. "No worse than the shit weed we used to buy at uni."

Ari looked at me, then shrugged, wiped off her own pipe and tried it.

"See, it's fine. Besides, smoke's like...cleansing, right?" Carla said, waving at me. "They're self-cleaning."

I didn't believe that for a moment, but I also didn't want to sit there and be a buzz kill. I gave the pipe a quick clean on my shirt and sucked in a lungful of smoke. The urge to cough was immediate but thankfully it didn't last long. I'd never thought of smoking as being anything like riding a bike before but apparently once you knew how you didn't lose the knack.

It wasn't too bad actually. I'd never liked the taste of cigarettes – even though the smell of them, unlit, was so rich and lovely. I had no memories of my maternal granddad, who'd died when I was two, but I'd always

125

been reminded of him when I opened a new pack and released that scent. This smoke tasted floral, medicinal almost. It reminded me of the health-food shop I'd worked in whilst I did my undergraduate degree; that same mix of aniseed and dried green things.

"Nice," Ari said, after a while. "Did you know, mugwort's used for lucid dreaming? And telling the future. I wonder if it'll still be in our systems when we go to bed tonight?"

"I hope not," I said, without really thinking about it. "I don't want to think about the future."

I jumped a little when Ari put her arm around my shoulders. "Only good dreams for you. I'm a witch, I can do that. Besides, mugwort's also used for protection and warding off evil. So you'll be safer than ever after a few puffs. Trust me."

I managed a small smile and distracted myself with another puff. I didn't believe in magic, but perhaps one of the herbs in the blend was some kind of natural sedative because I was starting to relax a little. Even if it wasn't real and just the result of Ari's reassurance, or placebo effect, I wasn't going to turn down a little bit of peace.

Unfortunately the buzzing of my mobile broke the fragile sense of calm I'd been fostering. Not many people had my number and none of the options were good – Nick, using a number I hadn't yet blocked, someone from the university or my mother. Still, I took it out and looked at the screen. Mum calling. Great, it was as if she knew what I was up to and wanted to register her disapproval.

"Shit," I said, mostly to myself.

"Who's…Oh," Carla glanced at my phone. "Do you need to get it? Or can you decline and we'll just pretend she never called?"

Carla and Ari didn't know a lot about my mum. I hadn't shared much with them when we were at uni or since moving back in with them. Both of them however had apparently picked up on something, probably when I took phone calls around them. A few weeks ago I'd been talking to Mum on my mobile in the kitchen. When I was done and hung up, Carla had whistled and Ari had said, slightly more diplomatically, 'she asks a lot of questions, doesn't she?'. To them it must have sounded like an interrogation. My end of the conversation was mostly weak justifications, 'Yes', 'No' and 'I will, I promise'.

My phone stopped vibrating and I had nearly breathed a sigh of relief when it started going again. Mum must have hit redial right away. She wasn't one to take no for an answer. Or even no answer, for an answer. The sigh still came but it was more aggravated than I'd intended.

"I should probably answer. She'll just keep calling until I do. Or she'll start sending a million voicemails asking if I'm OK because she's so worried." I winced at the venom in my own voice. I felt as if the smoke had loosened my tongue. I didn't normally talk much and I never volunteered information about things back home. It was too embarrassing having to admit just how much control Mum had over my life and how lonely my world had been before university.

"I'll just be outside," I said and got hurriedly to my feet. I answered the phone as I was picking my way out of the dome and nearly tripped over a girl's knee as I did so.

"Hey, watch it!" she snapped, brushing dust off of her denim shorts and glaring up at me whilst her friends gave me side eye.

"Shit, sorry," I muttered.

"Language, Joan," Mum said, sounding scandalised. "I taught you better than that."

I winced. She was the only person who used my real name – my Christian name, as she insisted on calling it – I'd tried going by 'Jo' at school and she'd squashed that with the help of my teachers. She'd been so against it that the name was permanently ruined for me, even once I got another chance to use it. Jody was meant to be a more modern version of 'Joan' – according to the net – and I'd started using it when I left home to go to university the first time.

"Sorry, Mum. I tripped. Everything OK at home?" I said, keeping my voice down in case anyone overheard me. What kind of woman got interrogated by her mother over the phone at a festival for God's sake? Just me apparently.

"Oh, fine. Good. As to be expected," she said, with so much forced casualness that I felt my entire spine tense. "It's been quiet here and you hadn't rung me in a while, so I was worried about you."

I'd phoned her two days before leaving for the festival. It hadn't even been a week yet. Though to be fair back during my first time at uni I'd rung every other day, sometimes every day. I hadn't really had anyone else to talk to, even with Ari and Carla I'd felt like I was putting on a front. Pretending to like what they liked so they wouldn't get sick of me. As much as Mum piled on the pressure to 'make friends and join in' she at least knew me for who I was – she just didn't think who I was, was enough.

I'd gotten down to a phone call every two to three days whilst I was with Nick but that was mostly because I was caught between the two of them, trying to keep him and my mother happy was like trying to balance plates. Plates that were adept at loading on the guilt and shouting at you.

"I'm actually away at the moment, sorry," I said, trying to pick my way through the truth without giving her too much ammunition. "Signal's a bit rubbish so I might have to go in a second if it drops entirely…"

"Away where?" She was on it like a crow ripping into roadkill.

Why had I said anything? She just made me nervous and I'd given myself away. "Just away with some friends for a few days. Quick break to celebrate the end of term. I thought you'd be pleased I was being sociable."

She sounded more disapproving than pleased. I could imagine her in one of her pink or mauve fleeces, with her arms folded across her chest, leaning against the kitchen wall with the landline cord twisted around her finger. "What about Nick? You've just left him to fend for himself? I'm surprised at you."

Fend for himself, like he was a pet I needed to feed and take care of. Mum had a lot of ideas like that. When I was choosing my GCSE subjects she'd insisted on Food Technology so I could 'make a proper meal for my family in the future'. It was the same reason she'd taught me to sew on buttons, polish shoes and clean an oven. All part of the plan to secure me a future free from loneliness; if I could make a perfect shepherd's pie I'd surely always be surrounded by my husband, children and friends aplenty. Even at the time I'd wondered why I couldn't just learn these things so I could do them for myself. Apparently it was only worth the effort when it was to win other people over and keep them happy so they'd stay.

Sometimes I pitied Mum. She'd spent years with my dad and me, doing what she was raised to do – being a good wife and mother. Then he'd died and she'd been left with nothing much to show for it. No friends, no career, just a little girl to take care of and bills to pay. Any friends she'd had were pre-marriage and she hadn't kept in touch. Maybe she'd thought she didn't need them anymore. Maybe they'd been too busy with their own husbands and children and just drifted away.

Maybe that was why I said it then. That old mix of pity and irritation at the back of my mind pushed me into it. Or perhaps that was a cop-out and I wanted to say it, to prick her back the way she was always pricking me, drawing tiny amounts of blood every time she opened her mouth.

"We broke up, actually," I heard myself say. "Nick and I are no longer together."

The phone line hummed into the silence. I could sense her shuffling her deck of reactions, choosing carefully, making sure it was just the right thing to send me spiralling.

"Oh…Joanie."

A classic. The disappointed tone caught me right

130

between the ribs like a physical blow. Those two words said a lot of different things:

I knew you'd ruin it

I knew it wouldn't last

I told you so

You should have listened to me, you know I'm always right.

And the classic – *don't you think it's time for you to come home?*

"Do you need any help with the rent?" Mum asked, with a sigh. "I might be able to pick up a few extra days and I can always cancel my coach trip to Cornwall…"

"It's fine, I moved out of the flat and I'm not paying that much in rent now," I said. "Because I left him, so he's still there. Sorry, I meant to give you my new address but, it's fine for the moment I'm having everything forwarded."

"Oh, well…are you sure moving was wise? What about your degree? Where are you staying – are you in campus housing again? What if something had happened? I wouldn't have known where you were!" Mum was on a roll now and it didn't seem as if she planned on stopping.

I shut my eyes and dug the nails on my free hand into my palm. The barrage of questions buzzed around me, swarming through my head. Each one was accompanied by several more unspoken, pointed, queries – *why didn't you tell me this? Why did you leave him? Why didn't you try harder to keep him? Why haven't you come home? Why why why?*

My mouth tasted like burned flowers and my head was swimming. I wasn't in the right state of mind for

131

this. Whatever 'properties' those herbs had, making it easier to talk to your mother wasn't one of them. Maybe Ari could mix up a spell to give me a spine. Or just get me a cocktail so I could forget this whole conversation ever happened.

"I'm fine, Mum," I said blinking back tears of frustration which felt as sharp as glass. "I moved into a house share with the girls I lived with in first year. I'm actually saving money. It's all going fine. I'll text you the address later, when I'm back home."

"This is your home, Joanie – here, with me," Mum said, managing to sound both sad and aggrieved. "It'll always be here, waiting for you."

Didn't I know it? Waiting for me like a mousetrap, luring me in to never let me go again.

"I know," I said. "I've actually got to go now, Mum, sorry. Love you."

I hung up whilst she was saying goodbye and turned my phone off. I wouldn't need it again unless Carla, Ari and I split up, and after last night and this morning's awful experiences, I wasn't letting that happen again any time soon.

Chapter 12

"Hey, you were gone a while, thought I'd come out and check...oh, Jody," Ari said, when I immediately burst into tears upon hearing her voice. She wrapped an arm around me and shepherded me around the side of the dome so that we were between it and the next one along. There was nothing there except a load of electrical cords and bare dirt. At least we were mostly out of view of the crowds. Not that anyone seemed to be paying us any attention. We were only on the second day and apparently crying girls were already just part of the scenery. Like rubbish and drunk people passed out on the ground.

"Is everything OK with your mum?" Ari asked. "Has something happened? D'you need to go home?"

I shook my head, wiping my face with my hands. Ari smelled of herbal smoke and sun cream, it was weirdly comforting. "It's nothing like that. She's fine."

"OK...what's got you so upset then, eh?" she asked. "Did she um...give you a hard time, like before? About the festival or...Nick?"

I sniffed, upset and humiliated and wishing I'd never

133

answered the phone at all. "She wanted to know where I was and I ended up telling her about Nick. That I left. Not that he...not everything else."

Ari seemed to digest this for a moment, still lightly patting my shoulder.

"Do you feel like you can't tell her, about everything else?" she said, finally.

I nodded, struck dumb by a fresh wave of tears. I couldn't really put into words what it was I wanted. Part of me was crying out for my mum, but not my actual mother. I think what I really wanted was the idea of a mother, and just then Ari was the closest thing to a nurturing presence. At least she wasn't judging me, blaming me. I just wanted someone to hold me and tell me I was going to be OK. Was that so much to ask?

"Oh, hon, it's OK. You don't have to tell her everything right now. Or at all, even," Ari said, holding on to me and swaying slightly, calming me. "You can keep it between us three if you really want to. I'm sorry we started talking about the police and stuff this morning. It felt like the right thing to say but...I thought afterwards, actually we don't know how hard this is for you and it should be about what you want. Not what I think is the right thing to say."

I gulped air, trying to steady myself. "Thank you. It was...it helped, a bit. It was good to know you guys were there for me. I just...I don't know how to tell her." I shook my head, frustrated. "It's not that...it's more like..." I gestured helplessly.

After a few beats of silence Ari said, "Is it more like you don't know how she'll react?"

I shook my head and swallowed down the lump that had risen into my throat. "It's not that. It's that I do know how she'll react and I don't think I can stand it. I want to be wrong about it but...I don't think I am. Every time I turn to her for support I feel stupid when she doesn't say or do the right thing. Because I should know by now that she's not...who I need her to be. She never has been."

Ari sucked air in through her teeth, glanced around as if for help. I couldn't blame her, that was a lot to dump on her and I felt awful for having done so. I bit my tongue and resolved to keep my emotions more firmly under control. I didn't want to scare Ari or Carla away.

"Do you want to get a drink and talk about it?" Ari asked eventually.

"No, no I don't. I don't want to ruin any more of the festival...can we just talk about it when we're back home? For the next couple of days can we just pretend everything's fine?"

"Not sure you can do that, or that you should," Ari said. "It's OK to be upset, Jody. It's not ruining anything for you to just feel your feelings, you know? Maybe if you get it all out you'll start to feel better."

I knew she was probably right but I didn't want to take the chance that it would just make things harder to deal with. Ari and Carla could reassure me all they wanted but that only made me feel worse. Paradoxically the more they tried to tell me I wasn't ruining their trip the more I felt like a burden.

"Should we get Carla and check out whoever's playing at the moment?" I said, to change the subject. "I've never heard of any of the people on the posters."

Ari looked at me for a moment, clearly not fooled one bit by my sudden change of topic. Still, she let it go, apparently deciding she'd pushed me enough. "Yeah... me neither – I think they're probably fairly indie, regional. Last night was pretty good though. I liked some of the covers they did."

"I didn't realise they were covers," I admitted. I wasn't much into music. What I liked I'd liked for a long time – songs I'd heard on holiday in my teens and albums I'd bought at fifteen with my pocket money. Mum's musical tastes were just as sparse as mine but I'd taken possession of her collection of *Now That's What I Call Music* albums in my teens. Consequently most of my favourite songs were at least twenty years old.

"Yeah, it's a bit weird now I think about it. Small bands I've never heard of, but they're covering some really recent songs," Ari shrugged. "I don't know, maybe the organisers are hoping to get away with not licencing anything. I don't know how that stuff works."

"Hey," Carla appeared at the end of the passage between the domes. "There you are – I thought you'd ditched me. Are you OK, Jody?"

"I think we should strike that question from our lexicon for the rest of the trip – yeah, Jody?" Ari said, giving me a gentle nudge.

"Yup," I nodded, hoping that if they stopped asking I could try and keep a lid on things, at least until we got home and I could sort through everything in private. It at least felt possible for me to do that now, which was an improvement on before when I'd just wanted to hide and let whatever happened, go on without me.

"We were about to ask if you wanted to head over

136

to the stage," I said to Carla, who was still looking between Ari and I with mild curiosity. "See if whoever's playing is any good?"

"Sure. Sounds like a plan, I'm all blissed out and ready to vibe," Carla smiled, stretching her arms over her head and attracting attention from a passing group of guys. Intentionally or not, I wasn't sure. She didn't so much as glance their way as we left the domes anyway.

We headed over to the stage area, stopping to buy some drinks on our way. The bars were no less busy than they had been before. If anything the lines were longer. People must have used up their contraband alcohol on the first night and were now stuck buying drinks. Still, standing in the queue gave me some time to settle myself and people watch instead of obsessing about my mum.

As we wandered away towards where the music was being played, sipping on sticky pink cocktails I noted the size of the crowd by the stage, which was smaller than last night. It was still fairly early and people were probably scraping themselves back together after the night before I decided. Besides, the pyrotechnics and light show wouldn't start until it was dark again. Right now it was comparatively tame.

The act on stage was a girl group, three women in sparkly silver outfits. Two with tinsel wigs. The music was upbeat pop but it wasn't in English so I had no idea what it was about. It sounded like it was German. It was a good song and if I was alone in my room I'd probably have thought nothing of dancing to it. But in broad daylight amongst all those strangers I felt stiff and awkward. Ari and Carla had no trouble dancing to it though. Everyone else there was, so why was I still feeling so tightly wound and anxious? I couldn't seem to stop myself.

I was still in my head after twenty or so minutes of trying to look like I was having fun. So much so that when someone grabbed my shoulder from behind I whipped round in shock and nearly dropped my drink.

"Sorry!" the girl from that morning, Evie, said. "I thought you were Roisin."

"You haven't found her yet?" I asked, though obviously she hadn't if she was still looking. Much less grabbing me.

"Haven't found her, no," Evie was saying. "I've asked around, given out my number, even managed to track down a security guard out by the front gates and told him about her but no one's called me yet to say they've seen her. Just a bunch of prank calls and some well wishes."

"Sorry. I hope you find her," I said. "Let me know if there's anything I can do to help." Though what that would be I had no idea. It just felt like the right thing to say.

"Yeah, thanks. I'd better find her," Evie sighed, "can't exactly leave without her." With that she left me standing there, my insides like dirty snow – messy and grim. I turned back to Carla and Ari, managed to get their attention by catching their hands as they danced. They pulled me into their routine, twirling me between them until I struggled to a stop.

"What's up?" Carla asked, raising her voice over the music. She glanced at Ari. "If we're allowed to ask?"

Ari rolled her eyes. "You can ask, just not all the time – right, Jody?"

"I just ran into Evie again," I said, still turning over our brief conversation. Something in it was needling me, a stone in my shoe that I couldn't shake.

"Has she found her friend?" Carla asked.

"No, but she grabbed me because she thought I was Roisin and I thought that was weird, kind of? Do you think we look a bit alike? As in, could you mix us up if it was dark and you were maybe a bit drunk?" My heart was hammering as I realised what felt wrong, what had my skin prickling. It was mad, paranoid, but nevertheless it was what I was thinking.

Carla and Ari exchanged one of their familiar 'Jody's losing it' looks. Then Ari shrugged.

"I suppose. Yes. I wouldn't even have to be drunk to be honest – when I saw her picture this morning I thought you could be related. Not like twins or anything but cousins, sisters even."

"Why?" Carla asked. "What are you getting at? And why do you look so freaked out right now?"

"It's just, when I saw Evie just now and she thought I was her friend, Roisin, I realised she went missing last night. Which is when I saw, or thought I saw…Nick," I said, already feeling stupid even as I tried to explain. "And maybe…that's connected? Like, perhaps he tried to corner her or something – thinking she was me – and she freaked out and left the festival too fast to tell Evie about it?"

"Jody," Ari said, after a second of surprised silence. "I thought we agreed it was probably just some guy who looked like Nick? Now you're saying what, that

139

he came here and he did something to that girl because she looked like you and he got confused?"

I felt the weight of her doubt like a physical pressure. It made me flush and trip over my words as I tried to justify my theory to her and to myself.

"I-I'm not saying he came here intending to do something like that," I said, wilting further under her disbelieving look. "But, he was always unpredictable, like even he didn't know what he was going to do. If he saw her and thought she was me, especially if like Evie said, she was with some other guy…maybe he flipped out and scared her enough that she just ditched the festival."

Again they were silent, the sounds of the stage and the crowd swamping us. I was shunted to the side slightly by a wind milling arm and nearly lost my footing. When I righted myself, Ari and Carla were still staring at me. Their expressions held a mix of concern and pity. I knew before either of them spoke that they didn't believe me. Really, I shouldn't have expected them to. It was an insane idea. So why couldn't I let it go?

"Jodie…" Carla said, finally. "That sounds…"

"Crazy," I said, so she didn't have to. I felt embarrassment flare up the back of my neck, adding to the heat of yesterday's sunburn. Yet I couldn't shake the feeling that there was something to it. I wasn't just paranoid, it felt very much like someone was out to get me. Or maybe that was my anxiety talking, using my trauma against me? It was hard to tell, I needed someone else to decide for me. Someone who would listen and not immediately try to dismiss everything to make me feel better.

Someone who wasn't either of my housemates.

"He won't even know we're here," Carla said, clearly trying to reassure me. "I thought about it after we talked last night and there's no way. None of us told anyone where we were going, right?"

I nodded reluctantly and saw Ari do the same, even as she ducked away from a girl riding her boyfriend's shoulders through the crowd. I desperately wanted to get away from the concert and talk about this somewhere else.

"And our socials are private so, even if we posted about it, which I haven't – Nick wouldn't be able to see it. So, how could he know where we are?" Carla finished, looking pleased with herself for constructing this neat parcel of logic. "The best he could have done, or the worst I guess, would be coincidentally winning tickets and coming here and then randomly spotting you amongst like, a bajillion people, and then confusing you with someone else and scaring her. But that's...I mean unlikely isn't even the word, right?"

"But it could still have happened," I protested, weakly even to my own ears. "And what if he did find out we were coming here and he didn't need a ticket – he could just get a boat and..." I cut myself off, I was being ridiculous and I could see it on their faces.

"Still, hardly likely is it?" Carla pressed. "Jody, I know that it freaked you out and it is really sketchy that Evie hasn't managed to find her friend yet but it's just not possible for it to be related to Nick. He's not here, OK?"

I wanted to argue, but I nodded, defeated. She was right, they both were. There was no way for Nick to

141

know where I was exactly. Him being at the festival at all would take some doing, let alone him being involved in the disappearance of a girl whose friend just happened to ask us about her. I was being ridiculous and I felt like it.

Still, I couldn't silence the part of me that knew, unshakeably, that Nick was anything but predictable – I'd never been able to see the worst of his behaviour coming. The last time I'd assumed I knew his limits, he'd tried to coerce me into a threesome and trapped me in our flat. I'd learned the hard way not to put anything past him. But my friends obviously didn't have the same experience as I did. I couldn't make them understand just how far Nick might go to teach me a lesson.

Carla gave me a sympathetic look and put her arm around my shoulders, encouraging me to dance. I felt even less like dancing than usual but, I tried. Ari twirled and raised her drink up high before downing the whole thing. I promised myself that I was done bringing up Nick. It wasn't fair on Ari and Carla and it wasn't fair on Evie's missing friend either. If she was in real trouble the last thing she needed was for me to start muddying the waters with my own issues. I only hoped that Evie had managed to get her face out there to everyone. Someone at Lethe had to know where Roisin was. She couldn't have just vanished.

Chapter 13

After a nice, lengthy break from the chaos near the stage to queue for some food and more drinks, we came back in the evening. It was the same sort of mix of European bands we'd never heard of before performing their own stuff with covers sprinkled in. I wasn't a great judge of music but it sounded good to me. We'd managed, with some trial and error on quantities, to balance the disgusting free booze with some bottles of fizz from the bar. It was at least a drinkable mixture, after you got the first two down at least. Consequently I was feeling fairly chilled out, all things considered.

Night crept in and stole the heat of the day away. I was glad of it, as it had become overbearing as the day wore on. The night was balmy and the stink of rubbish died down without the sun beating down on us. It didn't get too cold – it felt as if the heat of the day was radiating out of the compacted ground under us. Warm as a freshly baked cake.

The stage lights flashed pink and lilac over us and white, starry pyrotechnics fizzled overhead. Everyone around us was having fun, cheering and shrieking for the bands or the pretty explosions. I wasn't sure. I was just blurry enough around the edges to not worry that there were people around, to just sway to the ballads that came on as the night progressed. It was lovely, magical even. I wasn't sure if it was the booze or the herbs from the hookah, or if Carla had finally despaired of me enough to spike my drink with beta-blockers, but I was actually relaxed. Every so often I'd be struck by the thought that I was having fun, and get surprised all over again. Proud of myself.

As we stumbled towards our tent after the final song I was actually giggling. We had our arms around each other like characters in *The Wizard of Oz*, skipping down our own dusty yellow dirt road. I didn't even feel that tired which was amazing in and of itself. The alcohol had dulled the aches in my feet and back from standing for hours. It felt like I could carry on all night. Still, when we passed a cluster of tents where a party seemed to be in full swing, my stomach flipped over. I could feel Carla pulling towards the voices and music, dragging me with her.

"Oh, Carla, come on – I'm exhausted," I lied, not wanting to get caught up with a bunch of strangers. I was feeling relaxed for the first time in ages and I didn't want to ruin it with awkward socialising away from the roar of the music and the anonymity of the crowd.

"Just a quick one," she insisted, having caught the eye of a guy amongst the happy, dancing throng. "You'll sleep better."

I looked to Ari for support, but she was nodding her head to the dull thump of the music and fishing the half-empty water bottle of booze out of her bag.

Unless I wanted to head back to the tent on my own like the party-pooper I was, I was staying for a drink. Or two, judging from the way Carla was prowling after the guy that had caught her interest. It didn't seem like this would be over soon. I'd just have to make the best of it and try to stay out of everyone's way.

I turned back to Ari but found her gone too. She was a few metres away, talking to two girls in the same kind of dark clothes as her. She'd found her people. Unfortunately that meant I'd lost mine.

I was looking around for a handy corner to stand – sort of a hard ask in a field – when I noticed someone looking at me. He was standing by a folding table topped with cans and cups. The neighbouring tents must have dumped all their booze there to share out. It was the guy from that morning, not the furious one who'd grabbed me but the one who'd rescued me. He lifted his hand and gave me a casual wave, then invited me over with a nod of his head. The back of my neck flushed but I went anyway, the alternative was too awkward to consider.

"Hello again," he said, once I got within conversational distance. "I'm glad you didn't decide to leave after what happened this morning."

"Me too, actually," I said, surprising myself. Despite having cried a lot since we'd arrived and the fact that I currently felt more out of my depth than ever, there were moments where I'd actually had fun today. I hadn't thought that could happen in a place like this. A few days ago I'd never thought I'd have fun again.

"Is this your first festival?" he asked, offering me an unopened can of cider from the table, which I took automatically despite not being a cider fan. At least it gave me something to do with my hands.

"That obvious is it? Yes, it is. I'm not usually one for gigs or camping or travel so this is a lot of new stuff for me." I opened the can to stop myself rambling on any further, but he laughed like I'd told a joke.

"I know what you mean. It's such a weird combination of things isn't it? Especially here with the beach and the 'activities' they have. I've never seen anything quite like it." He held out his hand. "I'm Andrei, by the way. We didn't really have time to talk this morning. Are you here with friends?"

"Jody. And yeah, I'm here with my friends, Carla and Ari."

He nodded. "Good, I was worried you'd be on your own after that thing this morning. I'm here with my brother, Ivan. But he's always off doing his own thing. I only really came to keep him out of trouble – which is obviously going really well, because I haven't seen him in a while."

I laughed. "Well, you tried."

"I did," he smiled. I noticed that his teeth were slightly crooked on one side. That more than the curly dark hair, tattoo and ripped t-shirt made him appealing. A small touch of the adorable. I pushed that thought away and felt my neck burn all over again. What had gotten into me? Was it the alcohol or the fact that he'd rescued me, twice now if it was possible to be 'rescued' from an awkward social situation.

Andrei gestured to the people around us, now dancing to several different tracks on different phones. "I sometimes feel like I'm missing something when

I'm somewhere like this. Or like I got an extra bit of something – too much self-awareness maybe, or perhaps I just take myself too seriously."

"I get what you mean. I hear 'dance like no one's watching' and I think, 'OK, but how' you know?" I said, trying to make a joke out of it, even though it was true.

He nodded, waved a hand in a 'there you go!' gesture. "I'm always telling myself 'no one cares that much about you' but it never seems to sink in. Have you been to the beach yet?"

"Yeah, it's a bit…" I was still looking for a diplomatic way of putting it when he broke out another blinding smile.

"A bit shit, right?"

I laughed. "Mmmhmm. I wasn't expecting it to be so…industrial. All the bricks and concrete and stuff."

"And the smell," Andrei said. "I've caught it a few times now, around the camp. Like rotting garbage?"

"Yes! What is that about?" I said. "I thought that on the first day. The festival had barely started and there was this smell like the bins were already full and had been for ages."

"It's the island," Andrei said, looking pleased with himself for knowing this. "I was talking to some local guys at the beach earlier. This island, or whatever it is now that there's a bridge connecting it to the land, it used to be a landfill."

"A dump?" I frowned, disgusted but also worried. "But that means we're like, on top of tonnes and tonnes of rubbish, all rotting away and making gasses and stuff? Is that even safe?"

"Who knows? I think they do build on them. I've heard of it but I'm not sure about just dumping earth on top and letting people camp here. If we can still smell it maybe it's not buried deep enough. Still," he took a drink from his own can. "The tickets were free."

"The prize of a lifetime," I said, eyebrow raised.

Andrei laughed. "It's lucky though, both of us ending up here. When you think about how many people wanted to win tickets." I felt my heart flutter a little. Was he flirting with me? He was smiling a lot and we were very close together. I was terrible at judging this kind of thing. Maybe he was just a bit drunk and being friendly? He was definitely too good looking for me. A pang of realisation hit me; he was probably interested in Ari or Carla and had seen me with them. I was used to being the 'approachable one' in the group. It had been that way before, when we went out at uni.

Yet, as we talked a while longer about everything and anything – the music, the weather, the bus situation and the likelihood of the festival happening again next year – he didn't bring up Ari or Carla once. He was just talking to me. I got the feeling he was glad to have someone to talk to, just like I was. Someone who wasn't part of the crowd or the party. Someone in a quiet corner that wasn't a corner.

"Sorry," I said, smothering a yawn. "Late nights catching up with me. I'm sort of an early to bed person."

"Same," he said. "I was up for hours this morning before Ivan woke up. Very boring to be awake with nothing to do. I should have brought a book or something."

"I did actually bring a book but it's hard to concentrate, even in the tent." I yawned again and winced, glancing around for the others. I couldn't see either of them. The party had filled out some as more people drifted past, distracted from their tents by the noise and bustle. The competing music hadn't stopped people from dancing, little knots of gyrating bodies rubbed shoulders with static clumps of chatting people.

As much as I was enjoying my talk with Andrei I was also dog tired and my feet had already been sore that morning, now, as the alcohol wore off, they were actively throbbing. There was nowhere to sit down, unless you counted the floor. The problem with there being nothing but tents around, meant there wasn't even a wall to lean against.

"If you like I can walk you to your tent?" Andrei offered. "If you'd rather not go alone."

"Oh...um..." I heard my mother's voice telling me to never, ever, let a man walk me home alone. Heard Carla telling me to never let any guy, even one I worked with or from uni, know where I lived until I knew him well. I knew it was one of those rules, the unwritten ones we're all supposed to know. But when I thought about the man from that morning, grabbing me and about Nick possibly being out there somewhere, it seemed like a rule worth breaking. There were so many people moving past in the dark, so few lights and all those shadows between the tents.

"I understand," Andrei held up his hands. "Don't worry about it."

"No, it's fine..." I said, accidentally talking over him and rolling my eyes at myself. "Thank you, if you're alright leaving the party for a bit I'd really like you to walk me back to the tent. Just in case."

Andrei smiled and put his drink down on the folding table. "No problem at all."

As we crossed the bare patch that the party had formed in I looked around for any sign of Carla and Ari. I thought I saw the top of Carla's head in a huddle of people across the way but there was no way to catch her eye. I'd just text them from the tent to let them know where I was.

Away from the party I started to have doubts about what I was doing. It was easy to trust a virtual stranger when I was surrounded by people and noise and the light from so many torches, lanterns and phones. On the dark path between empty tents I felt my skin prickle with unease. When I looked at Andrei however he was walking quite casually, hands in his jeans pockets and looking up at the stars.

"One thing that's good about this place, there's less light pollution than in the cities," he said. "I can't remember the last time I saw a sky this clear, isn't it beautiful?"

I looked up and realised he was right. Back home in Dorset I was used to being able to see the stars from my bedroom window and on the way home from evening choir practice with Mum. Since moving to London I'd missed seeing them, both because of the light pollution, the tall buildings and the fact that I was usually in a rush to get from one place to somewhere else.

"It's lovely, isn't it?" I said. "I've missed seeing the sky like this." When I looked back down Andrei wasn't watching the stars anymore. He was watching me.

"I'm glad I ran into you again," he said. "There wasn't much time this morning to talk. Not really the environment for it either. But tonight has been nice. Really nice."

"I've had a good time too," I said, struggling to come up with words that didn't sound stupid or stumble into babbling.

"Would you like to, maybe…sorry, I'm bad at this," Andrei laughed nervously at himself. "You probably have plans with your friends but, I'd like to do this again, while we're here. If that's OK?"

"I'd like that, yes. Definitely," I said, heart picking up speed in my chest like a stone rolling downhill.

"Good." Andrei blessed me with another smile. "That's…I'll come by tomorrow maybe or just keep an eye out for you around, we could get a drink or… something?"

"Sounds good." We'd arrived at my tent and I stood in front of it awkwardly, wondering how I looked to him and what he was thinking. I hadn't thought about anything so nerve-wracking as romance since before Nick and I got together. I'd hardly had to think about it even when Nick arrived on the scene, he'd steamrolled over me – gifts, dates, feeding me endearments and wrapping me up in his world without me ever stopping to feel scared or worried that I might make a fool of myself. Which, in the end, had only made it worse when Nick did make a fool out of me. When he ripped it all away like the set-dressing it was.

"I'll see you then," Andrei said. For a moment it felt like he was going to lean in for a kiss. He seemed to sway slightly on his feet. I was caught between letting it happen and wanting to step back to give myself some space. In the end though he just smiled again and took a few steps backwards before turning around and walking away. Like he was reluctant to stop looking at me.

I watched him go, chewing my lip. What was I doing? This wasn't what I'd come to the festival for. I'd wanted to get away not get involved with anyone. Yet here he was and it felt somehow safe, because in a few days he'd be leaving the festival the same as me. He'd head back to his home and I'd go back to England. There was a finality to that which felt reassuring. The choice wouldn't be up to me. It was, in fact, pre-decided.

I unzipped the tent and got in, secure in the pocket of darkness. After dashing off a quick text to the group chat between Carla, Ari and myself I got changed for bed and laid down in my sleeping bag. I didn't have the focus necessary to read and I was suddenly not as tired as I'd thought I was. My skin was buzzing and I kept catching myself smiling at the dark canopy overhead. Sleep wasn't quick in coming but for the first time in a long while, that was more from excitement than fear.

Chapter 14

I woke up briefly when Carla and Ari crawled into the tent. Without looking at my phone I had no idea what time it was but it felt very late. Or possibly early. The air that rushed in with them was cool and damp, dew scented. There was something about the quiet outside too which reminded me of early starts in Dorset. So early that there were no cars around and every house was dark. It made me almost unbearably homesick.

"G'night," Carla mumbled, tumbling into her sleeping bag still fully clothed and made-up. Ari made a token effort with a makeup wipe before cosying down in her bedding, mouth still lipstick stained and eyeliner smudged onto her cheeks. I shut my sticky eyes and fell back asleep within minutes.

I didn't wake up again until bright sunlight was filtering through the nylon canopy overhead. By then the entire tent smelled of warm socks and our breath, a musty but domestic smell. It was already getting too hot inside the tent and I was damp with sweat.

I pulled on some shorts and a hoodie inside my sleeping bag to get dressed, because it would be colder

153

outside. Then I crawled out into the mid-morning rush. It was the latest I'd managed to sleep in for two weeks. Spending most of the day at the concert and having a few drinks had really tired me out. That or the herbal mixture we'd smoked had done something after all. Either way as I boiled some bottled water to make tea and rehydrate some porridge I found myself humming a song I'd heard the day before. Things were looking a little brighter than they had yesterday. I felt more rested and a little bit more relaxed than I had since we arrived.

"Ugh, how are you so chipper?" Carla asked, creeping into the daylight with a face-full of yesterday's makeup. One of her fake lashes was stuck to her cheek like a squashed fly and she scratched at the spot with a wince as it came free.

"I think you had more to drink than me," I pointed out. "Tea?"

Carla shook her head and for a second it looked like she was actively repressing a retch. I decided that trying to talk to her would only make things worse. After a few minutes of lying like a landed fish on the blanket Carla dragged herself into a sitting position and took a bottle of water for herself. I finished eating my porridge with a plastic spoon and stuffed the pot into a plastic rubbish bag we'd staked to the ground outside the tent. It was already so covered in yellow dust that it blended in with the dirt.

"Just popping to the loo," I said.

Carla gave me a limp thumbs up and put her sunglasses on.

As I headed in the direction of the portaloos I wondered what we were going to do today. I didn't feel as anxious as I had when we first arrived, like I had to fill every moment with something or else I'd be boring. Perhaps Ari and Carla would want to hang around the tent for most of the day to recover from last night? That was fine by me. I could even, I thought, go to look around the domes by myself. Just to get a drink or maybe have a go on the arcade games we'd seen in one of them. Nothing crazy, just half an hour or so of alone time. I thought about running into Andrei and quickly distracted myself, feeling butterflies in my chest. It was a big change, feeling like I could go around on my own. But somehow my encounters with Andrei had given me a little confidence back. Not everyone out there was unkind or scary. The thought of seeing him again brought a small smile to my face.

I was still smiling when I looked up and saw Nick.

My smile froze and then crumpled, a bitter taste filling my mouth.

It was impossible. I knew it was impossible, and yet my body, my mind, immediately went into panic mode. Everything in my head ground to a halt, the thoughts, the feelings, and my ability to walk. I froze on the spot and just stared as he crossed the path ahead of me and disappeared into the surrounding tents.

The moment he was out of sight, I blinked. Already I was scrabbling to reassure myself. It was just a man who looked the same. The same muscular body type and hair colour, height and swagger. Even the t-shirt was one I'd seen him in before – but then again how many bearded, well-toned guys in Jack Wills t-shirts were there? Thousands. Probably more than a hundred just at the festival.

And yet…that same horrible jolt of recognition as I'd felt in the crowd by the stage. Part of me was screaming that I'd seen Nick. Right here. My heart was like a trapped bird flinging itself at closed windows. I could feel sweat turning cold all over me. He was at the festival and I'd lost sight of him. Where had he gone?

I looked around, struggling to pick out the colour of his t-shirt or the flash of the ring around his neck in the sunlight. If seeing him was a shock to the system, not knowing where he'd gone was sickeningly worse. I felt like the ground was moving under my feet. The sky above spinning.

"Nick…" the word spilled out before I could stop it. I was still looking for him. Had to find where he'd gone. I took one step and then another, almost without thinking. I followed him. I had to prove it to myself – that he was here, that I wasn't going crazy. I needed to see where he'd gone, what he was doing here.

I was shaking as I picked my way through the tents, watching out for guy ropes and potholes in the parched earth. There were people all around, sitting outside their tents or walking between them as I was, but I kept my eyes on him as much as possible.

From the back it was even harder to tell if this was Nick or not. Parts of him looked familiar – the shape of his shoulders and the way his joggers were rolled down at the top, the mole on the back of his arm and the buzzed hair was the right colour. But was it his left arm or his right? Was that how I remembered it? The truth was I'd almost avoided looking too closely at Nick even when we were still together. They way you're not meant

156

to look a strange dog in the eyes in case it takes it as a challenge.

So I followed him and felt myself stop breathing every time he twisted slightly, as if he was about to turn around. Was he playing with me? Did he know I was there and he was just torturing me, knowing I wouldn't stop following him now that I'd committed? I trailed behind him all the way through the campground and paused once we got near the showers and the toilets. Nick, or, not-Nick, walked between two portaloos and vanished.

I waited a few seconds but he didn't come back out. What was he doing back there? Luring me out of sight so he could grab me? I moved hesitantly, circled around to the end of the row of portaloos. I stuck my head around the last one in the line, ready to jump back if needs be. But he wasn't there.

There was, I realised, a gap in the metal security fence panels. On the other side the dirt field continued, no longer the campground but some kind of backstage area. It was all reels of cable, trailers, piles of rubbish bags and vans. I caught a glimpse of him again between two stacks of wooden pallets, still walking away. What was he doing?

Was I really going to follow him back there? I couldn't see anyone else around. What if he caught me? I'd be all on my own, defenceless, just like when we'd lived together. I hesitated but the idea of going back to Ari and Carla with yet another paranoid story spurred me on. I had my phone on me if I got into trouble.

If I could just get a picture of him front on, without him seeing me, then I'd be able to zoom in and see if it really was Nick. I'd come this far, I couldn't leave without knowing if I really was losing it or not. Without being able to prove it to Ari and Carla once and for all.

My legs felt ever so slightly numb as I walked down the row of plastic portaloos and ducked through the gap in the fence. It was just a panel of metal wire but it might as well have been a stone wall hundreds of feet high for how it felt once I was on the other side. Like I'd crossed over from one world to another and almost immediately I felt a new weight settle in my chest – an awareness of the danger I was putting myself in. Still there was no turning back for me in that moment. I had to know.

I followed him through the narrow spaces between trailers and vans, trying not to trip over stray rubbish and the rubberised electrical cords that were snaking all over the place. The hum and sputter of generators helped to cover the sound of my footsteps as I scrunched my way over the dusty ground. The man turned one corner and then another, moving quickly and with purpose. He knew where he was going, but what he was up to I couldn't guess. The further we went the less sure I became that this was Nick at all. I'd only seen a glimpse of him from the side after all. What was I doing, chasing after him?

A brown rat darted across my path and I nearly yelped in shock at the sudden movement. I flinched back more out of surprise than anything. I'd never had an issue with rats or mice – they were generally harmless, intelligent animals. Insects were the things that bothered me. Still, that second of hesitation was all it took for me to lose sight of the man at the next fork in the path.

I reached the point where the foot-worn track split into four and looked each way, listening. I couldn't hear him over the sound of all the generators and refrigeration units humming away. Through a gap in the side of a nearby tent I could see huge chest freezers which were probably packed with the stuff being deep-fried all over the festival site. The two nearest me had padlocks on the lids.

Where had he gone? I started down one path and found no sign of him, retraced my steps and tried another. All avenues exhausted I sat down on a pile of wooden pallets out of sight of anyone passing by and put my head in my hands. Damn it. Now I'd never know if it was him or not.

God the others were probably right. I was cracking up, being paranoid. Was it not a massive coincidence that the moment I was thinking about another man I thought I saw Nick? It was probably just my own screwed up sense of guilt and fear playing tricks on me. Making me feel like I was being disloyal to the shitty human being who'd sent me running here. That was what being with Nick had done to me – he was inside my head, not just twisting my words but twisting my thoughts until he could punish me for things before he even knew about them. Things he'd never know about. Even now that we weren't together anymore.

I rubbed my hands over my face where grit and dust had stuck to my nervous sweat. Time to go back to the tent and try to let go of whatever this awful feeling inside was. That's all it was, a feeling. A phantom. There was nothing to worry about, nothing to fear here except the things I'd brought with me. And there was no escaping those apparently, no matter how far I travelled or how much 'fun' I put myself through. Nick would be right there, inside my mind.

I got up and started to pick my way back through the windblown rubbish and electrical cables. I'd barely gone a few steps before the toe of my shoe caught in some trash and sent an empty coffee cup and some Styrofoam containers flying. I winced, worried about the noise, and was about to carry on when I heard a sound – a quiet, soft little squeak.

There were refuse sacks piled along the edge of this part of the path, stacked against the rusting side of a trailer. The sort of thing you saw serving burgers and chips to drunk idiots in the town centre at one in the morning. I followed the sound and moved a few pieces of torn cardboard from on top of one of the rubbish bags.

It was a rat. A common brown one, greasy and damp from crawling through the refuse. It was stuck to a glue trap. I winced just to look at it. They were foul things, glue traps. Even poison was kinder than trapping an animal like that and letting it struggle itself to death.

The rat was still alive, probably only recently trapped. It might even have been the one that had scared me, made me lose track of Nick, or not-Nick. Whichever it had been. It was fully stuck though, its entire body matted down to the glue. To get it off I'd need a lot of time, oil and patience. Even then the stress of it on the poor thing's tiny heart…it was probably a lost cause already.

As I looked down at it the rat twisted its head, probably sensing that it was being watched, smelling me, wondering if I was a predator. Perhaps it thought I was the one who'd trapped it like this. I felt tears scratching at my eyes at the idea. As stupid as it was. I couldn't stand the thought that it might think I was responsible for its pain. It was something that bothered me about treating all animals – not being able to explain that I was trying to help – but in a work setting it was easier to overcome.

I felt so helpless that I couldn't stand it. I had to do something. Casting about I retraced my steps until I found a wooden pallet stacked with cardboard containers, each one supporting a collapsible plastic jug of cooking oil. Industrial sized for the many deep-fat-fryers of the festival. I struggled to twist the lid off of one, and picked up an empty coffee cup from the tide of rubbish. I pressed down on the top of the jug and oil glugged over the rim, messy and bland-smelling. With the cup brimming over I went back to the rat.

"I'm sorry," I said, stupidly, as I snagged the edge of the glue trap with my fingers and carefully dragged it until it slipped off of the rubbish bags and onto the ground. The rat was twitching, trying to get away but stuck fast as ever. My breathing was ragged, pre-emptive guilt already curdling into a solid mass in my chest. This was probably going to hurt him, but I couldn't just leave without trying to help. I poured the oil over the struggling rat, trying to keep its eyes and ears free of the gunk. It was panicking, fighting, and I had to hold it with one hand as I rubbed the oil into the glue, loosening it. Slowly, the fur started to lift and though

161

my legs were burning from kneeling, I didn't give up. I kept working at it until the rat slipped free and shot out of my hand like a fully wound-up toy, rushing off and out of sight.

"Bye then," I said, the corner of my mouth lifting. I'd managed to accomplish something, even though it was something small. That rat – no matter what some people thought of it – had escaped a drawn out death because of me. My Dad would have been proud. He was the one who'd always secretly tripped the traps Mum put in the shed, so no mouse or rat got their neck snapped. Instead he'd hide capture traps around the side where she couldn't see, and take the mice and rats out to the fields to release them. I used to go with him in the evening after work, waving goodbye to the scurrying animals. I smiled at the memory.

The shifting of the rubbish bags nearby made me jump. Another rat bounded out, running for its tiny life. One of the bags pitched off of the pile and rolled across the path. It wasn't done up tightly enough and slimy stinking rubbish spilled out; green-grey mouldy bread, plastic coated in gloopy blood and egg shells left to ferment under black plastic in the hot Grecian sun. I coughed and stepped back.

That was when I saw the hand.

A scream died in my throat, strangled to death before it got past my lips. The hand clearly belonged to a woman, one with bitten nails with chipped red polish on them and a tiny tattoo of a butterfly. It was attached to a pale arm which snaked from between two of the rubbish bags. The skin was so pale it was greyish, deep

162

bruises in the shape of fingers around her wrist, caging the butterfly in.

I stumbled forward and felt for a pulse on instinct. I could feel one but wasn't sure if it was hers or my own. Her skin was hot and sticky. I flinched away, wiping my fingers uselessly on the dusty dirt. I had no idea what I was doing. The smell of hot rubbish was suffocating and my throat was closing up, my stomach rebelling. Still I dug my hands into the rubbish bags and dragged them away, letting them fall anywhere.

It wasn't until I exposed her face that I realised I knew her.

It was Evie.

The girl who'd mistaken me for her missing friend.

Her green cap with the peace sign was in the rubbish pile with her, I vaguely realised that her expensive looking leather jacket was missing. My mind was all over the place. I tried to feel for a pulse again, at her throat this time, but could barely distinguish if what I felt was the pounding of my own heart echoing in my fingertips.

"Evie?" I tried to shake her awake, but she just flopped against her bed of rubbish. I looked back down the path towards the main festival site and realised how far away we were from help. If I wanted to get Evie to someone who could do first aid, I'd have to carry her.

"I'm going to try and lift you, OK?" I said, locking my feet on the hard ground and stooping to get my arms around Evie's shoulders. She was so limp. I felt a ball of ice form inside my chest, almost burning me with cold. This wasn't right, was she...was I too late?

"Help!" I yelled it so loudly that I felt the back of my throat fray. "Help me!"

I heard footsteps running towards me and only then remembered how I'd come to be where I was. The man who I'd followed. The one who looked like Nick, was Nick, I still wasn't sure. Every muscle in my body froze as I looked up the row and held my breath, waiting to see who'd answer my call.

Chapter 15

Several people came running after I screamed for help. None of them were Nick. There wasn't even a guy who looked like him. He'd simply disappeared, where and to do what I had no idea. Which felt a little strange, after all if it wasn't Nick, up to no good, why wouldn't he come running, to help? But I couldn't speculate further, I was too busy trying to help Evie.

A guy in a polo shirt and apron arrived first. He looked like he was from one of the catering vans. Hot on his heels came a woman wearing one of the 'Lethe' festival t-shirts and another man, deeply tanned and shirtless, a tool belt around his waist. All of them were out of breath and wide eyed as they stumbled into view. My screams must have sounded truly horrifying.

"What's happened? Jesus! What's the matter with her?" The woman dropped to her knees and started pulling Evie up into a sitting position. The rubbish around her shifted, a new wave of stink wafting up and making me choke. I took hold of one of Evie's shoulders and tried to help the woman lift her. Evie felt sticky, like she was covered in dried sweat, or juice from the rubbish bags.

"I found her like this, I don't know what's wrong," I babbled. "I don't know how to check for a pulse properly, do you...?"

"Has she taken anything?" The woman interrupted, as between us we managed to lift Evie's torso off the ground, before I lost my grip and she slithered back onto the rubbish bags. One of them split up the side, scattering maggoty noodles and gloopy sauce. My stomach rebelled and I looked away, tried to breathe through my mouth. The two men were frozen in place, watching us and clearly unsure what they could do to help.

"I don't know," I panted. "I don't even really know her – maybe? What do we do?"

"Help me get her up," the woman snapped at the two men, who were still standing a few feet away, helpless and frozen as I'd been when I first saw Evie lying in the rubbish. "There's a medical tent through the fence, over that way."

The catering guy and the man with the tool belt were talking to each other, I assumed in Greek, but they clearly understood what the woman in the t-shirt was telling them to do. They moved together and between them got Evie off the ground. With her held between them by her shoulders and legs they followed after the woman as she hurried through the warren of narrow paths, conferring under her breath on a walkie-talkie. I stumbled after them and, remembering my phone now that the first searing panic was over, I called Ari. It was instinct – I needed someone to tell me what to do, to take charge, and she was it.

"Hey, where are you?" she asked as soon as she picked up, I could hear Carla still talking away in the background. "You've been gone ages."

"I found Evie passed out on the ground. She needed help – she was unconscious," I gasped, nearly losing my footing over an electrical cable. "Drugs they think. Or something else. I don't know."

"Wait, what?" I heard rustling and scuffling as she moved, heard her shush Carla. "Evie's collapsed?"

"Yes, she was passed out when I found her! We're taking her to the medical tent. Can you come and meet me? I...I don't know what to do."

"Sure, of course we're – we're already on our way," I heard her hiss something at Carla and then there was wind blowing past the phone, making the line crackle. They were on the move. "Who's 'we'? Who's there with you?"

"I don't know – a woman and two guys from the backstage bit."

"Backstage?" Ari sounded confused and concerned in equal measure. "What were you doing backstage? Like at the concert or..."

"It's not important! I'll tell you later," I said, as the path ahead broadened and I spotted the medical tent just beyond the metal security fence. The woman in the Lethe t-shirt was already dragging the fence panel – made into a gate with cable ties – open so that the men could carry Evie through. Beyond the fence the endless streams of festivalgoers didn't stop but they slowed, looking at what was going on. Their eyes slid

167

over Evie's unconscious body and they grabbed at each other, whispered, looked away. Like it was bad luck to even see her. No one stopped to ask if she was OK or to offer help, even if it would have been useless. I was still surprised that no one seemed to care that much. Maybe this was just a normal thing at festivals? I didn't know.

"I've got to go," I said. "We're near the beach I think. The green medical tent just past the froyo stand."

I hung up before Ari could say anything else and reached the metal fence just in time for the woman to hold out an arm, trying to bar me from the medical tent. Behind her I saw the two men carry Evie into the tent and let the door flap fall closed behind them. Moments later, they returned empty handed and rushed off, presumably back to their jobs. Clearly eager to get out of this situation as quickly as possible.

"We'll take care of her from here," the Lethe woman said briskly. "We've got first-aiders on site and we can get an ambulance through if necessary. She'll be fine."

"I want to make sure she's OK," I protested. "Can I go in, or wait somewhere?"

The woman frowned, dust sticking to the sweat on her upper lip. "You said you don't really know her."

"That doesn't matter – I'm still worried about her," I said. "The friend she came with has gone missing, as far as I know there's no one else to check on her. I can prove I've met her – we exchanged details, I've got her number in my phone."

I could hear people moving around in the tent, talking to one another. I heard plastic packaging rip and glass chime against metal. They were treating her. She'd probably throw up and be fine, right? That was how I'd handled accidental medication ingestions with pets, if you got whatever they'd swallowed out fast enough they'd recover. Most of the time. And this was a festival; they'd have all sorts in there to deal with overdoses and alcohol poisoning. They were prepared for this. So why was the knot of panic in my chest refusing to go away?

"OK, then she can call you when she's recovered then, can't she?" the woman pointed out, turning from me to look at the medical tent, chewing her lip. Was she worried? Did she know something I didn't? After all she had to have seen her share of overdoses working at the festival.

It registered with me for the first time that the woman in the t-shirt was British. I noticed that above the Lethe design on her top the words 'Volunteer Steward' were printed in a plastic transfer, already flaking. She'd probably taken this job to get free access to the festival, having not been able to win a ticket like everyone else. I got the feeling that she wasn't exactly thrilled to be caught up in this situation, she wasn't doing this job because she wanted to be, that much was clear.

Digging deep, I found a reserve of stubborn resolve. "Can I at least give you my number, so you can ring me if she needs to go to hospital? Or if something happens?" I asked as a last resort. "Just in case she needs someone to help, what with her friend being missing." I stressed that last word but it didn't seem to register with her. Twice now I'd mentioned a missing girl and twice I'd been ignored. She really didn't give a shit.

The woman nodded, but she seemed more resigned than anything. "Sure, read it out."

I did and watched as she took a pen from her pocket and wrote it on her hand. What was the bet that she'd wash that off later and forget all about me? About Evie?

"Jody!" Ari appeared next to me, catching herself with an arm around my shoulders. The pair of us nearly tumbled into the t-shirt woman. Carla arrived at my other elbow, panting and wheezing a little. I remembered her asthma and hoped that all the dust and the running wouldn't give her an attack. The last thing I wanted was for someone else to end up in the medical tent.

"Is she in there?" Ari asked. "Can we see her?"

"It's only patients allowed back there. There's not much space," the woman explained, gaze flicking between the three of us. She looked more than ready to be done with us. "There's nothing else you can do at the moment – thank you for alerting us to the problem."

"You're not going to let us make sure she's OK?" Carla said, clearly appalled.

"You didn't say it was patients only before," I said.

"It was implied, and she'll be fine," the woman said. "I have your friend's number now but I really don't think you need to worry about anything. We've had so many drunk girls through here, or people off their faces. Now that she's under professional supervision she'll be fine."

"I gave her my number already," I told Ari and Carla. "You will call, if anything happens? And remind Evie to let us know she's OK?"

"I will," the woman said, insistently. "Go on, don't let this ruin your day just…let us get on with things."

I still had my doubts and was about to start arguing again. However at that moment her walkie-talkie blipped and she rolled her eyes and pressed a button. "Jessica here, what's going on?"

"Erik's heard about the situation and he's on his way down. Wants you to keep everyone there. Together," said a voice on the crackly radio.

"Erik's coming down?" the woman – Jessica – echoed, glancing at us. "OK…I'll make sure we don't lose anyone. You guys'll stay put for me, won't you?" she said, once the radio went quiet.

"Who's Erik?" Ari asked, sounding very annoyed with Jessica now. I didn't really blame her, she'd been quite dismissive and this sudden turnaround wasn't exactly endearing her to me. Though I supposed she was probably dealing with some shock herself. She'd said they'd had a lot of people through the medical tent but how many of them had been found outside the festival boundary and buried in rubbish? What had Evie been doing out there to begin with?

"He's the organiser, for the festival," Jessica said. "I haven't actually seen him since the day before all this kicked off. He's some kind of property developer. Him or his company or some of his investors own the island."

"Which used to be a landfill," I said, to Ari without really thinking, remembering what Andrei had told me.

"Really?" Jessica's eyebrows drew together. "That explains some of the weird smells you get where the earth's all cracked open. It's rank – they should be

171

paying me to breathe that in. Oh, there he is – Mr. um…Erik!"

A man in a cream linen suit came barrelling through the crowds of passing festivalgoers. He had a deep tan and crinkles around the eyes, his bald head gleaming in the sun. His clothes were rumpled and he certainly had the look of someone who was in charge of a festival – slightly wired looking and clearly very stressed.

"Hello, Jennifer is it?" he asked her and Jessica nodded, apparently without thinking as her cheeks turned red as she realised she couldn't go back and correct herself without looking foolish.

"And one of these ladies is the one who…" Erik looked at the three of us, one grey eyebrow raised.

"Jody found her," Ari said, after the pause had gone on slightly too long, with me failing to introduce myself. Everything was just starting to press down on me now that the adrenaline was fading and knowing this guy was so important had stuck my tongue to the roof of my dry mouth.

"Thank you, Jody. I'm sure the poor girl is also incredibly grateful you came across her when you did. I just need to look in on things here – Jennifer, why don't you take Jody and her friends to my temporary office and I'll speak to them in a moment? If that's alright with you?" He asked the question of me, not Jessica and I nodded. With a crisp, professional smile, he ducked into the medical tent. I heard him greeting the people inside in English before switching seamlessly to Greek and rattling off what were either questions or instructions.

172

"It's this way, follow me," Jessica said, sounding even more put upon now that Erik was out of earshot. I wondered how long she'd been on the clock for. Maybe she sounded so done with everything because she hadn't stopped working since the festival started. I didn't want to believe that she was really just indifferent to Evie's situation.

"Why do you think he wants to talk to us?" I asked Ari as we followed Jessica through the throngs of brightly dressed, tanned, festivalgoers.

"Not sure. Maybe it's like a 'thank you' thing? Or a 'please sign this NDA thing'?" Ari said, eyebrows rising towards her hairline. "Either or...both?"

"Right...you don't think he maybe wants me to talk to the police?" I asked, feeling nervous. What if the police asked me what I was up to back there? I'd have to make something up. There was no way I could tell anyone about seeing Nick again. I'd sound insane. God, if Carla and Ari were there to hear it that would only make things worse. But wouldn't the police be able to tell if I was lying? They might think I was hiding something to do with Evie.

"The police?" Carla asked. "Why? Was she not just drunk or high? Had a bit too much, you know? No harm, no foul."

"If it is 'no harm'," Ari pointed out. "She might be really fucked up. Whatever she took must have been strong, or really nasty. No one knows the dealers here and that stuff gets cut with any old rubbish."

Carla looked a little abashed and I remembered the pill she'd taken.

"What was Evie even doing outside the festival?"

Ari mused. "Looking for Roisin, or doing a deal for the drugs, maybe? She was lucky you came by really, after she took the stuff where no one was there to help."

"She was buried under some rubbish," I blurted. Now that I'd mentioned the police I realised the implications of where and how I'd found Evie. "She didn't do that to herself."

Carla and Ari exchanged a look, but didn't seem to have anything to say to that.

"Here we are," Jessica said, stopping so suddenly that I nearly walked right into her. We'd come to a stop outside a shipping container similar to the shower block. This one had an air-conditioning unit on the outside, chugging away in the dusty air. The doors were in the centre of the longest side, glass, but with blinds over them.

Jessica opened the doors and waved us inside, clearly not planning on waiting with us. Not that there was much room inside. Carla and Ari led the way into the chilly metal box and the door clicked closed behind me. Part of the room inside was blocked off with boxes of t-shirts and plastic cones, a giant tub of vomit sand – a teetering pile of stuff that had no home anywhere else. On the other side was the 'office' part of the office. We three took our seats on camping chairs between the two areas, jammed in almost knee to knee so there was room for the door to open. The festival noise was cut down by half with the door closed, almost as stunning as total silence. Both my housemates were looking at me with identical expressions of confusion and worry.

"Tell us everything, from the beginning," Ari said.

I nodded, already trimming the pieces of my story in my head, removing anything about following Nick. Even as I started to tell them how I'd 'gotten lost' I was still not sure who I'd seen. It had felt like him, made my stomach churn with fear and my skin prickly. But what if I was just as deluded now as I had been at the concert? How would I even know?

Chapter 16

"And you're sure she was…alive?" Ari asked hesitantly, once I finished describing how I'd found Evie. Her face creased in concern.

"I…" that was the thing, I wasn't entirely sure anymore, especially now that I'd told the story over again, thought back on it. She'd been so still, so unresponsive. Had I felt a pulse? I couldn't remember if it had been mine or hers. If she'd been warm because she was alive or because of the hot sun and the fermenting rubbish. I couldn't even be sure if I'd seen Nick or not, either time. I couldn't trust any of it. I couldn't trust myself.

"I'm not sure," I said, honestly. "It was all so fast and everything just sort of…happened."

"They took her to the medical tent," Carla said, looking between the pair of us like we were both nuts. "They would have said, right? If she was…if she hadn't made it."

"Right," Ari said, not sounding fully convinced, to my ears at least. Perhaps she was thinking, as I was, about how the first-aiders might have been trying to avoid a panic or a scene.

The office door opened and Erik came in, bringing a swirl of hot dusty air with him. The office suddenly felt very small with him in it. I hadn't really appreciated how broad he was before. Like a club bouncer, albeit a friendly one. Erik greeted us with an affable smile and rounded a flat pack desk, which, along with several plastic crates of files and wires, took up one half of the space. He sat down hard on a squeaky office chair and reached under the desk for something.

"Water?" he offered chilled plastic bottles to us and I heard the door of a mini-fridge thunk shut under the desk. We all took one and as soon as I took a sip I realised how horribly thirsty I'd been. My mouth was coated in dust and my throat still felt raw from yelling. I hadn't had any plain water to drink in ages and it had been so hot we were probably all dehydrated.

"Right, well – thank you for meeting with me. I wanted to thank you properly for your quick thinking, Jody," Erik said. "Thankfully the girl – Evie? – is going to be alright. She's been transferred to hospital for observation, apparently she had taken something. Something quite nasty. But she should recover now, thanks to you." He gave me a warm smile.

"So it wasn't an overdose – it was bad stuff?" Ari asked, raising an eyebrow. "Are you warning people? Do the first-aiders know what they're dealing with?"

Erik's forehead creased with a serious frown and he steepled his fingers on the desk.

"One of the medical staff said whatever she took was probably cut with something unpleasant – they couldn't tell me what but you hear news stories; cleaning products, other medications, chalk, even rat poison.

She'll be alright but we've had a few incidents like this over the past two days. It looks like there's something nasty being circulated but, we'll be putting out some warnings, trying to make people aware and we have brought in more staff to keep an eye on things."

"That's, good?" I said, because it felt like he was waiting for a response. I glanced at Ari, whose shoulders relaxed a little now it was clear something was being done.

"Glad to hear something's being done," she said.

"I hope it wasn't anything too awful," I murmured, thinking about what I knew of commercial rodenticides from my veterinary training. Pets swallowed them by accident all the time and the results were often fatal. If it was rat poison she'd ingested, Evie wasn't out of the woods yet.

Erik nodded. "I hope so too. I'd like to offer you something, Jody, as thanks and also to make up for what you witnessed. I know it must have been distressing. I don't want your experience of the festival to be completely coloured by this incident." His expression was kindly, he sort of reminded me of my dad, when he'd break bad news to people at his clinic. His eyes held the same kind of soft, understanding look.

"I really don't need anything..." I started to say, but Carla nudged my foot with hers and I shut my mouth automatically. To my surprise, Ari also shot me a look. I'd have thought she'd agree with me that this wasn't the sort of thing that needed rewarding. It was just the right thing to do. Besides he was probably only talking about some free drink vouchers or a VIP pass or something. Nothing to get excited over, for me especially.

Erik opened a desk drawer and removed a lock box. He flicked through its contents and pulled out an envelope, handed it to me over the desk. I took it, expecting to feel laminated passes inside, or ravelled lanyards. But I could tell from the feel of it that it contained money. The edges of notes peeped out of the top as I lifted the flap. It wasn't just money. It was a lot of money. My insides squirmed. I felt his eyes on me like a physical pressure, willing me to take it. They no longer reminded me of my dad. It was like he was trying to force me to accept the money from the pressure of his gaze alone. Or was that all in my head? I glanced sideways and found Carla and Ari looking at me with the same intensity.

I felt suddenly as if I was surrounded by crows, their sharp beaks hovering over me.

"Thank you," I managed, letting the hand with the envelope fall into my lap. "I hope Evie will be OK. I'd like to be able to visit her in hospital before we go home if you know which one she was taken to."

"Jennifer said she has your number, I'm sure she'll be in touch to offer her thanks too," Erik said, leaning his forearms on his cluttered desk. "Thank you again."

It was clearly our cue to leave and we trooped out of the air-conditioned icebox into the full Greek sunshine, still clutching our bottles of water. The odour of rotting rubbish and weed was even more noticeable after being shut out for a while, the air newly hot and suffocating.

When Carla and Ari didn't immediately start asking questions or talking about what we'd just witnessed, I could feel something was off. They were bothered by something but weren't telling me what. We made it a

179

whole ten feet before I couldn't stand the tense silence anymore.

"What's going on?" I asked, touching Ari's arm to get her attention in the stream of people filing between the beach and the amusements of the festival.

"What do you mean?" Ari said, eyes darting to Carla as if for support.

"You both really wanted me to take the money, practically snatched it up yourselves. But…it's weird, isn't it? To accept this much cash for just doing the right thing. It's weird of him to even offer."

"Not necessarily," Carla said. "He's obviously minted, being able to put this whole thing together, owning an island. To him it's probably like chucking fifty quid to the person who found your cat."

"If he does own it," I said. "And it's a landfill, remember?"

"How much did you get?" Carla asked, ignoring my protests and peering hopefully at the envelope. I started to open it, thumbing the notes inside.

"Not here!" Ari interjected. "Back at the tent. You never know who's skulking around looking for stuff to steal."

"Not the iPhone again, Ari," Carla sighed. "Let it go! Though…maybe you have a point, we'll go through it when we get back." She glanced between me and Ari. "We should tell her."

"Tell me what?" I asked, my stomach suddenly sour. "Have you been keeping something from me?"

Just like Southend, I thought. It was happening again. The pair of them keeping secrets, manipulating me. Deciding what was best without even asking me what I wanted.

We were approaching the gates to the campground now and there were fewer people about. Most of them were probably over near the stage or hanging out where they could get drinks and have fun. There wasn't much to keep people in the tent city during the heat of the day. A dusty haze spread between the tents and the colourful nylon canopies seemed to radiate heat back at the sky. I already felt heavy and exhausted just from walking from Erik's office. Though perhaps that was the adrenaline wearing off and the shock starting to kick in.

"I'm not sure..." Ari began.

"Please just...tell me," I interrupted. "I have a right to know if it's to do with me."

"Well, I wanted to tell you when we first got the email," Carla said, somewhat smugly, which suggested the pair of them had argued about it. "Ari was the one who didn't think you could handle the stress of it at the same time as coming here."

"Jesus, Carla!" Ari glared at her. "It wasn't like that, I...look, Jody, I just thought it could wait until we got home because otherwise you'd be thinking about it the whole time and it wasn't like we could refund the airfare, not on budget tickets. So..."

"What's happened?" I asked.

Ari sighed, looking even guiltier. "We got an email through from the landlord a few days before we were due to fly out – he misspelled your email and we were going to forward it on but then we thought..."

Carla cleared her throat pointedly.

"Fine, I thought," Ari continued, clearly irritated. "That...it just seemed like we'd be worrying you for nothing. Especially with all the pre-trip jitters you had going on. It just seemed easier to save it for when we got back. It was only a few days difference it's not like any of us could do much about it in that time anyway."

"What did the landlord want?" I asked, a horrible feeling settling in my chest. They'd hidden something from me – they'd basically lied to me. And it was about the house, which immediately sent my anxiety skyrocketing.

See, they had a point, a traitorous voice in my head muttered.

It didn't matter though, if they'd had a reason. Did it? They'd still lied to me, and not for the first time. Back in our university days together when we'd all gone on that girls' trip to Southend, I hadn't wanted to go. It sounded like a nice idea in theory but I didn't want to be an unwanted hanger-on or to spend reading week club hopping and getting day-drunk on the beach. Especially as my go-to activity in a club was hovering in a corner, wishing I hadn't come out.

But when I'd told Carla I didn't really feel like it and they should ask someone else instead, she'd been so upset. She told me that if I didn't go they wouldn't have enough people to cover the cost of the holiday home they'd put a deposit on. That no one else was free and it would ruin the whole trip for everyone. Ari had backed her up so in the end I'd gone along.

Just like I'd feared the trip turned out to be a wasted reading week of being around drunk or hungover girls and standing stiffly in clubs and pubs wishing I could just go home. I could tell everyone was getting annoyed with me for not joining in, for being the one to shush them because I was worried about complaints from the nearby holiday homes. The entire time I was worried about the work I wasn't getting done and trying my hardest to look like I was having fun and didn't care about uni. It was Hell and it cost me money I could have really done with saving.

The worst part was, I'd found out later from one of the other girls that she had a friend who'd wanted to go, but couldn't because I'd taken the last spot. Carla and Ari knew the other girl too. They'd just lied to me to get me to go, thinking they knew best. Wanting me to join in, no matter what a terrible time I was having. Just like my mother. I'd felt a complete idiot for trusting them at the time. Not that I'd had the courage to confront them. I'd done my best to pretend it had never happened and eventually managed to forget about it – until now.

Was this the first time they'd lied to me since? How would I ever know unless they told me, or I managed to overhear something I shouldn't? I wanted to trust them but, just then I was reminded of all the reasons not to.

"The landlord's putting the rent up from this month – by three hundred quid," Ari said, reluctantly. "He said something about the interest rates. I guess rents are going up everywhere but....yeah, three hundred between us, starting from the end of this month."

"What?" the shock of it was almost physical. I felt ill. "He can't just do that, we have a contract...right?"

"Unfortunately he can do that. We're month to month," Carla said. "I've been out of contract for a year now. Reading between the lines it sounds like he's expecting us to move out. It was all very 'if you don't like it you know where the door is' – you know? He

183

probably wants to sell or divide the place up even more to cram more people in."

"But we can't find somewhere else to live in like, two weeks," I was still processing, trying to hold onto something solid. Which wasn't easy with the knowledge that I could no longer afford my rent hanging over my head. Where was I going to find an extra hundred pounds a month? Especially with the threat of losing my bursary hanging over my head because of all the lectures I'd missed. Not to mention Nick demanding money from me too.

"Exactly, so we probably need to pay it," Ari said, as we reached our tent and she collapsed onto the blanket. "Which means recouping some of the money we just paid out on this trip so we can pay this month's rent and scrape together enough to find somewhere new. We were going to try begging our parents but this money means we can save that option for when we're really screwed."

"The deposit's going to be the big thing," Carla said. "I doubt he's going to give ours back, not fully. Maybe not at all. You know what they're like – it'll be 'someone walked over this carpet too much, that's a hundred quid you'll never see again'."

They were acting as if I'd already let it go, forgiven them for lying to me. That, more than the lying itself, rankled. All three of us were sitting on the blanket now, a witches' circle around the envelope to protect it from view. I lifted the flap and flicked through the notes, checking the denominations.

"It's…a thousand euro," I said, slightly stunned. A reward, that's what Erik had made it sound like. But seeing that amount of money, holding it in my hand, it only felt like one thing – a bribe. But for what, and why?

"That's what...nearly nine-hundred quid?" Carla said, ever the fastest with maths.

"About that, yeah," I said. "Do you not think that's like, too much?"

"Not enough I'd say," Carla said. "I mean, it'll help us cover three months of the increased rent in the worst case scenario, right? But after that we'd better have something else in place."

"I don't think that's what Jody means," Ari put in. "Is it?"

Something about her tone made me feel chastised. She sounded irritated with me for the first time since I'd met her. I looked up from the envelope of money and found her watching me steadily, unblinking.

"Jody, we need this money. We can't really afford to look a gift horse in the mouth here," she said.

"But doesn't it feel weird?" I said, stressing the final word. "You were right there with me, wondering if Evie was...if she was dead, when I found her. Now the festival organiser just hands over a thousand euro and you're happy to say it's a reward?"

"Yeah, like Carla said – he's loaded. Besides, if he was trying to cover up a death I think he'd give us more than a thousand euro. If it's a bribe, it's a shitty one," Ari said. "And he's going to issue warnings – it's not a cover-up, you're being paranoid. Again."

Was I? Or was this reasonable suspicion and anger over them lying to me? I was almost certain that it was justified, that Erik had been acting weird. But sitting

185

there looking at the two of them I felt my resolve weaken. My denials, when they came, were weak.

"But he said this had happened to other people. Is he just handing out a grand to everyone who gets their wasted friend to a medical tent? Because that sounds unlikely," I said, embarrassed and annoyed at her accusation.

"Obviously he's not doing that," Ari sighed. "But you found Evie when no one else was going to – right? She wasn't just pissed and in need of a sit down and some water with a volunteer. She was unconscious, maybe overdosing and you saved her life!"

"That's right," Carla said, nodding along to Ari's arguments. "Jody, I'm sorry but…do you think you're feeling this way because you're kind of down on yourself, at the moment? I mean, it was a really amazing thing that you did. You deserve a reward."

Was she right? Was this horrible squirming sensation in my belly just another variation on the feelings I'd had my entire life? The thought that I wasn't worthy, that anything good happening to me was suspicious and that nothing I ever did was good enough?

I thought of Evie lying in those rubbish bags and of seeing her carried into the medical tent. If Ari was right and I had saved her life, maybe that was worth recognition, even a reward. But an envelope full of cash? It just all seemed so sketchy, not even trying to hide the blunt truth of what was going on like with a prize or a gift-card. I'd found a girl on the edge of death, a girl who I still wasn't one hundred per cent sure hadn't been dead, and I'd been paid off.

"No," I said. It came out weak, barely audible. I

cleared my throat. "No. I don't like this. Something's wrong with this entire situation, with this place...I want to go home."

Silence greeted my words, broken only by the occasional footfalls of a passer-by on the packed dirt path. Ari and Carla exchanged wary looks.

"I don't want to leave," Carla said. "So...if you're going...you're going without me."

"And me, sorry," Ari said, not meeting my eye. "We came all this way, I'm not leaving the festival just because some girl took some bad drugs and you want to turn it into some big scary plot because you're still freaking out about Nick."

The unfairness of that pricked me and I felt my spine stiffen. "I'm not freaking out – I'm reacting normally. You're the ones who're trying to make this all mean nothing. You don't want anything to be wrong so you're trying to make me feel crazy."

"Jody...*that* sounds pretty crazy," Carla said. "We're not trying to fucking... gaslight you, or whatever, we just don't agree with you. I mean, first there was the Nick thing and now you think that...what? The festival organisers are bunging people hush money to keep quiet about people going overboard on the drugs? It's a festival! That's what happens. I know you've never been to one but trust me – this isn't weird."

The Nick thing. I felt my face go hot when she mentioned him. I was immediately grateful that I hadn't mentioned seeing him again. That'd just be giving them more ammunition to use against me. Ammunition was right as well. I was definitely under attack.

"I don't agree," I said, simply. "And it's not the same

187

thing. I was terrified that Nick might show up again – I still am. That's why I thought I saw him, or that's what you said anyway. But this isn't about being afraid, it's about seeing the red flags and they're everywhere. This place is wrong in so many little ways."

"Like what?" Carla asked. "The bus not coming? The shit booze? A few half-arsed attractions? That's just…teething problems. This is the first Lethe festival. It wasn't going to be Glastonbury was it? They're working things out and it feels more authentic, not like Butlins. I thought you knew what you were signing up for?"

I looked at Ari, hoping she'd see that I was struggling with Carla. That I couldn't hold my own against her when she was being overbearing like this. But Ari was just watching me get steamrolled.

I was suddenly struck by the reality of our relationship. They'd helped me so much, propped me up and comforted me, but really we'd only been getting to know each other again for a few months. They weren't the same girls I'd been at uni with. It had been a long and eventful two years. They were adults, virtual strangers. It was quickly becoming clear to me that I didn't really know them that well at all. Certainly not well enough to predict how they'd react to the kind of situations which would test even well-established friendships – like going abroad together or coming into money. Certainly not both at once.

Apparently the only thing that had remained consistent since uni, was their readiness to lie to me. To manipulate me. I was so tired of being manipulated. Of feeling stupid and grateful and unworthy. I just wanted to feel safe.

The only thing I wanted in that moment was to get away from the festival. To get out of this argument before it went too far. To be by myself so I could calm down and get myself together. Before whatever it was that we had in the way of friendship was damaged beyond repair. I was painfully aware that they were all I had. Without Nick, with every word I exchanged with my mother feeling like a thrown knife, this was it for me. The truth was, I needed them more than they needed me.

"Look, if you want to stay here, that's fine. I can try and get an early flight back by myself," I said. Even as I did so I wondered if that would be possible, if I had the money to do it without using the 'reward' and whether I could afford to stay at a hotel near the airport if not. Hell, I wasn't even sure where I'd find a taxi to take me even that far. Without any through traffic past the festival gates, I might end up having to walk until I found signal.

Carla and Ari looked as if their thoughts were running in a similar vein to mine. Perhaps they were wavering at the thought of sending me off all alone?

"Come on, Jody – just stay. It's not worth the stress," Carla said.

"Yeah, it's only another day."

"I'd really rather just not be here," I said, and crawled into the tent, started sorting through my bag and packing things away. I felt ridiculous even as I did so. Was I really going to upend everything for the sake of bailing one day early? I heard the pair of them whispering and then the nylon canopy shushed against someone's body. It was Ari. She watched me pack for a minute, then sighed.

"What about the money?"

I looked at her, hurt that she was apparently more worried about the envelope of cash than what was going on at the festival, than me. I shrugged.

"I'll take my third of it, OK?" I said, though it was technically all mine I didn't want to piss them off any more than I already had.

"Jody, can you just...can we just forget this happened?" Ari asked, sounding genuinely chastened. "It doesn't have to be a big deal."

"I don't want it to be. I just don't want to stay here either." I found the plastic pouch that contained all the important stuff I didn't want in my handbag during the festival. I frowned at the lightness of it and quickly undid the zip.

"What is it?" Ari asked.

"My passport," I said, tearing the rest of the stuff out of my bag in the hope that I was mistaken. "It's gone."

Chapter 17

"It has to be here somewhere," Carla said for the second time in ten minutes.

Between the three of us we'd searched every inch of the small tent and every bag at least twice. All our stuff was in a mess, clothes unfolded and screwed up again, small pouches opened and dumped out, I'd even flicked through the pages of my book and left it splayed open on the floor. My passport was nowhere to be found. I'd started the search already in a panic and now I was absolutely frantic. My hands were shaking as I went through my handbag for the third or fourth time. It couldn't have just evaporated into thin air. Like Carla said, it had to be somewhere.

Only apparently 'somewhere' was not here, and passports couldn't get up and walk off on their own. Which left one possibility niggling about the back of my mind – someone had taken it.

"Is anything else even missing?" I asked, my voice coming out shrill and too loud in panic and suspicion. "It looks like all my other stuff is still here. Nothing else has been touched. Have you lost anything?"

"I can't see that anything else is gone, no," Ari said. "Carla?"

"All present and correct. Why?"

Both of them sounded far too casual for the nightmarish situation I was in. I needed someone to panic with me, so I knew I wasn't overreacting. So I could feel like I wasn't alone with whatever happened now that my passport was missing.

"Well, it seems obvious that if it's not here that means someone took it," I said. "And isn't it weird that they'd come in here and take just my passport," I said, frustrated with the pair of them, still going through my bag. "Whoever 'they' are. You've both still got yours." That was the first thing they'd looked for once I made my discovery. Both their passports were exactly as they'd left them – stored a lot less safely than mine in their suitcases.

"Besides," I added, growing more and more suspicious with each passing second. "Who would steal a passport? Why not cash or our phones or the booze? Something someone would actually want at a festival? They didn't even take my debit card to use with it."

"Yeah, I don't think anyone would steal just a random passport, Jody…but that probably just means it wasn't taken, it's just lost," Carla said, raising her eyebrows at Ari. "I mean, you're right – who's going to steal just a passport, nothing else – and just one passport at that when there's three in the tent if that's all they were interested in."

Her agreement that the theft made no sense only made me more frustrated that she didn't agree that someone had in fact stolen my passport purposely.

Both of them were acting like just because it was weird, that meant it couldn't have happened. But I was sure that I hadn't just lost my passport. It had been in its place in the tent since we arrived. Someone had to have done something with it. We were in a tiny tent, there were only so many places it could be and we'd checked all of them. Twice. Three times even. Every suitcase, every pocket and bag.

I'd even sat there and remembered all the way back to the airport. I remembered specifically putting my passport back in the plastic pouch that contained my boarding pass for the flight out to Greece. I remembered the sign I'd been looking at as I did up the zip, remembered how it had stuck and then closed neatly. I'd had my passport when we arrived, I was certain of it. Had seen it as I'd hunted in my bag for cash to pay the taxi driver.

Which meant that someone had specifically taken it. Taken my passport and nothing else from the tent. So it wasn't just done on a whim. Someone was targeting me, specifically. They had come into the tent to take my passport and then left without even being tempted by any of the small valuables lying around like jewellery and phones. My list of suspects wasn't long, I felt my heart thumping along unevenly as I considered the possibilities.

"Do you think it might be...him?" I said, curling my arms around myself protectively.

"You mean, Nick?" Carla said, a trace of annoyance in her tone. "Come on, you can't just blame him for everything that goes wrong. Even if he deserves it. You'll drive yourself nuts."

"I just mean, what if he's trying to trap me here – you guys will have to leave me behind if I haven't got a passport – won't you? You've got tickets for the flight home you can't afford to replace. And you can't miss work, can you Carla?"

"Well, no but, come on, Jody," Carla said, sprawling into a sitting position on the ground sheet, clearly done with uselessly searching. "Let's say Nick is here – which, I know you think you saw him but…come on – number one, how would he know you were here? And two, what are the chances of him just coincidentally also getting Lethe tickets? But putting that aside, even if he happened to come here at the same time as us, why would he mess with you when there are people everywhere and he has a whole festival to distract him? And even if he was here, which again – he isn't! – why would he steal your passport to keep you here? Why not, I don't know pee on your sleeping bag or steal your clothes. The kind of petty awful shit idiots like him do to get back at women."

"She has a point," Ari said. "For the sake of argument let's say his plan is to strand you here in Greece while we have to head home. Well, then he'd have to stay here to get at you, wouldn't he? What would be the end result of that, except him spending more money to stay on here and follow you around… what, indefinitely?," Ari said briskly. "It makes no sense."

"Unless he was just doing it to get back at me and he wasn't planning on staying to watch," I pointed out. "Or he could have somehow found out that I was here and maybe he knew someone who was already coming to the festival and he just asked them to fuck with me however they could."

"And they'd do that just because he asked?" Carla said doubtfully, chewing one of her painted nails. "They'd have to be pretty good friends and you said it yourself, Nick's an arsehole."

"And he has arsehole friends from work, from the gym – it was one of them he was trying to get me to sleep with, in case you've forgotten! I wouldn't put this kind of thing past them. And if one of them took my passport it's probably either in the sea or a bin or... somewhere else I'll never get it back in time."

Carla actually seemed to consider this, even though I sounded borderline hysterical to my own ears. "But how would he know you're here? We didn't announce it online, it was all so quick anyway we barely had a chance to tell anyone. We haven't posted anything since we got here either."

"Well, if he has friends who just happened to be here they might have recognised Jody, just while we were walking around," Ari said, sounding like she was reluctant to add strength to my theory as she fiddled thoughtfully with her necklace. "We've been trying to reason it out like he was trying to follow Jody but what if it's all more coincidental than that – just a crime of opportunity? Someone here knows Nick, told him about seeing Jody and Nick asked whoever it was to follow us to the tent and find a way to fuck with us."

Carla was nodding, clearly on board with Ari's theory, like it was easy to believe. Perhaps too easy, when they hadn't exactly been falling over themselves to believe me about seeing Nick before. Why was this suddenly more plausible? Didn't it take more of a coincidence for Nick's friend or whoever to randomly be at the festival instead of Nick choosing to come after me?

"What's wrong?" Ari asked. "We're agreeing with you. Haven't you been telling us that Nick was up to something since we got here?"

I nodded but couldn't meet her eye. I picked my book up and smoothed it closed, tucked it away into my suitcase for something to do. The horrible squirming feeling in my stomach refused to go away. Why were they agreeing so easily with this one theory? Especially such a convoluted one, involving his friends who had taken my passport but apparently passed up the opportunity to do any of the horrible shit Carla had suggested. Wouldn't Nick's mates have enjoyed throwing my clothes out into the dust or leaving shit in my suitcase or something equally awful? Unless the point was to have the theft of the passport go unnoticed until it was time to leave and thus too late to do anything about it?

I thought of the Southend trip and how Carla and Ari had both lied to get me to go with them, because they'd wanted me to 'have fun' and 'get away for a while'. What if this was the same kind of thing?

What if this was...*them*?

When I couldn't stand the squirming feeling any longer I picked up a pillow like a shield and clasped it tightly in my lap. After taking a deep breath I asked the question that was buzzing around my head like a fly, refusing to leave me alone.

"You wouldn't...take my passport, would you?"

"Jody!" Carla was aghast. I looked up and found that both she and Ari were looking at me with twin expressions of horror. Ari still had her necklace between her fingers, frozen, mid-twiddle. "How could you think that?"

"That's a really shitty thing to say, Jody," Ari said, dropping her necklace. "Why would you even think… is this about the money? You think we'd try and screw you over for a few hundred quid, after everything you told us since we got here?"

I felt my face go hot. They were right, it was a shitty thing to accuse them of, when they'd been so supportive, but was thinking it and saying nothing any better? And, more to the point, hadn't they done something like this before?

"I was just thinking maybe, when I rang you and told you about Evie…you might have thought I'd want to leave right away and so you hid my passport before you came to meet me, so we'd have to stay for the rest of the festival and you could just 'find it' again on the day we were due to leave," I said, all in a rush. "Not to be horrible or anything just…you might have thought it was for the best. But, it's freaking me out so…if you do have it, please can you give it back now and we can just forget it ever happened?"

Strained silence greeted my words. I'd hurt both of them, I knew that. But I still wasn't sure if they were being honest with me or not and that hurt too.

"Look," I said. "I don't want to fight about it but… it's not like it would be the first time you've done something like this, would it? I know you both lied to me, back in uni – about the Southend trip? When you told me I had to go so there'd be enough people to pay for the house. I know there were other people who could have gone. People who would have actually enjoyed it."

Carla scoffed. "That's...that was years ago, Jody. And it wasn't really a 'lie' it was just..." she looked to Ari for support.

"We wanted you to come with us, and you'd already agreed to. We just didn't want you to pull out because you were nervous," Ari said.

"But you did still lie," I pointed out, feeling miserable even as I said it. "So...what's to stop you from lying again, now? If you thought it was going to do me some good?"

Carla just looked at me like she didn't even recognise me. I felt uncomfortable and squirmy under her gaze but I couldn't let it go. It felt like we were deadlocked; me accusing them and the two of them horrified that I would. Finally, Ari shook her head and sighed, breaking the standoff.

"Look, we're all under a lot of stress right now so... let's just drop this and...we don't have to talk about this again, OK?" she sighed and I thought it was over, but then she spoke again. "But for the record Jody, neither of us would lie about something like this. Neither of us has your passport. And if you can't credit us with a little bit of trust after the last few days..." she glanced at Carla, who folded her arms across her chest. "Then you probably need to find somewhere else to live because this isn't going to work if you think we could do something like that to you, now, after everything you've told us about Nick and the rest of it. We're your friends, Jody. We'd never do that to you."

My insides turned cold. I looked between her and Carla but neither of them wavered. They were serious. I'd accused them of a pretty heinous lie to be fair, even so, their reaction was extreme. So much so that it made me wonder if they were trying to push me to drop the issue for good by as good as threatening me with homelessness.

Or, I told myself, maybe it's because they're so offended that you'd even think it, after everything they've done for you. After they heard you out about Nick and all the rest of it. I looked at them and wondered if that was it. If I'd hurt them so deeply that they didn't even want to be around me anymore.

Yet, even with both of them looking so upset and Ari's words still ringing through my head, I still wasn't completely convinced. There was a part of me that whispered they were trying too hard, being too sincere. I wanted to be able to trust them but I wasn't sure I could trust anyone anymore.

"Fine...let's just...forget about it and try and work something out," I said eventually.

Both Carla and Ari seemed to relax at that, though I still felt as if the subject was far from dropped. We were all just avoiding the gaping pit I'd opened up between us. Tiptoeing around it and hoping none of us pushed the others in.

"I don't know how I'm going to get home," I said, eventually, trying to move the subject on slightly from accusing them of theft. "Do I need to get an emergency passport or something? Is that a thing?"

Both of them seemed to revert back to their normal selves as the topic of how my passport had vanished was left alone. Ari took out her phone and attempted to get online for about the hundredth time since we'd arrived to look up the procedure for this kind of thing. She tutted when the internet refused to load.

"I don't know. We'll probably have to get in touch with the embassy or something. That sounds right – doesn't it?" Ari said.

Carla nodded. "We can probably get the number at the airport, there might be someone there who can help."

"We can't leave it that late, surely?" I said, aghast. "It could take days to sort out. Weeks even!"

"It might still turn up," Carla argued. "In the meantime, you should stay with us. There's no point wasting money just to go stay in a hotel when your passport's probably still somewhere in the tent. We'll probably find it once we start packing everything up."

My suspicions flared again, even brighter than before. My friends weren't nearly worried enough, I thought, about the time crunch we were under here. I was freaking out, wondering if I'd be able to get home. Wondering how on earth I could afford a new ticket if I missed our flight, never mind days, maybe weeks, of hotel accommodation. Ari should have been talking about packing up the tent and going to the airport now to find someone who could help us. I'd have expected Carla to be going from tent to tent asking if anyone had working internet so we could look up contact numbers and get things sorted. But neither of them were really offering anything in the way of actual help.

Which felt very much like a sign they knew, for

certain, that my passport would be 'found' in time for us to leave. Because they had it.

"I say, we enjoy what's left of today and tomorrow and then sort things out when we leave here for the airport," Ari said. "By then we'll have probably found your passport anyway – it'll be in the last place we look. It'll turn up when we're emptying out the tent. You'll see."

She sounded sure about that. Too sure quite frankly. I didn't want to start the argument all over again but I did want to search the tent without them there. For all I knew they were moving my passport around between the pair of them, like a game of keep-away. I just had to convince them to leave me be for a bit.

"You two should go and enjoy the music, soak up some sun," I said. "It's been kind of a…full-on morning. I think I need to get my head together a bit. By myself."

Ari exchanged a look with Carla, one I couldn't read. Was she trying to tell her she thought I suspected them? Were they worried I might make a run for it even without my passport? Or was this just a 'one of us should babysit Jody' look?

"If you're sure?" Carla said.

I nodded, trying to look and sound like I was embarrassed by my freak-out and just needed some space. "Yeah, I'll read for a bit or something. Just try and relax and catch up on some sleep maybe. Bring me back some lunch, yeah?"

"Sure," Ari said, still not sounding completely convinced. "Text us if you need anything else, OK?"

The pair of them quickly changed into more concert-ready clothes and popped to the toilets. Whilst they

201

were away I went through their handbags, feeling lower than shit for doing so. No sign of my passport. I checked the pockets of the clothes they'd just changed out of. Nothing there either. They couldn't have it on them anymore, surely? Carla was wearing a maxi dress with no pockets and Ari's tiny black denim shorts didn't have pockets big enough to hide a passport. Unless they'd managed to shove it into their bra or something I was fairly sure neither of them had it on them at the moment. Which meant it was somewhere in the tent still. The only places I hadn't searched personally were their suitcases.

After they returned from the loo I waved them off from the front flap of the tent and set my phone timer to fifteen minutes. Whilst I waited, in case they came back for something, I found Evie's number and rang it, hoping she'd pick up and tell me she was recovering in hospital. That she was doing OK and had heard from Roisin after all. Unfortunately it went straight to voicemail. Maybe they'd taken it off her at the hospital and turned it off? Or it had run out of battery and she didn't have a charger. What if it was still somewhere in the rubbish where I'd found her? I sent a text anyway in the hope that she'd see it when she woke up. *Hi, it's Jody. Hope you're doing ok, will keep an eye out for Roisin. Let me know if you need anything.*

That done, I tried to read until the alarm went off and once I was sure neither Ari nor Carla would be coming back I started to search the tent all over again. I went through their suitcases, their pockets, even the bag linings and their bedding. I opened their makeup bags and lifted the ground sheet and went through the snacks they'd brought in case my passport was tucked between the packets. Nothing.

Finally I sat back on my heels in the tent doorway, sweating and deeply ashamed of myself as I surveyed the chaos of our shared space. It wasn't there. I'd just broken Ari and Carla's trust in me for nothing and still, I had my doubts. I couldn't tell anymore what was paranoia and what was reasonable suspicion. A throbbing headache had started up behind my left eye and I desperately wanted to be at home, in my own bed. I wanted very badly to have never come to this festival. Though if I was wishing for things perhaps I'd go back even further – wish I'd never come to London, wish I'd never met Nick. Wish I'd never been born quite frankly. It wasn't as if I had much to show for my time on earth was it? And precious little of that was positive.

"Hello again."

At the sound of a man's voice I turned and nearly fell over in my rush to see who was behind me. For a fraction of a second I was horrified that it was Nick. But it wasn't. Andrei was standing on the path, a clean white t-shirt on over black jeans with a chain connecting to his wallet. He smiled, shy but pleased looking. I blinked at him, in all the horror of finding Evie, losing my passport and hurting my friends, I'd let him slip from my mind. Now, seeing him, I felt a flutter of hope, here at last, was a distraction from the mess I'd made for myself. Someone who wasn't going to look at me like I was nuts.

"I was going to go get a coffee," he said casually. "I'm sick of making it over a little stove...I was wondering if you wanted to come with me?"

Just then I wanted to be anywhere but in that tent. Anxiety be damned. I nodded. He could have suggested going to dig a hole down to the landfill under our feet and I probably still would have said yes. It didn't matter what we'd be doing, I just wanted to feel normal for a while. To stop thinking about Nick and conspiracies and all my past mistakes.

"Sounds good. Um...let me get my bag," I said, marshalling a smile.

I grabbed my handbag and did a quick check of the tent to see if it was obvious that I'd gone through it. As far as I could tell it looked just as it had after our first search – disorganised and messy.

Together we walked through the campground towards the entrance to the amusement area, where the bars, food kiosks and entertainment domes were already buzzing with activity. The air was still morning fresh and not as hot as it had been, I wrapped my arms around myself and rubbed at my goose bumps, wishing I'd brought a cardigan. Andrei let the silence lie for a while but then nudged me playfully, making me jump.

"So, not at the concert today?" he asked casually, nodding in the direction of the stage, from which music and cheering rose and fell as a distant roar.

"No," I said. "I wasn't really in the mood. I think maybe the lack of sleep's getting to me."

"Same. Too tired – last night went kind of late and sleeping on the ground isn't exactly my idea of rest."

I could have just agreed with him and let the conversation drop but I found myself telling the truth instead. It wasn't that I wanted to talk about it, I just needed to know if I was being weird or not. I needed an outside opinion. "I'm sort of stressed out because my passport's gone missing."

"Shit, really?" he came to a halt. "Do you want me to help you look for it? Are your friends off trying to retrace your steps?"

"I've already checked the tent and I never took it anywhere else, but thanks anyway. My...friends, are off having fun because I told them to go without me." I felt my face burn. I'd lied to them, betrayed them.

But what if they'd betrayed me first?

"That was nice of you," Andrei said, a slight frown on his face. "But it's kind of irresponsible of them to go off and leave you behind. Don't you need to get a new passport if you want to get home after the festival? It might take a while to sort that out, right?"

"They think I'll find it again before it becomes an issue," I said, hearing the bitterness in my voice with a wince. "I hope they're right because I definitely can't afford to get stuck in Greece, even for an extra day. Never mind weeks."

"I hope they're right too, it would be pretty awful to end up stuck so far from home... Expensive too."

We were well into the amusement area now, moving between the crowded domes. It made further conversation difficult and I settled for following Andrei towards a coffee kiosk with a bright yellow awning, wedged between two domes. I was turning his words over, feeling more suspicious than ever. If Andrei, a stranger, was this worried about the passport situation why weren't Ari and Carla? The only reason that made sense to me was that they knew I'd find my passport in

205

time, because they had it. But if that was true, where were they keeping it?

"For what it's worth," Andrei said, after appearing to be in deep thought for a while. "I know someone with a flat in town, if you need somewhere to stay."

"If a hotel is going to be expensive, I can't imagine how much a flat would cost," I said, with a wince.

"My uncle used to let it out on an app for holidays but it's empty most of the time now. Probably cheaper for you than a hotel, especially if I ask him for you – he likes me, I used to work for him in the summer as a teenager," Andrei said whilst we queued for our coffee.

"Oh, that's really nice of you...I'm probably fine," I said, still thinking about my housemates and how they were probably off somewhere congratulating themselves on tricking me. "It'll work itself out, I'm sure."

"I hope so." Andrei smiled at the guy behind the counter. "Americano please, and a...?"

"Oh...same for me please," I said, caught off guard and defaulting to just copying his order. I flushed at how pathetic that was, I couldn't even order coffee without someone to tell me what to get.

"I'll get them," Andrei said, as I fumbled with my bag.

"You don't have to," I said, my face flaming even more now.

"It's the least I can do. Sounds like you're having a shitty day."

"It's getting better." I shrugged, just happy to be away from the messy tent and my own thoughts.

Andrei favoured me with a smile and I immediately

felt my face turn redder. I hadn't meant to sound like I was flirting. Had I?

"Shall we walk down to the beach?" he asked, after paying for the coffees. "Such as it is."

"Sure," I accepted one of the cups and followed him into the crowd.

Chapter 18

We were sitting on the same large chunk of concrete that Carla had sunbathed on a few days ago. The beach was a little emptier now, probably because most people had been there and realised it had very little to offer. Unless you were on a scavenger hunt for eroded construction materials or needed to meet a quota for collecting take-away containers. The breeze off the water was nice though, even if it did smell like petrol and damp rubbish. Across the water the city was blindingly white and sparkling as the sun hit the glass of several high-rises. Comparatively the festival felt like a shanty town on a prison island, cut off from civilisation.

I'd long since finished my coffee and the whole sorry story was spilling out of me into the companionable silences that stretched between us. It was good to be able to tell it all to someone who just...listened. Who didn't try to tell me what was real and what wasn't. Someone who didn't try to fix things or talk me down, but just let me get it all out. Well, most of it. I hadn't told him about Nick, but everything else, I'd put out there. It was like giving a confession. I just needed him to hear it.

"And now," I concluded, picking at my cuticles, "I don't know if I believe that they don't know where my passport is. They might be doing it again – manipulating me. Trying to do the same thing as my mum and making me stay here 'for my own good' so I 'join in' with everyone else and 'have fun'."

"You really think they'd do that? Steal your passport just to make you stay an extra day at the festival?" Andrei asked, head tilted to the side as he considered the idea. Even though he didn't know Carla or Ari he sounded like he didn't want to believe the worst of them. It was oddly reassuring to know that I wasn't giving them too much credit when I tried to convince myself they hadn't done it. "Maybe they're just downplaying it going missing to stop you from getting too stressed?"

"I'm not sure, that's the problem," I told him. "The more I think about the last few days the less sure I am about everything. Anything. I can't even trust my own friends." My own eyes, I thought, but didn't say. Twice now I'd seen Nick and twice I'd doubted myself afterwards. That didn't say a lot about my ability to tell fact from fiction. Maybe Ari and Carla were right about me. I was losing it.

"They're your friends, right? They wouldn't do such a horrible thing."

"I'm not sure we are friends, not properly. We just lived together before, and again now. Maybe we have different ideas of what 'being friends' is. I mean…isn't it childish to have best friends at my age? To think that we should be close and honest and take care of each

209

other instead of just being women who live together and share the occasional pizza. And maybe they don't think it's a horrible thing they've done. They might have decided it would be good for me to stay for the rest of the festival – this could all be a terrible attempt at an intervention." As I said it I felt a burst of annoyance and a flood of shame. Did they really think I needed to be lied to, manipulated, in order to be somewhat normal?

"Hmmm," Andrei said, worrying his lip with his teeth. "Perhaps, but then that means they care, at least? Doesn't it? They want you to have a good time. They're just not doing it the right way."

"I suppose. But does it matter why they did it if the fact that they did it at all makes me not want to see them ever again?" I said, frustrated and upset with them, with myself. With everything.

Andrei nodded slowly, looking off towards the horizon. "I get what you mean. I suppose it doesn't matter why someone does something if it hurt you anyway."

"The worst part is I can't know for sure," I said, scrunching my empty coffee cup in my hands until the plastic lid popped. "I mean if I'm already struggling to believe them about the passport thing how can I believe them about their intentions if it turns out that they did lie? I suppose actually the worst part is having to see them again later, spend the night in the same tent and wondering if they're sharing these...looks, behind my back."

Again I felt embarrassed for dumping all of this on a virtual stranger, especially as he'd already done so

210

much for me. Saving me from that awful guy and being so nice at the party. But maybe it was because he was a stranger that I found it so easy to confide in him. I just wanted someone to tell me that I wasn't crazy, that what I was feeling was valid. Ari and Carla had done their best with the whole Nick situation but they'd also left me feeling too embarrassed to tell them when I thought I'd seen him again.

"You could stay in my tent," Andrei said, so quietly I almost didn't hear him.

I looked at Andrei and was surprised to see that he was avoiding my eyes, clearly anxious over what he'd just suggested. One hand twisted the chain on his wallet.

"I could sleep in my brother's tent," he continued. "Ivan's spending all his time with a girl he met so it's just sitting there empty. I'd offer that one to you but he spilled most of a bottle of rum in there and it still stinks."

"That's...you don't have to do that," I said, my insides fluttering regardless. "I can just suck it up and go back to my tent."

"I wanted to offer, you seem like you could use a break. And look if you don't feel safe where you are you should get some space. Even if it's just for one night." He looked so earnest that I felt myself wavering.

The idea of avoiding further conflict with the others was tempting. Even if it made things worse afterwards I was not above making a decision based on my short-term comfort. It was basically all I'd been doing since leaving Nick. Every time I stayed inside instead of going to a lecture, hid away in my room instead of hanging out downstairs. I wasn't completely blind to the damage

I was doing to myself even as I did it. But it was worth it at the time to feel safe. To feel in control.

The mental image of Evie, pale and limp amongst the rubbish bags, flashed before me. Was that what she'd been doing? Living for the now and not thinking or worrying about the future? Alright so I wasn't on such a steep trajectory down to rock bottom, but I could feel it waiting there. I'd been trying to slow my slide but nothing seemed to be working. Coming to the festival was meant to be me giving myself a chance to reset. If anything it had made things worse.

"That's a really nice offer, I'm just not sure I should," I said. "There's a lot going on and, I don't think I've been making the best choices to be honest. Not for a long while. After everything that happened today I think I should probably stay put and not make things worse."

"Everything?" Andrei asked, frowning in confusion. "More than your passport going missing?"

I realised then that I hadn't told him about Evie. I'd been too focused on myself and the argument with my friends, all my insecurities. I'd forgotten about the girl I'd found half dead, like she wasn't worth mentioning. My face went hot with shame. I was being so self-absorbed and selfish. No wonder my friends were sick of me. My chest hurt at the thought of going over it all again none the less. Going back to that moment of total fear and panic. Still, I found I didn't want to brush him off, or lie.

"This morning I was in the backstage sort of…out of bounds bit of the festival…"

"Why?" Andrei's face scrunched up in confusion.

"I was…" I couldn't explain about Nick just then. Especially as I'd avoided mentioning him so far. "…I saw a rat stuck in a trap and I wanted to help."

Andrei's expression softened. "That was kind of you. You could have gotten hurt back there."

I shrugged, feeling bad to have half-lied to him. "Turned out to be less of a silly thing to do than it seemed. I tripped on some rubbish and found a girl unconscious in a pile of plastic sacks. It was really scary and luckily there were people around to hear me scream. They carried her to the medical tent. That's why I think my friends might have wanted to take action to keep me here – because they thought I'd freak out and immediately want to go home. Which I did. But that's normal right? You'd be pretty freaked out if you found someone like that?"

"Anyone would be! My God – is she alright?" Andrei asked, face aghast and disgusted, as if he couldn't believe what he was hearing. Just like me, he was shocked and shaken by what I'd seen. "What'd happened to her?"

"They said it was something she'd taken – either just the drugs, or they were cut with something dodgy. They said they'd had her transferred to hospital, that she was stable." I frowned, looked out to sea. "I didn't see an ambulance though. Or hear one even. You'd think it would have caused a stir…though I suppose by then we were in Erik's office. The organiser."

"Maybe it came quietly? To keep from causing a panic," Andrei suggested. "Or they took her out on a stretcher so they wouldn't have to get a vehicle all the way through the festival?"

"Maybe…I tried to check up on her but her phone

must be off. That or it's out of battery. Maybe I should ring the hospital? Do you know which one the nearest hospital is?"

Andrei shrugged helplessly. "I'm not sure. My uncle lives here, I don't. I'd look it up but my phone isn't working properly – no internet since we got here."

"Me either. Which is weird, right? Unless it's because this place used to be a landfill. Could be there's no infrastructure out here. God, I wish I could find anything out for sure." I pressed my palms on the sharp concrete, frustrated and confused. "Why am I the only person who thinks all this is weird? I swear to God! All Ari and Carla do is make me feel crazy."

"Hey."

I looked down when Andrei took my hand, fingers curling gently around mine to keep me from hurting myself on the concrete.

"You're not crazy," Andrei said. "Even if there's nothing weird going on, it's not crazy to question things because you're concerned. It's just how you feel and there's nothing wrong with that. But, now you've told me and together we can deal with it – we can make a plan for if you can't find your passport and everything will be OK."

An actual declaration of undying love would not have hit me harder. Comparatively that would have felt generic, overplayed. This was altogether different. It was like he'd reached into the most secret depths of my mind and pulled out the one thing I'd always needed to hear from someone else. Not wanted, but needed. Needed the same way a child needs their parent's love, or air. Like hearing that I wasn't wrong or bad or weird, had slotted a piece back into place inside me which I hadn't known was misaligned. I'd just been living life with it hanging askew, hurting me.

I felt tears springing to my eyes. Everything I'd ever needed to hear, had just fallen from the mouth of a stranger. It was simultaneously the most understood and loneliest I'd ever felt. I wasn't alone anymore though – Andrei believed me and he was going to try and help me. Just knowing I didn't have to do it all on my own was such a relief. I hadn't realised just how cut off I'd felt since starting to doubt Ari and Carla. Him turning up and listening, wanting to help, had given me back some stability.

"Jody," Andrei said quietly, "I really think you should take my tent. Just for tonight. To get away from…everything that's bothering you. I think it would be good for you."

I nodded, sniffed hard to try and control the quavering of my mouth.

"Can I give you a hug?" Andrei asked, voice so soft it was nearly swallowed by the sounds of other people on the beach, the hiss of the waves and the ever-present pounding of the music.

I nodded and he put his arms around me, squeezing so carefully that I felt my resolve crack a little. The scent of coffee and damp grass clung to him faintly, and his clothes held the warmth of the sun. It was so comforting, just being held. I blinked and two tears slid down my sunburned face. We stayed like that for a moment, him awkwardly hugging me whilst my arms remained at my sides. Then, with a sudden rush of bravery, I hugged him back. I felt his spine unknot as if he'd been waiting, tensely, for me to reciprocate.

After a long moment we parted and Andrei gave me a small smile.

"You should let your friends know where you'll be," he said. "I can come with you to get anything you need for the night. We can just hang out for the rest of the day if you want? Take it easy?"

I nodded, felt the dried tears pull tackily on my cheeks as I smiled. "Thank you, Andrei...you're being so nice and, God I've been a total mess, haven't I?"

Andrei gave me a soft, sympathetic look as good as any hug. "You're allowed to be a mess. Especially after the day you've had. But I promise, tomorrow everything will look better. It'll be easier. So don't worry."

I wanted so badly to believe him. To turn my problems over to someone else for a while and stop thinking about everything that was weighing on me. There were warning lights flashing – part of the old machinery my mother had installed and maintained in my head to keep her one and only child safe. She'd guarded me relentlessly, her insurance policy against old age, against loneliness. But it was so easy to just reach over and flip a switch, shut them off. They'd been flashing for so long anyway, practically my entire life. I couldn't trust those warnings. All I heard were klaxons and alarms and warning bells. They'd become part of the background noise of my head.

"I'll walk you back to your tent?" Andrei offered, standing up and brushing grit off of his jeans and offering me a hand. I let him pull me to my feet. Together we retraced our steps through the crowded amusement area. I cast a look towards the medical tent and found myself checking the dusty ground for tire tracks, but there were none. Though of course all the people walking past would probably have erased any that had been left even half an hour ago.

I didn't catch sight of Carla or Ari anywhere. I wasn't sure if they were still at the concert or if they'd ended up grabbing some lunch and were currently looking for me back at the tent. I hoped it was the former. The coward in me didn't want to see them again until I'd had a chance to sleep on everything that had happened today.

Thankfully when we reached the tent it was empty and just as I'd left it. I didn't take my whole bag with me, just put what I'd need for the night into my sleeping bag and rolled it up. I found a receipt in my bag and scrawled out a quick note, just in case the others came back before I had a chance to text them. *Staying the night with Andrei (from the party) see you tomorrow.*

I followed Andrei back to where the party we'd met again at had been. There was still a little sort of clearing preserved between the tents, though there was more rubbish in it now. I'd noticed it around the edges of the path too, along with the smell of unwashed clothes and old food left to stink in tents. The festival was ripening rapidly into a kind of slum.

"It's those two," Andrei said, shepherding me towards a pair of red tents off to the side. They were both small pop tents and he quickly unzipped one and started moving his stuff from it into the other one. There wasn't much, I supposed men travelled lighter than women did in general, so that made sense. If

217

he'd managed to smuggle beer or something in it was probably all gone by now.

"Get settled in and we can grab some food, talk over a good plan for what to do next, yeah?" he said, tossing an armful of wrinkled clothes into the other tent. He looked so nervous about the state of the place I found myself smiling. It was sort of nice to be around someone just as anxious as me, if not more so.

I quickly stashed my things in the vacated tent and zipped it up. Whilst Andrei attempted to sort things out in his brother's tent I took out my phone and sent a quick text to my housemates, complete with a picture of the tents and a description of where I was. I said I'd be back the next day and not to worry but I just wanted some time to myself.

"Ready?" Andrei asked, draping his arm over my shoulders, warm and solid. "Shall we see if we can get something edible from the stalls? My treat."

"Thank you. Not just for the food – for everything. For today," I said, the back of my neck going hot as I felt myself rambling.

"You don't have to keep thanking me," he said, nudging me with his hip. "It's no big deal."

I wondered then if he had any idea what the past hour had meant to me. If he'd ever know just how deeply he'd managed to dig down into my heart. I even wondered, in my innocence, if he knew just how grateful I was.

Chapter 19

That day divided itself in my memory – half-horror story, half-perfection. Nightmare and dream. There was the discovery of Evie, the loss of my passport. All the uncertainty and paranoia and the argument. Some of the worst moments of my life so far. Then there was Andrei and the slow slide of the day towards sunset, hours I was busy committing to memory even as it was happening. It was an afternoon when being with someone else was the easiest it had ever been for me, and by extension all my worries seemed less daunting. Minimised by his presence. The problem of my passport and the argument with my friends no longer insurmountable.

Andrei and I had lunch as we walked around the attractions. He got me to play arcade games with him and we shot zombies and drove rally cars like teenagers stuck in the same seaside resort town. I insisted on buying his next drink and we sipped rum and Cokes as we explored the rest of the domes, glancing in at a silent disco, body painting and a UV lit rave with only about five people in it.

Through it all Andrei nudged me and muttered little comments and jokes that were just for the two of us. I found myself laughing more than I had in ages, responding to him in kind with jokes and stories about my life. It felt so easy that I started to wonder if I'd been kidding myself all the years I'd thought this kind of thing – friends, casual fun, being around people – was difficult and not for me. Maybe I'd just been trying with the wrong people.

I only checked my phone when we stopped to grab dinner and headed to the beach again to eat. I was surprised to see that I had texts from both Ari and Carla. I'd assumed they'd both be giving me the silent treatment. They'd put mostly the same thing – asking me if I was sure, if I was OK and telling me to be careful. Carla had added a line which basically amounted to 'I hope you're over this mood tomorrow' but cloaked in nicer words. I put my phone away without responding. There wasn't anything more to say, I would leave things to calm down, as Andrei had said. There was no message from Evie or anyone else. I told myself she was asleep at the hospital, recovering and had just not seen my text yet.

The sun started to go down as we sat on the beach, picking at pittas, salad and kebabs with plastic knives and forks. I wasn't sure if it was the nicest food I'd had since arriving at the festival or just that I didn't care that much about it because I was too focused on Andrei.

There were a few groups lingering on the sand, playing music from Bluetooth speakers and lighting small bonfires in hollows they'd dug into the sand. The air smelled of salt and wood smoke and I could hear the popping and cracking of the driftwood as it burned. It was almost idyllic enough that I wasn't concerned about how many people were openly doing drugs. Including one group where a few people seemed to have actually passed out on the rubble strewn sand, half-deflated balloons in hand.

"People really are getting away with anything, aren't they? Fires, music…drugs," I said, trying to sound light. "I suppose anything goes when there's no security around."

"Mmm, there's a positive side to it," Andrei said. "The freedom to have a campfire and relax out there. But yeah, you've still got the drugs and theft issue… Sorry, didn't mean to bring that up again. The passport thing."

"Don't worry about it. Besides, people steal all the time at festivals. Ari had her phone taken at one ages ago. You were right earlier – it's not like I'm the first person to ever lose my passport. The embassy will know what to do and I'm sure it won't take long to get a new one." I tried to internalise it as I said it. He was right after all, there were processes in place for exactly this sort of thing. Still, there was that worry at the back of my mind, about money and where I was going to stay whilst a new passport was arranged. Would the embassy pay for that?

I was also thinking about whether or not I'd have a room to go back to once I returned to England after the others had already made the trip. What if they took the delay as an opportunity to find a new housemate, or move in somewhere together, just the two of them?

"Yeah, it's not great but it's not like you can't get another," Andrei agreed. "As for stealing...I didn't bring anything with me I can't afford to leave behind, that's how you've got to do it. You should remember for next time."

I nodded. "Good advice, but I'm not sure I'll be going to any more festivals after this one," I admitted wryly. "Far too much hassle so far."

"That's a shame," Andrei sounded like he meant it. "They're usually a lot of fun."

"I don't think it was ever going to be my thing, not really. But, I can't say it's been a great experience. All things considered." I winced, hating how negative I sounded and hoping I wasn't putting him off.

"I get that. Still, I think you should let yourself have fun now and again. It suits you."

He took my hand in his and I felt my pulse speed up. I'd never just held hands with someone before – with a man – just to enjoy being connected. Nick had only grabbed mine to lead me around. Holding Andrei's hand felt nice, comforting, like a grounding tether instead of a lead to be dragged along by.

For the rest of the afternoon and into the evening we just sat and watched the fires burn, listening to the many different songs playing across the sand. From the smell of things, people were toasting marshmallows – the waft of burned sugar was unmistakeable, joining the smell of wood smoke and weed lingering in the air. Over the water the far-away lights of the city sparkled and the occasional boat passing in the dark showed flashing red lights. The distant music of the festival and that coming from the tinny speakers mingled with conversations and the rush of the sea. A sort of festival themed lo-fi atmosphere track.

Lost in the shadows I could forget about the rubbish and the bricks and concrete piled up on the beach. I could imagine that it was beautiful. I could imagine that I was beautiful.

It wasn't a surprise when Andrei kissed me, I'd felt it coming, or wished for it. I couldn't tell. Even though I felt it coming my heart still sped up as he nudged his way towards my mouth, nose brushing my cheek. He gave me plenty of time to turn away, to ask him to stop. I didn't. Instead I held my breath and silently urged him forwards. I let him put his arms around me and when he kissed me I kissed him back.

He was the first man I'd kissed since Nick. The only other man I'd kissed in my life. And the difference was so stark it made my eyes prickle. Andrei was so patient, so gentle. He kissed me like it was for its own sake, not as a demand for more. He was the first to pull back, to smile at me as if asking if it was alright that he'd kissed me. He looked so relieved when I nodded that I wanted to kiss him again immediately.

"I don't want to move too fast," he said, after we broke apart. His voice was quiet, reserved for the world we'd built between us on that beach, in the space between us. A private space just for the two of us, where no outside worries or cares existed.

"Me neither," I said, mouth dry, lips tingling. "I'm pretty tired too though so...shall we head back?" I didn't mean it as a come-on, it really had been a long day and I was a bit overwhelmed by everything. Especially knowing I had to deal with the passport issue if it turned out my friends weren't hiding it from me. It felt weird to be hoping that they were lying to me after all, rather than the alternative.

He kissed me again, on the forehead this time. "Good idea. You've had a lot to deal with…early night and we can deal with everything tomorrow."

As we walked back through the darkened festival grounds I saw them as beautiful for the first time. Really beautiful. The coloured lights spilling out from the domes, the scents of herbal smoke, frying dough and cinnamon sugar, incense and so many different kinds of perfume. Sounds of laughter and music as everyone relaxed into the evening. Without the heat of the sun baking the scent of hot rubbish into everything, it felt like the night was breathing fresh air over us. A touch of a chill to the breeze and the crack of pyrotechnics bringing flashes of light overhead.

When we reached Andrei's tent we stood outside, like he was dropping me off at my door after a date. Which I suppose he was, sort of. Only it was his tent and I was just borrowing it for one night. My last night at Lethe Festival. Maybe everything would be better in the morning, just like Andrei had said. If all went well I'd be headed home tomorrow, away from my suspicions, back in the safety of my room at home, where Nick couldn't get to me. Perhaps I could even forgive Ari and Carla once they gave me my passport back. If they had it, which I was still almost positive that they did.

Did I really want to shut myself in my room again? No. For the first time I wasn't sure it was even necessary. With the whole of London to hide in, what were the odds that I'd see him again if I went out? Maybe I could get Ari or Carla to go with me the next few times I did just in case. I didn't want to go back to being a shut-in, out of fear that Nick might decide to show up again. I wanted to live my life again. Cautiously, sure but not drowning in paranoia as I had been.

My lips were still buzzing from Andrei's kiss and there was a fragile little hope in my chest that maybe this would chase away the last hint of Nick. Out of my mind, out of my life. I didn't just want to know for sure that Nick wasn't following me. I wanted to believe it. The trip to Greece had really opened my eyes to how different those two things were. Maybe this day with Andrei was finally causing a change. Maybe.

"Good night then," Andrei said, taking both my hands in his. "I'll see you in the morning, OK?"

"OK," I echoed.

He leaned in slowly and kissed me again, light and hesitant. Pyrotechnics went off in my belly, sending sparks through my bloodstream. I sighed when he drew back.

"OK...I'll see you in the morning," he let go of my hands reluctantly.

I crawled into his tent and zipped up the door. After I unrolled my sleeping bag I checked my phone and found no new messages. Whatever the others were doing they weren't talking to me about it. Still no word from Evie either. I frowned. Tomorrow I'd make sure to go to the medical tent and find out which hospital she went to, to phone them directly. Even if my passport really had gone AWOL and I had to deal with that mess – I would find the time to check on her. She didn't have anyone else that I knew of. I wasn't sure if that friend she'd been looking for had any idea something had happened to Evie. Roisin, that was it. If she was flighty enough to go off on her own without warning, the odds of her realising something was up with her friend were very small indeed.

I got changed in my sleeping bag and laid awake, looking up at the red nylon ceiling. The tent smelled like Andrei's cologne and I kept kicking my feet in the sleeping bag – too nervous and gleefully excited to settle down. Then I'd remember something I'd said or done around him and clench my hands in embarrassment. Or else start worrying about what my friends were doing, if they were still angry at me, talking about me behind my back. Or were they worried about me? Wondering what I was doing and if I was OK? Common sense assured me it was the latter, but my paranoia told me it was the former. That they were sitting somewhere talking about how much they hated me.

In the end I broke and typed out a group text to both Ari and Carla – an apology for going off at them. I swallowed the worry that they were bashing me and added some stuff about Andrei and the kiss – as if pretending we were all friends again would make it so. I even wrote about how I felt like I was finally leaving Nick behind me. But I didn't end up sending it. I started to imagine their responses, ranging from still annoyed about the argument to asking for more details and, perhaps, telling me I was being crazy again. Jumping into kissing someone I'd only just met. Considering that they wanted me to have a good time and be normal, they still treated me a bit like a little sister, I realised. As if I was naïve or somehow less intelligent than them.

Was I being unfair? Maybe. I just didn't want to get into all that. I wasn't looking for more of what my mum already gave me – over-protectiveness and self-doubt. Tonight at least, I just wanted to be.

It was late and I was half asleep when I heard the sound of a zip slowly crawling open. I looked towards the front flap of my tent but even in the dark I could see that it was firmly closed. The sound was coming from nearby though, to the left of me – Andrei's tent. A few moments later I heard someone speaking and Andrei answering back in fast-paced Russian. Low and tense like they were arguing or trying to solve a problem. It sent a warning prickle down my spine. A feeling which only intensified when I sat up, making my sleeping bag rustle and both men – because it was definitely Andrei and another guy – went quiet. Both of them silent at the same time. As soon as they went quite I felt my skin tighten, as if I'd been caught doing something wrong.

Was it just paranoia that whispered to me to keep still? Or instinct?

Did I even know the difference anymore?

I froze anyway, listening intently. After a few seconds of complete silence, Andrei spoke again. Even quieter and quicker now. There came a rustling and the sound of crumpled plastic, the whisper of paper shuffling together. Then I heard footsteps scuffing through the dust, heading away at a brisk pace. I waited for Andrei to settle back into his tent, but instead I heard him get up and come to the front of my tent.

Lying there I could just about make out his outline as a light flashed somewhere outside – probably someone's torch moving about as they came back to their tent. He stood there, motionless, then tapped on the taut nylon with his fingers. A sort of knock.

I was holding my breath, but why? What was I afraid of? What had I actually heard? Just two men talking. I hadn't even understood the words. Still, there was that familiar sense that something was wrong. The sense that had been going off a lot lately, about the festival, my friends, Evie's continued silence. How much of it was real, and how much just a nerve Nick had hammered until it couldn't stop firing.

"Jody? Are you awake?" he whispered.

I didn't say anything, though I had no reason to pretend to be asleep still. No reason to be afraid. I knew that, I told myself that. I just didn't want to cause a problem or make Andrei feel awkward. That's what I tried to make myself believe anyway, despite the roiling in my stomach.

Whatever Andrei had been talking about with the other man outside, he obviously hadn't wanted to be overheard. They'd been speaking Russian and had gone quiet when they heard me. Perhaps it was his brother, stumbling home to find Andrei in his tent. He might have fallen out with his festival hook-up and wanted to spend the night where Andrei was currently sleeping. That would explain why he'd sounded so tense, bordering on annoyed. It made sense.

So why was my skin still crawling?

"Jody?" Andrei repeated, slightly louder. "I'm sorry if we woke you up…it was just Ivan."

He wasn't showing any signs of leaving. He'd probably come in to check on me if I didn't say anything. I wasn't sure why that idea made me feel a little panicky.

I couldn't tell anymore if I had any reason to be afraid. I just was and it wasn't going away, no matter how hard I tried to reassure myself. The fear was too strong to deny.

"Does he want his tent back?" I asked, trying to sound freshly woken and groggy. It was instinct, to try and play dumb. Part of what Nick had drilled into my head, that there was a certain safety in appearing not to notice bait. Because that's what it felt like Andrei was doing – baiting me into admitting that I'd heard. That I found this strange. Trying to feel me out, decide how he was going to play this.

He offered an easy chuckle. "I told him he's out of luck. He can go back to his new friends or sleep in one of the domes. He's messed me around enough," Andrei said at a more normal volume, sounding more relaxed now. "By the way I was thinking, because I couldn't sleep but...tomorrow if you can't find your passport, I can get us a taxi to the embassy in the city. Take you on to my friend's place afterwards? It'll be no problem. I might be staying on a while anyway – we could do something together. Go out for dinner maybe?"

Despite the stuffy atmosphere in the tent and the sleeping bag wrapped around me, I shivered. I'd been trying to ignore the warning bells but they had just gotten louder. As if Andrei had opened a door and let the full, deafening power of them in. Friend. Not uncle. His story had changed hadn't it? Or was I misremembering?

I'd turned a perfectly nice person into Nick in my head. Anything was possible when I was this scared, this paranoid.

"That sounds good," I said, automatically. "We can talk about it tomorrow, OK?"

"Sure…good night, Jody."

I listened as Andrei went back to his tent and settled in, rustling in his sleeping bag. When he went still I laid back down and shut my eyes, but sleep was the furthest thing from my mind.

His friend's place. That's what he'd said just now. But before I could have sworn he said it was his uncle's. I was more and more sure every time I thought back. I could hear him saying it, unless that was just my memory playing tricks on me again? Still, that one little inconsistency triggered a barrage of questions that I hadn't wanted to ask myself. Questions I'd been actively supressing. Starting with why was this man being so helpful? Sure, maybe he was just trying to be nice and part of me wanted to believe he was being romantic, dashing, playing the hero to win me over. But it was hard work to convince myself that I wasn't being delusional. The fact that I wanted so much for it to be true was counting against him, paradoxically. I wanted to trust him so badly that I didn't trust myself to see the truth.

I got out my phone, hiding its light in the sleeping bag. I was thinking about texting the others, though they were probably asleep. If I couldn't trust myself then the only option was outside validation. But then I wasn't sure if I could trust them either, given that they'd lied to me about the landlord and were possibly holding my passport hostage. Who did that leave? No one. Or my mother. It was hard to say which option saddened me the most. Or which would provide the least help.

230

I settled on no one. At least then things couldn't get worse. Talking to Mum always seemed to make things feel worse.

Tomorrow I was going to have to turn down Andrei's offers of help. I knew that. I didn't feel too sure about his intentions anymore. If I was being honest with myself I'd had my doubts since he'd first mentioned this flat. I'd just been ignoring them. Forcing myself to look past the red flags. Tomorrow there would come a moment where I'd have to turn him down definitively and I didn't want to be alone when I did it.

I couldn't just get out of the tent and make a run for it. Andrei would hear me, he'd want an explanation. If he followed me he might confront me before I got back to the others. I didn't want to chance that. I wanted someone there in case...in case things went like they had with Nick, when he'd brought that 'friend' of his back to the flat. When the pretence of choice was suddenly stripped away, and the hand closed around my wrist. When his casual smile turned hard and his eyes said 'you're going to do what I say...or I'll make you anyway and then you'll regret it'.

It would have to be the girls. I didn't trust that they hadn't stolen my passport but, if they had done it, I also didn't think they'd done it to hurt me. That was just a by-product of them trying to do something nice in an admittedly extreme way. They were trying to do what they thought was best and that would have to do. I'd known them longer than Andrei, years longer. And though they had lied before, had hurt me, I did at least trust they'd not set out to do so. They'd seen me through the worst of my post-Nick spiral. When it came down to it I knew deep down that they wouldn't let Andrei get me if he went nasty. They'd be there for me, argument or no. That's what friends were for. They wouldn't let our falling out change that.

I hoped so at least.

Chapter 20

I didn't sleep well, for obvious reasons. A light doze was about all I could manage and every time someone walked past or shouted to a friend half a field away, I jolted awake. By the time the morning sun pushed back the shadows in the tent I was running on nothing but adrenaline, even as doubts started to creep in. Was I really right to be afraid of Andrei? He hadn't done anything but be nice me. It was just a feeling I had. Was I really going to run away from a nice person based on a feeling?

Yes. I was. I had to. When I thought about staying my anxiety spiralled. I had to get back to my friends. I just had to try and keep it together until then. My only comfort was that I'd done more with less. Hadn't I managed to get away from Nick with only fear to fuel me?

I quickly dressed and shouldered my handbag. The sleeping bag and pyjamas I could afford to leave behind as a sort of ruse. In case Andrei wondered where I'd gone off to, he'd hopefully be reassured that I was intending to come back. As it turned out, this was a good idea. As soon as I unzipped the tent and climbed out, Andrei left his tent and smiled at me.

"Good morning – sleep well?" he asked.

"Yes, thank you," I said, marshalling my face into a smile. "Just need to pop to the loo. Back in a second."

Andrei smiled back easily. "Sure…when you get back we can get coffee or something and work out what to do first about the passport situation, OK?" he said, effortlessly casual. So casually in fact that I started to doubt myself all over again. Was I really about to run out on him without explanation, just because of a slip of the tongue?

I knew I was still going to do it. Despite what I wanted to believe I knew that there was something not right about all this. I couldn't will that feeling away any more than I could simply stop being afraid of Nick. It was just there, a part of me for the time being. A part I had to listen to, because it was screaming at me to be careful and to get out of this situation.

"Sounds good. I'll see you in a bit," I said as brightly as I could and dashed off towards my tent. With any luck the others would be awake and I could apologise for my part in our argument. Once that was out of the way I was sure they'd own up to anything they'd done, give me back my passport, and then we could leave together.

If they didn't have my passport, well, then we'd figure that out together. They wouldn't just abandon me to my fate.

Unfortunately once I reached the tent I found that they were indeed awake. They were also gone. Inside the tent I found their bags packed and ready to depart but they weren't there. They'd probably gone to get some food.

I was put out and not a little bit anxious to find my friends missing when I needed them the most. Though part of me felt like I deserved it for abandoning them the day before. I did notice though that they had packed my bag up too. Maybe they weren't as angry with me as I was worried they were? Then again maybe they were just being passive aggressive. Was them packing for me a sign that they had my passport, and expected us to leave together as planned? My mind was churning it all over as I sat in the tent, trying to come up with a plan.

I wasn't sure what to do. Did I stay put and potentially leave myself open to Andrei coming to see where I was? The tent was definitely one of if not the first place he'd check and I wasn't feeling particularly safe there. My other option was to go in search of the others and hope I found them before Andrei found me. No small feat in a crowded festival that was already a hive of movement and noise. Though if I texted them I could at least find out where they were or ask them to come back to the tent.

After zipping myself into the tent to give myself a tiny sense of security, I fired off a text and waited for an answer. The one I got was less than helpful – a bounce back for both numbers. Something was messing with the signal, maybe the concert or some other source of interference. I tried calling them three times and it wouldn't go through. By the final attempt I was almost in tears. I desperately needed them and it felt like I was being punished for running off and leaving them after our fight. Not by them, but by fate. I'd brought this on myself.

Finally I realised I had no other option but to head out of the campsite and try to find my friends on foot. Even if it meant potentially running into Andrei whilst I was alone. Not to mention the possibility of Nick maybe being out there too, a fear that was still creeping about at the back of my mind. There was also the worry about something being up with the festival itself, some evil lurking just out of sight that I couldn't name or even really articulate. I had never in my life felt less safe. But I had to go. I changed my clothes to try and keep myself hidden from Andrei, and also stole a pair of Carla's massive sunglasses before tying my hair up, wishing I had a hat to hide it under. It was the best disguise I was going to come up with. Once I was ready I quickly left the tent and headed for the food stalls by a route that didn't take me past Andrei's tent. It was more circuitous but hopefully safer for me. My heart was in my throat as I looked over the crowd, every head of dark hair made me jolt unpleasantly, thinking it was him.

I was nearly at the gates to the food stalls when the PA system sprang to life with a whine, making me jump and clench my fists in panic. I hadn't heard it used since we'd arrived. It was probably for emergencies only though, judging from the announcement that rang out over the festival grounds.

"Attention everyone! Just a quick reminder that there have been reports of unusually potent drugs making the rounds at the festival. There have been a number of incidents already and we don't want anyone to have a bad time on the last day so, please do keep yourselves and your friends, safe. Thank you."

The announcement was met with a few mocking voices, and muffled groans as those still sleeping were disturbed by it. I passed one or two groups of whispering girls exchanging shocked looks. Most people didn't react at all. I supposed that for seasoned festivalgoers such announcements were white noise at this point. That and most people were probably still asleep and had missed it, or woken up to the tail end. What good was a warning that most hadn't heard?

What it had done was reminded me about Evie. I still hadn't got any replies to my messages from her but then again the phones were being weird. I thought about yesterday, which already seemed so long ago. How could I be sure that there really had been an ambulance? That she really was in hospital? I felt so alone and frantic in the crowd that I wasn't sure what to believe anymore. Was Evie safe? Were any of us safe here?

Just then I caught sight of Andrei and instinctively hid behind a group walking past. He walked by, looking this way and that. Looking for me, I realised. I watched him head into the food area. There was no way I could go through there without him seeing me now. I had to find a way to get hold of Ari or Carla without going into the crowd where Andrei could get at me.

The answer came to me as I peered down the row of tents. Backstage. When I'd followed Nick, or whoever he'd been, I'd ended up behind the security fence. I'd be separate from the crowd but able to see into it. I'd also have plenty of places to hide if I was spotted. I turned and started to pick my way through the chaos of tents in the direction of the shower block, where I'd been able to get out of the fence before.

Since I'd been back there someone had made an attempt at securing the fence. Was that because of me specifically or just a coincidence? Either way it wasn't a great attempt – just a few plastic cable ties threaded between the metal bars. Still it was enough to give me some trouble. I dug around in my bag for anything I could use. Unfortunately I'd taken my manicure scissors out before we left for the airport. I did have some really cheap nail clippers that had come in a Christmas cracker a few years ago though, and those had made it through the bag check. Even I'd forgotten they were in there. It was a bit awkward but I managed to position them so I could snip through three of the four cable ties. The clippers sheared apart on the third cable tie and I had to sort of force my way through a gap which hinged on the final one. After I'd crawled through the fence I got to my feet and tried to remember the way I'd gone before.

Every pathway looked the same and I couldn't tell one pile of rubbish from another. Things had been moved around since the day before or I'd just not remembered them clearly enough. Perhaps a little of both. I wasn't sure I was on the right track until I spotted the empty glue trap lying on the ground, curling at the edges like it was dying in the sun.

It was exactly where I'd left it, too shocked at my discovery of Evie to dispose of it properly. Flies had gathered on it, sticking to the glue trap and buzzing angrily as their fellows crawled around nearby.

Thankfully no other rats had stumbled into it. I swallowed the hint of bile that crept into my throat and stepped over the grim signpost. Bugs creeped me out more than any animal. Even that tiny movement disturbed the flies and I waved them away, trying not to panic as they hit my face and hair. I carried on, following the route Evie had been carried down yesterday morning. Only yesterday, but it felt like a lifetime.

I turned a corner and saw the metal fence ahead, with the swarming crowds beyond. I moved between generators and piles of pallets, looking for any sign of Carla or Ari amongst so many other, similar, women. The happy, brightly dressed crowds felt so far away, so alien to me as I scurried through the rubbish backstage. The whole festival really was a paper-thin fantasy – teetering on top of a landfill. Literally built on trash.

After following the length of the fence as far as I could, almost to the beach, I turned and went back. Still no sign of them. I hid myself around the corner of a catering van with its shutters closed and crusted with rust. As I watched the crowds stroll by I started to worry. What if they were already back at the tent, having found some breakfast? What if they'd left without me? They could be anywhere and just waiting for them to pass me by wasn't going to be good enough.

I took my phone out before remembering the failed texts from earlier. As I looked at the screen I saw that the battery icon was only one third full. I hadn't had access to the power banks last night. Damn it. The signal strength was looking good though, I noticed. I tried another text to the group thread and watched as it failed to go through. Maybe it was because my friends were also within the festival? There wasn't just interference with sending the message, but with receiving it.

I looked down at my previously sent messages and my thumb hovered over Evie's contact info. Could I maybe get a call through to someone outside the festival? Evie had Ari's number from where they'd shared details. If Evie was awake and I was able to reach her, she might in turn be able to tell Ari to get back to the tent or meet me somewhere. I didn't want to bring Evie into this or worry her when she was recovering, but I didn't have many options.

Also, then at least I'd know she was alright and that she really had been taken to get some help.

I selected Evie's number and sighed with relief when it connected, but then a robotic voice told me that the number I was calling was currently unavailable. Evie's phone was still off or out of battery.

OK, so forget trying to get in contact with the others via Evie. I could still make sure she was alright. The only other relevant number I had was the EU wide emergency services number. I'd saved it for the trip, specifically. I brought it up and pressed 'call', went through the automated menu and finally got put through to a person. It wouldn't take long, I just had to know.

"Hi, I'm really sorry...my friend was taken to hospital yesterday and I can't find the number for which one it is. Can you tell me the nearest hospital to..." Where was I? I didn't even know the name of the island I was on, or peninsula, landfill, whatever. "...to

Lethe Festival," I finished, feeling myself go hot with embarrassment.

The operator didn't sound too happy with me, but after some rapid typing they rattled off the name of the hospital and a number, which I repeated to myself even as I was dialling it, desperate not to forget. The automated menu which came on the line was in Greek, so I hammered the hash button until a real person picked up – a trick I'd learned when I temped at an insurance call centre. Once the woman on the other end confirmed she spoke English I gave Evie's name and a brief description of what had happened to her.

"Is she at the hospital? She would probably have turned up yesterday morning or early afternoon?" I asked, picking at the rust on the catering van nearest to me, the red flakes crumbling to the ground as I chewed my lip.

I heard her typing and a mouse clicking tetchily as she attempted to find what I was asking for with the bare minimum of information. Finally she sighed.

"No one by that name was admitted yesterday."

I clenched my fist in frustration. "Is there any way to check other hospitals?"

"No...but she would be here if she came from the festival, like you say. There's no hospital closer than us. The next nearest is another forty-five minutes away, and it's right in the city so it's busier than we are. An ambulance would have come here, definitely."

My stomach clenched, empty and swimming with bile. All that 'wrong' feeling crystallising into a single, sharp point in my guts. "So...if she's not with you, she's not in a hospital at all, is that what you're saying?"

"I'm not sure, but it seems like it," the hospital operator said. "I can check to see if she was perhaps treated and discharged without being logged on the system?"

"Does that happen often?" I waved a fly away as it buzzed into my face, blinking rapidly.

"No it would be against policy but…" I sensed her helpless shrug in the way she sighed. "I don't know what else I can do."

"Don't worry about it. I'll…I'll think of something." I hung up and looked out at the crowds of smiling, tanned festivalgoers. Something was very wrong at Lethe and I had no idea what, or who was responsible, never mind how to warn my friends. I was all alone and well out of my depth, running from one, possibly two different men – neither of whom I was certain was even after me. I couldn't handle anything else but what I did know, what I was absolutely sure of in that moment, was that something bad had happened to Evie. I trusted that even if I trusted nothing else. Evie was in danger, because something about the festival was wrong. I needed help and there was only one place I could think of to turn to.

I quickly tapped at my recent call log and selected the emergency services number again, then brought the phone back to my ear.

"Hello? Police please."

Chapter 21

"What I'm trying to tell you is that I don't know what happened to her," I explained, to the third person they'd put on the phone in the past ten minutes. My shoes were wearing a trench into the dusty ground as I paced back and forth in frustration. "I don't know what drugs she took or where she is now, I just need someone to come to the festival and make sure that they're telling the truth about what's going on here."

I was beginning to regret ever calling the police. This was proving to be a waste of time. I needed to find Ari and Carla and this quick attempt to check on Evie was spiralling out of control. Still, I didn't give up. I had to at least try and make them understand. Not just for Evie's sake but for mine – I was right at the heart of Lethe and it had never felt like a less safe place to be. Without any security on site, the police were my only hope of back-up.

"I'm not sure I understand what crime you're concerned about," the man on the phone – his name and rank already having slipped out of my panicked grasp – said. His tone was perplexed but polite, as if I

243

was a crazy person he was trying to talk down. Maybe that's what he thought I was. Some perpetually stoned festival-chaser panicking over their missing friend and unable to string a coherent story together.

I'd gone around in the same circles with the previous two police officers I'd spoken to. I couldn't give the details they wanted, even things like Evie's last name were beyond me. What it boiled down to was that I only knew Evie had taken something bad and I'd been told she'd gone to hospital, but the one hospital I'd contacted had no record of her. The police didn't seem too concerned, given that I had no real claim to Evie and didn't have any useful information for them to act on. I couldn't even say for sure that she was missing.

I tried one last time, hearing the desperation in my voice. "I just want to know that she's OK. That she really is recovering and they did send her to hospital."

I heard voices in the background, a busy office with people calling out and phones ringing. There was a distinct sigh on the line as whoever I was speaking to attempted to marshal some patience. I wasn't the only one hovering close to losing my temper, though on my end it was fuelled by desperation.

"I'm sure if you call around you will find the right hospital," he said, already sounding like he was holding the receiver away from his face, ready to hang up on me. "If you have any further concerns, don't hesitate to…"

I hung up and suppressed a growl of frustration. I was on my own. God, why hadn't I lied to get someone to at least come to the festival? I could have told them about all the drug dealing going on – not that it seemed anyone would care. For a moment I considered calling back and hoping I wasn't recognised, making up a wild story about a gun or something to inject some urgency into the police. But then doubt crept in and shredded that idea before it was fully formed. They'd soon find out that was a hoax. Even if I rang the police again and tried explaining to someone else, what would happen once the police came? They'd come in, ask the same questions I had and get the same answers. They'd be satisfied with those answers, with no reason not to be. Still no closer to finding Evie than I was right now.

I was scanning the crowd fruitlessly for signs of my friends when I spotted Andrei.

My heart jumped painfully, but it only took a second for me to register that he wasn't looking my way. He was standing right by the security fence, looking around the medical tent. What was he up to? Was he still looking for me or was this about something else? About Evie?

I ducked further behind the edge of the catering van and watched around the edge as he stalked off, clearly irritated. What had pissed him off? Maybe he'd been checking to see if I'd gone back there to ask questions? I crept out from behind the rusty metal van and followed him along the fence, keeping myself hidden as much as possible behind catering vans and generators.

Eventually I saw Andrei head towards the organisers' cramped little office and go inside. No knock, nothing. He went in like he owned the place. What was going on? What was he after and why? I tried to remember if I'd seen anything in Erik's office that Andrei might want but I was drawing a blank.

I couldn't get any closer, the security fence perimeter was too far away for me to get a better view of the office. Instead I backtracked a way and waited for Andrei to come out. Twenty minutes later and I was still waiting. There was no sign of movement and I was starting to get restless. This was wasting time. The festival was ending soon and many people were probably already on their way home on cheaper, painfully early flights. I still didn't have a way of getting home and no way to contact my friends. Was I really out here chasing after a conspiracy of some kind, instead of frantically trying to track down my friends and my passport?

All my worries from the previous day came screaming back to the forefront of my mind. Familiar anxieties which told me I was being crazy, that I was making all of this up, that my friends would never forgive me and had probably already taken their things and left without me. A voice in my head whispered that Andrei was the first decent man I'd met since leaving Nick and I'd ruined that too. Just like I'd ruined my training, my friendships, my future. The voice sounded like my mother, so soft and yet so insistent and devastating. An iron bar wrapped in a feather pillow.

I paced away from the fence, trying to walk off my anxiety, and found myself on the outer edge of the backstage area. The fence was between me and the water, rubbish piled high against the metal wire in plastic sacks. Piled to one side I saw the broken remains of the yurts we'd seen on our first day. I looked over the fractured poles and the dusty canvas, and stumbled to a stop. The yurts weren't the only thing in the pile.

246

There was another tent there too, only this one wasn't broken. It was pitched, the top of the canopy scattered with empty cans and Styrofoam containers as if in an attempt to hide it.

A tingle ran up my spine, telling me that I'd found something I wasn't meant to see. At the same time it felt like something important. Something significant, simply because it was so strange. Despite the sense of having intruded somewhere dangerous, I couldn't help myself – I went closer, stepping carefully and quietly around the fallen bits of wood and rubbish that surrounded the yurt pile. I reached the tent and found the front unzipped a little way. Through the lolling corner of the door flap I could see that the inside of the tent was deserted. But it wasn't empty.

I reached for the zip and pulled it open as smoothly as I could. It stuck a few times and I noticed there was mud crusted into it. The whole tent in fact looked like it had been used and used well – faded by the sun and with a slightly crooked frame, as if it had been stored under something heavy. The kind of tent you'd find slumped by a public bin on a beach, not worth the trouble of packing away.

From the looks of things inside, it seemed as if whoever was staying in it had done just that – found the tent in the rubbish. Everything in the tent looked like something that had been thrown away, from the holey gym bag spilling cheap, washed out clothes, to the sleeping bag stained with foundation, fake tan and a streak of blood at the top. As if someone had gone to bed with a bloody nose. The clothes were women's and I stood there wondering what kind of woman would be out here, camped alone in a crappy little tent all this way from the main festival.

I was looking for further clues, turning the edge of the sleeping bag over with my foot, when I found a passport. I picked it up, wondering who on earth would come to a festival just to camp out in the rubbish, sleeping in a bloody, stained sleeping bag. Maybe they were homeless and had broken in? Or like me they were trying to get away from someone and going about it in a very extreme way.

I flipped to the photo page of the passport and stared. It was my picture. My missing passport. There I was, pale and washed out, unsmiling in the photo booth at the ASDA nearest to Mum's house. What the hell was it doing here? Whose tent was this and why did they have my passport?

I tried to make the pieces fit in my head. Someone was living out here in the out-of-bounds area of the festival. Squatting amidst the rubbish and apparently hiding from everyone and everything. Yet that same someone had apparently decided it was worth the risk to creep into the campground and into our tent so they could steal my passport. No money, no clothes or toiletries had been taken – things this person clearly needed. What was going on?

I ducked into the tent and started going through the bag in there, turning out the clothes and looking for evidence. It was all generic cheap stuff, the sort of thing you'd buy from a dodgy website and not receive for about a month and a half. Buried in amongst the clothes were random bits of jewellery, chains tangled together, a single earring caught on a hairbrush. At the bottom of the bag I found a plastic baggie with a teaspoon worth of white powder in it, and a few crumpled up notes. There wasn't much money there, maybe around thirty euros and some other foreign currency I didn't recognise.

"What do you think you're doing?" someone asked, in a soft Irish accent.

I turned towards the source of the voice, still clutching my passport. The woman was only a few feet away, dusty and greasy haired, but familiar, clutching a piece of broken yurt pole like a baseball bat.

I couldn't believe it. "Roisin?"

She blinked at me, her thin, pale face suddenly showing recognition. I obviously looked enough like my passport photo for her to know who I was. She looked very different to the picture Evie had shown us. That Roisin had been carefree and pretty, skinny and pale sure, but healthy looking. She looked practically ill now – her skin was greasy, grey around her neck with ingrained dirt and her face was carved deeply around the eyes and mouth. There were half-healed bruises around the tops of her arms, left bare in a tank top, and she was carrying a plastic bag bulging with what looked like half-empty bottles of water and food packages from the rubbish. The acrylic nails on her fingers were mostly broken or missing and she looked like she was on the verge of throwing up or passing out.

"Oh shit, it's you." She lowered the piece of wooden pole and her eyes flicked to the passport in my hands. "I'm...I need that."

"It's mine," I said, automatically clutching it closer, as if she was about to make a grab for it. Maybe she would, I had no idea what she was capable of. "Why did you steal it?"

Her eyes darted around, wide and desperate. For the first time I wondered if she was maybe on something right now – I had after all found what looked like drugs in the tent. Evie had been on drugs too, so maybe the pair of them had found the same sort of trouble waiting for them here. Though that still didn't explain the tent and my stolen passport. Roisin was clearly running from something, or someone.

"Why did you take my passport?" I asked again, taking a step back, away from her and the tent, so she couldn't corner me against the fence beyond her makeshift camp.

"To get away. Please – please just give it back," she said, her voice cracking in desperation. I flinched when she moved, but she just dropped the bag of rubbish she'd been carrying, which tipped over. Half-empty bottles rolled out across the dirt and she let go of the piece of tent pole, not seeming to notice or care as it thumped to the ground. She held her empty hands out, pleading. "Please, I need it!"

"Get away from what?" I asked, disturbed by how easily she'd fallen apart. "Do you know Evie was looking for you? Why were you hiding from her?"

"Was?" Roisin's gaze sharpened. "What do you mean, 'was' looking for me? Has she left already?" She looked strangely hopeful at the idea of being abandoned by her friend. I slowly shook my head and watched that hope be overtaken by something which was unmistakeably fear.

I held up my hands, trying to calm her with an

automatic gesture. "She overdosed on something, had to be taken to hospital...or, they said she was going to hospital. I don't know for sure where she is," I said. "Were you on something too? Is that why you're out here?"

"Shit," Roisin hissed, then. "Who said she was going to hospital? Did anyone go with her? Did you see her go?"

She was clearly panicking and that ratcheted my own anxiety up a notch. What was going on and what would Roisin do when I couldn't answer all her questions? Or worse, when I answered even one of them in a way she didn't like? She looked close to the edge of either a breakdown or a violent outburst.

"I didn't see her go to hospital, no. But I was there when she was taken to the medical tent to be treated, and the organiser, Erik, he said she'd been taken to hospital. Afterwards."

"Erik?" Roisin's voice shot up an octave, making me wince. "Oh God. Shit!" She crammed the edge of her thumb into her mouth and started gnawing on the jagged acrylic nail, eyes moving quicker than a rat over the rubbish around us, like she was hunting for a way out. Of what I had no idea; this conversation, the festival, the chain of events that led her here?

"Can you please tell me what's going on?" I said, surprising myself with how strained my voice was. I realised that I was shaking, her fear was contagious, adding to my own. "Please. What's happening? How is Erik involved?"

"I need to get out of here." Roisin crossed the space between us in moments, reaching blindly for the

251

passport in my hands. I snatched it out of her reach and she let out a sharp sound of frustration and panic.

"Tell me!" I snapped. "Or I'll go ask him myself!"

I wasn't prepared for her to tackle me to the hard, sun-baked ground. The pair of us crashed into the ramshackle tent, flattening it as we struggled to pin the other down. My elbow hit the ground hard and pain reverberated up my arm, making it momentarily nerveless. Roisin's jagged nails raked across my skin and I clenched the fingers of my other hand tightly around my passport even as I yelped in pain. Nothing else mattered. I had to keep hold of my passport.

After a few seconds of struggling though, Roisin grabbed my throat with the hand not trying to snatch the red leather case from me. I reacted on instinct and threw the passport as hard as I could, splitting her attention. When her head jerked in the direction I'd thrown it and her hand loosened its grip, I struck. I used both hands to try and subdue her arms, pushing her off me and onto the ground. She was painfully thin, weakened by our struggle, and as she tried to bat me away I noticed greenish yellow bruises in the crook of her elbow, pinprick scabs charting the path of a vein. I managed to hold her in place long enough to pin her down with my weight.

"Tell me what you and Evie were doing to end up like this," I demanded, once I'd caught my breath. "What does it have to do with Erik? My friends are at this festival... Are they in danger? Am I?"

Roisin looked up at me, eyes huge and wet as an injured animal's. Begging me to free her. I felt sick, remembered the rat's terrified, trapped gaze. How it had struggled as I'd tried to get it free of the glue, unable to keep it from hurting as I tried to save it. How cruel did I need to be to her, to be kind?

"If you don't tell me…I'll let him know where to find you," I said. "If you do tell me, I can give you some money. I can help you get away – but you have to help me first."

Roisin seemed to weigh these options and, caught between them, she finally stopped fighting me. Her eyes went flat and dead as the tension left her body, leaving her limp. It was as if she realised it was pointless, that she needed help, and just gave up. "OK…OK, I'll tell you. But you have to promise me that you'll get me out of here. Please?"

"I will," I said, though I had no idea if I'd be able to do any such thing. I would try, in whatever way I could, but I knew that might not be good enough.

Roisin let out a long breath, rolling her head on the dirty tent canopy as she considered where to begin. "Evie isn't my friend. Not really. She's…we sort of work together. For my boyfriend." Her mouth twisted bitterly. "He used to be my boyfriend."

"And it's to do with drugs?" I filled in, eager to get to what the festival had to do with this. "The drugs she was on, that…you're on? Is this about all the dealers here?"

She nodded. "There's a group of us, girls. We're meant to get guys interested in a party, sell them stuff. It's us who got it into the festival – smuggled it in."

"How?" I asked, remembering the bag checks we'd gone through.

"You don't want to know," Roisin muttered, eyes

darting away from mine. "But you can probably guess. I couldn't...I can't do this anymore. It's the same everywhere we go and there's no way out. He won't let me go." Her eyes teared up and she blinked hard, tears sliding over her dusty face. I felt my chest grow tight, unable to keep from pitying her even though she'd attacked me, stolen from me. She was so desperate and so trapped it made her easy to forgive. "My boyfriend got me on that stuff and now...he has my passport. All the money goes to him and he searches us so we can't keep anything for ourselves. I can't save up to get away, even if I steal from my customers – he takes that as well. He has us watching each other, men like Ivan following us, checking up on us. I can't even make a phone call and even if I could, who would I tell? I don't have anyone back home that I can call and he has people everywhere. Important people. If I go to the police or try to get a new passport it'll just mean trouble. He knows Erik – that's his boss. This festival, Lethe? It's not just about selling the stuff, it's about finding more girls. It's huge."

I thought of all the prize draws for the free, exclusive tickets. The overwhelming way women outnumbered men in the queue when we arrived. It had felt strange but I'd allowed myself to be distracted by my panic over Nick. Ever since we'd arrived the wrongness of it had been right there just beneath the surface like rotting rubbish. I'd just failed to see it clearly.

"So you ran away from this boyfriend and you, what? Followed me back to my tent to steal my passport, because you thought we looked enough alike that it would work?" I said. "How were you going to afford a ticket?"

Roisin sniffed, looking younger and even more helpless as she confronted the impossibility of her plan succeeding. "Evie, she and I shared a tent. I stole one of the spares and came out here to hide until I could sneak out on the last day, in the crowd. I thought by now I'd have managed to get hold of enough money to get a ticket back to Ireland or at least enough to get away from here, but almost nobody uses cash. I was going to try and steal from one of the stalls later but..." she gestured at me. I'd taken my passport back and now she was out of options.

Slowly it was all starting to click together for me. "Was Evie... Was she sent to look for you then?" I asked. "She wasn't just trying to look out for you. She was ordered to?"

Roisin shrugged a mozzie-bitten shoulder. "Yeah, probably. I don't know how she managed to OD. She might have been worried about what'd happen to her if she couldn't find me. Maybe she was trying to shake that off, took too much by accident," Roisin said. "Or... they did it to her. As punishment, for failing to get me back or because she tried to run too."

I thought about that, my skin prickling with cold sweat. "She was out here, when I found her. Buried in rubbish."

"Then they killed her," she said, her voice numb and her face a mask of despair. "She must have tried to run or steal from them...anything really. It doesn't take much to earn punishment. Girls disappear a lot, and Andrei gets so angry."

"...Andrei?" I repeated. "As in...a Russian guy? Quite...um, handsome?" I said, practically cringing as I said it, because all those doubts buzzing around like flies had finally settled on the rotten truth. Led me straight to it. The thing that had smelled off about him and which I'd ignored and pushed under everything else, until the stench was overwhelming.

If it was possible, her face paled even more. "You know him."

"I've met him he...he said he'd help me find my passport, or put me up somewhere until I could get a new one." I felt so naïve even saying it. How had I ever managed to convince myself that he was genuine?

Because you were desperate, a voice in my head whispered. *And he knew it, counted on it.*

Roisin looked up at me and a disbelieving laugh bubbled out of her mouth, her throat convulsing. It was so disturbing I jumped to my feet and backed away. She remained on the flattened canopy, apparently dissolving into hysterics.

I staggered back and watched as she clutched her thin arms around herself, sobbing with laughter until no more sound could come out of her throat. I considered running but I still wanted answers. Roisin continued to shake until, second by second, she went still. Finally, she pulled herself upright and looked at me, her expression both young and old at the same time.

"Oh...darlin' you don't know how lucky you are," she said, with a bitter chuckle that was drier than the dirt. "With me, he was the charming boyfriend who wanted to whisk me away on holiday. Show me around his home city." She climbed to her feet and crossed her arms around herself. "'Course, when we got there my passport got 'lost' and he told me not to worry – he'd get it all sorted. And while we were waiting, why not go to a few parties, meet a few friends? Try a bit of this, bit of that." She bared her teeth at me in a grim smile. "Two months later and he brought a new girl around. Same thing. Reels us in, gets us hooked and then has us sell the stuff, hold it, smuggle it – keeps his hands clean."

I thought of Andrei, charming, kind and sweet, how much I'd wanted his interest in me to be real. To be the person who'd made his eyes light up like that. Only it hadn't been love or even infatuation for him, had it? He'd been seeing money, opportunity. Just another desperate, sad woman who wanted so badly to believe in the romance he was peddling. I hated myself in that moment, but I loathed him more.

"Will you help me get away?" she asked, coming towards me again, head down like a stray dog begging me to be the first not to kick it. "Please? I know I don't deserve it, not after stealing, after trying to attack you but...please?"

"I don't know what to do," I admitted, quietly. Her desperation was so sharp I was near tears. I felt just as helpless as I had when I stood over that trapped and dying rat. Only I was in the trap right alongside her. I wanted so badly to help, but I was stuck in the same glue and there was no one there to free us. It was just the two of us and we had to work something out.

"If I can't go to the organisers, and there's no security...the police maybe but..."

"But who're they going to believe?" Roisin filled in for me, voice flat. She had obviously been down this road before. "I can't be sure who's part of this, how far it goes. He got us into the country, the drugs too. Maybe there are police in on it. Maybe if you call them, I'm just as dead as if you turned me in to him."

"Don't say that!" I felt my skin go cold. "No one is going to die. We just have to...I need to find my friends before Andrei does. He's looking for me and he knows what they look like, he might try and get to them too. Might think they know something or that he can use them to find me. If I can get them back here..."

"Then what?" Roisin demanded shrilly, clearly swept up in spiralling panic.

"Then..." I was grasping for a plan, trying desperately to access the part of myself that had handled everything when I got away from Nick. I gave myself a mental shake. That wasn't just a part of me, it was me. I wasn't useless, I wasn't stupid – hadn't I known something was wrong with Andrei? Felt that something was up ever since we arrived at this place? I hadn't known what, had misconstrued it through the lens of Nick, but my instincts had been right. I just hadn't listened to them. I had to trust them now.

"I'll get them, and then come back for you. We'll get out of the festival, hide you, and then get the police, but also contact the embassy or the UK police, so they know where we are. Even if the local police are up to something, they won't be able to make us, or you disappear if enough other people are involved."

Did I sound as unsure as I felt? I hoped not.

"God...OK. Alright," Roisin ran a hand through her greasy hair, sagging under the weight of hopelessness. "I suppose there's nothing I can do but wait here and hide until you get back, is there? Go and find your friends and I'll…I'll be fine." She gave me a look which was clearly meant to be brave. She just looked scared and lost. Still I tried to look like I believed her – to give her some confidence and strength.

"I won't be long," I said, knowing that I couldn't promise that even as I did so. I had no idea what was waiting for me inside the festival. "Be careful."

"You too," Roisin said, as I hurried away from her. "Please be careful."

The entrance near the medical tent was closest. I couldn't delay any longer in getting into the crowds and trying to find the others. Andrei was a risk I just had to take, ironic as I now knew the real danger he posed. I'd been afraid of him before, now I knew exactly what he was capable of and I had no other choice but to brave the risk. For my friends and Roisin.

Once I got into the crowd I made my way towards the concert space. If Ari and Carla were anywhere it was likely to be there. At least there I'd be surrounded by people, safe amongst the crowd.

Chapter 22

"Lethe Festival! Get ready for the ride of your life!" The headliner's voice came through the loudspeakers at deafening volume. Cheers went up all around me and I tried to run for it, shoving at the people around me. But my foot caught around someone else's and I felt myself start to fall. I tried to catch hold of something, of someone, to stop myself, but I hit the ground hard. The people around me shifted away, giving me space out of concern or annoyance, I couldn't tell. No one helped me though. Everyone was too focused on the returning headliner.

"This one's for all the lovely ladies of Lethe! Make some noise!"

The cheering intensified, joined by air horn blasts, whistles and chanting. I was scrabbling around trying to get to my feet, being nudged and bumped as the crowd began to dance to the music.

I felt two hands grip the back of my t-shirt and I screamed, my mouth instantly coated with dust. I flailed with my legs and arms, felt my foot catch something fleshy, kicking hard.

"Ow! Jody what the fuck?!"

I knew that voice.

I was rolled over onto my back and found myself looking up at Carla. She was clutching her thigh and wincing, behind her, Ari looked concerned and confused. Both of them were sweaty and covered in dust, breathless from dancing. But otherwise, completely fine.

"Jody, what the hell is going on?" Ari said. "We heard you yelling over the announcement. Is this..." she came closer as the music grew louder still, her face both pitying and resigned. "Is this about Nick again?"

"No! It's Andrei," I said, as I grabbed Carla's offered hand and got back on my feet, looking around for any sign of him, heart hammering. I couldn't see him anywhere but that didn't mean much. He was probably still there in the crowd, waiting.

"You mean the guy you dumped us for?" Carla said, clearly annoyed.

"We need to get out of here – I'll explain, please just..." I grabbed at Carla's hand in my desperation to just make her listen to me. "Please, just trust me right now. Something is wrong. We're in serious danger and it's not just Andrei – it's the festival."

Carla turned to Ari, who was already looking to her for her reaction. I felt sick watching them silently communicate. I'd seen them do this already – when I told them about Nick being at the festival, when I tried to share my concerns about Evie. It looked like the 'Jody's gone mad' look I'd become so used to and I felt my skin go cold as I anticipated their careworn sighs and their awful pity. I knew I'd have to leave them if they refused to come with me. It was too dangerous for me to stay. All I could do was warn them, I couldn't make them believe me.

"OK," Carla said, with a final glance at Ari. "Let's go then."

I was so surprised that I just stood there, speechless. Around us the crowd was churning, the music flooding over us. They believed me? Now, after everything?

"You…" I started to say.

Ari took hold of my sleeve and shook me slightly. "Look, we were…I think things got too heated yesterday. We shouldn't have let it go that far and…I didn't like how easily this guy talked you into going off with him, when you never normally would. So, if you say he's bad news, we believe you. Right Carla?"

"Agreed," Carla said. "Jody, come on. We can get to the back and follow the fence round to the exit. You can fill us in there."

I nodded, turned and started moving in the direction she'd pointed. The crowd thinned as we went and I kept my eyes open for Andrei, seeing him in so many people. By the time we reached the rubbish strewn area at the back of the field, where the stinking portaloos were either padlocked or cordoned off, I was sweating through my shirt.

"Right, what's happened?" Carla asked me. "What about Andrei has got you freaking out? Did he try something last night, because I swear if he hurt you…" her hands clenched into fists, her collection of stacked rings looking like knuckledusters.

"We'll get him for you," Ari said, sounding deadly serious. "We never should have just let you go off with

262

him, no matter if we were arguing or not. We let you down. It won't happen again, we promise."

"That's…" I wanted to thank her, to apologise, but I had to get everything else out first. "I found Roisin," I blurted, as the series of events that had unfolded since I last saw my friends crashed through my head like a wave clogged with rubbish. So many things, all tangled together and turning foul. "She's hiding, she's been hiding this entire time, waiting for a chance to get away from him. From Andrei."

"Slow down, what does she have to do with Andrei?" Carla asked, eyes round with worry. "He's just some guy."

"He's a drug dealer," I hissed, glancing around just in case any of the few people standing around decided to take an interest. "He has all these girls with him – ones he's seduced or groomed into it, girls he's gotten addicted – and he had them smuggle drugs into the festival and sell them for him. Roisin was one of them. And Evie. They're not really friends. They were just working together. And…I think he was trying to get me to go with him, get me to be part of it."

The pair of them gaped at me. Carla looked confused, Ari appalled. Hearing it all out loud I felt increasingly desperate. If my theory that Nick had followed me to Greece had seemed paranoid, this was on another level.

"And Roisin…told you this?" Ari asked. "When? How did you find her? Where has she been all this time?"

"I was looking for you two and I ended up in the out of bounds bit again – I found her tent and she had my passport. She stole it so she could travel on it, because

Andrei took hers. Look," I took it out and showed them. "See, I'm not making this up! I know you didn't take it because I just got it back from her. She needs our help to get away. Andrei's still out there somewhere looking for me."

"Why's he looking for you?" Carla asked. "Look, Jody, can you slow down and just…give us a minute? This is a lot. I mean…"

"There isn't any time!" I heard myself go shrill. "He wanted me to come with him to some flat he told me about. To 'wait for my passport to come through'. He was trying to…recruit me. The same way he did Roisin. He knows I know what he's really like – he saw it on my face. I know it. He was chasing me in the crowd, trying to shut me up or take me somewhere, I'm sure of it."

Ari took the passport from my hand and showed it to Carla. The pair of them seemed to actually believe me. At least, they looked as afraid as I felt so I assumed they were taking it seriously. Even if they only believed half my story, I could work with that. I just wanted to get them out of the crowd and away from Andrei. Finally Ari handed my passport back to me.

"When we were at the tent earlier, packing, we saw something kind of weird," she said. "Some girls – three of them, and a guy. He was taking money off them. We thought it was a dealer but…"

"It was a lot of money," Carla said quietly. "Like he was collecting it from them, I guess. Which fits with what you're saying."

"So you believe me?" I asked, half-relieved that they did and half-desperate to just get moving.

"Yeah...we do," Carla said, offering me a small, supportive smile.

"What can we do?" Ari looked between us. "Call the police?"

"Our phones haven't been working since this morning," Carla reminded her.

"I know," I said. "I tried to call you guys but it wouldn't go through. But I did manage to get a call through to the police and the hospital already, when I was out by the vans and the rubbish backstage. I think maybe there's less interference? Or maybe the towers are overloaded and we can't get calls through to anyone here. It could even be someone doing it on purpose." Even I had to acknowledge that suggestion was a little paranoid, which didn't help with what I had to say next. "Look, Roisin – she said not to get the police involved, that they might be connected to it somehow. At least some of them. She's not sure how far it goes, just that Andrei's involved and, so is Erik. The festival organiser."

"Jesus," Carla breathed. "I can't believe this it's just so fucked up...but he *was* kind of weird, we were talking about the money after you left and," she glanced at Ari. "Once we weren't so buzzed about having the rent and everything it started to seem a bit shady. A lot shady, actually."

"You had a point, is what she's trying to say," Ari said. "And we're sorry. For this and for Southend... We get why you thought it might be us who took your passport. We, uh... We didn't know that you knew about us lying back then, or that it bothered you but... we're sorry."

"It doesn't matter, I shouldn't have still been holding on to that," I said, feeling both grateful for and embarrassed by her apology. It wasn't the time for that. It all seemed so unimportant now that our lives and those of Roisin and Andrei's other girls were in danger. "As long as you believe me now," I said.

"I just don't understand why they'd need to do all this," Ari said. "I mean, he could be making tons of money off the festival if he really wanted – they could just sell tickets. What's the point of just giving them away? Just to sell drugs? Why not just do both?"

"The festival's just a trap," I said. "It's about getting more girls, giving them free tickets to get them here. And I mean, how much has been spent on it, really? It's land he already owned and it's shit land anyway. A few amusements, some bands we've never heard of. It was all about getting this place packed with people to sell to and girls to prey on." I stopped to catch my breath and steady myself. "We need to get Roisin out of here before we even think of tipping the police off. Or else she's convinced the same thing that happened to Evie will happen to her."

"But Evie's in hospital," Ari said. "Right?"

Oh God, I'd forgotten how much they didn't know. I looked around, there was no sign of Andrei. I took a deep breath, better to get it all out now.

"I rang the nearest hospital but there's no record of her. The more I think about it…the more I think either she was dead already when I found her or so near as it made no difference. I mean Roisin is convinced it was murder but, she's so afraid of him that she's convinced he could do anything to anyone. Maybe they just let

266

her die, because she was trying to run away like Roisin or because she failed at finding her. Maybe she did it to herself by accident and they just tidied her away like rubbish. The fact is, we don't know and it doesn't matter which – the end result is the same. Roisin is in danger, and so are we, because now we know."

"Gee, thanks Jody," Carla said shakily, but I could see that she was trying to make light to suppress her own panic. They'd already been in danger because of my connection to them. Knowing the truth couldn't make that much difference.

"Right, so, we get out of here – back to Roisin and then I think we should hide out until everyone starts to leave. We'll get lost in the crowd and escape from Andrei that way," I said. "Unless either of you has a better idea?" I asked, hopefully.

Ari looked at Carla and they both looked at me, then shook their heads. Somehow I had ended up in charge, and I had no idea if I was making the right decision.

"We'll follow your lead," Ari said.

A tiny spark flickered to life in my chest. They trusted me. That gave me the confidence I needed to make a move. I turned and headed towards the fence, intent on following it to the exit, Ari and Carla following after me. We'd just reached the wire fence when the music blasting from the speakers ended in a clamour of feedback and discordant notes. Without it, the noise from the crowd was even louder and clearer than before. I realised that the shrieks I could hear weren't from excitement – they were from fear. Panic.

A scream ripped through the air nearby and I turned with my friends. People were moving in all directions, stumbling and stampeding like ants under a rain of boiling water. They seethed up to the fence and I saw it wobble and sway as people grabbed at it in desperation.

The loudspeakers burst with sound and the headliner's voice came to us, strained and shrill. "Everyone, please calm down... Oh God is that... Someone's hurt!"

Their breathing was magnified, like the sound of a fake seascape. In and out, cracking. Until they took a breath and yelled: "Oh my God! Someone's been stabbed!"

Chapter 23

Panic. Sheer, bloody panic, overwhelmed the crowd in a matter of seconds. The initial movement spread and rippled out until everyone was running, pushing, falling over each other and screaming. The noise was immense, louder than the music and cheering had been. So many voices all combining into a terrible wail that never ended or paused for breath. A sound which raised the hair all over my body even as Ari grabbed one of my hands, Carla took the other and they both dragged me towards the single exit.

One thought ricocheted around my skull – we have to get out. Unfortunately it was the same thought that was in the head of everyone else around us. A hundred feet from the one gate out of the concert area we hit a wall of people – shoulder to shoulder, pushing and shoving and dragging each other back – but they didn't seem to be getting anywhere. The noise was getting louder as people fought to get past one another and everywhere the dust was rising under shuffling feet.

"There are too many people!" Carla yelled. "They're fighting at the front!"

Shrieks and yells of outrage and panic underscored her shout. Ahead of us someone was shoved backwards into a cluster of girls, knocking one of them to the ground. She screamed and I saw a foot land on her hair as her friends tried to drag her upright. This was turning into a stampede.

As I turned to my other side I gasped, too late to intervene as Ari caught a stray elbow to the ribs. She swore, shoving the offending person away. The elbower, a man lathered in sweat and clearly very drunk, collided with a woman and her boyfriend. A mini struggle broke out and Carla hauled Ari away out of it.

We were never going to get out of this panicky mosh pit at this rate. The crowd was too thick and everyone was too confused and frightened to get out quickly; looking for their friends, their family, or the knife-wielding attacker. We had to find another way out or we'd be trampled before we reached the gate. If Andrei didn't get to us first. I was certain he was the one who'd caused all this, blundering through the crowd with his knife.

Searching for inspiration I turned and looked back towards the area from which we'd just come. I spotted something across the dusty, abandoned field. An idea formed. Not a good one, but the only one I had.

"This way!" I shouted.

I tugged Carla's arm and she grabbed hold of Ari. The pair of them followed as I ran back to where the portaloos were arranged against the rear fence. Doubts were running through my head as I reached the one nearest the end. Would this work? What would I do if it didn't? I gritted my teeth and threw my weight against the plastic portaloo. It rocked, but rattled back into place almost at once, bottom heavy with tanks of waste, water and chemicals. Fortunately, as I turned to get the others to help, they were already catching on. They threw their strength in with me. The portaloo teetered and finally fell against the fence, forming a ramp.

"Climb! Go!" I panted, waving them forward, eyes flicking back to the masses of people. I couldn't see Andrei, but that didn't mean we were safe. I also didn't fancy finding out what it would be like to be mobbed by the crowd once they spotted a new way out.

Within seconds Carla had climbed up the side of the portaloo and hauled herself over the fence, dropping down over the other side. The fence bounced with the shifting of her weight and I could hear the plastic of the portaloo cracking.

"Come on!" she called back, staggering on the uneven ground. "It's easy!"

Ari gave me a doubtful look and then scrambled up the plastic box, which wobbled alarmingly as the fence began to buckle. As soon as Ari reached the top and dangled herself down, I hurried after her.

It was too much for the fence. The metal panel crumpled at the top, the connectors between it and the panels on either side sheared away as the whole thing plummeted to the ground. Ari squealed as she fell the few feet to the ground and I crashed down with the portaloo. When it hit the ground the wind was knocked out of me and I struggled to catch my breath. The stench of the chemical slurry seeping out onto the dusty ground didn't help matters. Carla was at my side in moments, dragging me upright. As she did so

I turned back and saw that other people had noticed what we were doing. Half the crowd still waiting to get out were headed our way at a run. We'd be swarmed in moments.

"Move!" Carla yelled, practically wrenching my arm from its socket as she dragged me towards Ari, shoving her onwards through the chaos in the amusement area. The folding chairs and tables around the bars had all been knocked over, stumbled through and kicked. As I watched a girl got her legs tangled in a chair and fell hard, crawling to her feet again with blood running down her forehead.

We'd landed nearer the campground than the actual exit would have taken us. If we'd been trying to leave we'd have lucked out. As it was I cursed to see the tents ahead of us as I realised we were further from Roisin than ever. We'd have to get to the backstage area via the campground instead of the medical tent gate. We'd never be able to fight against the flow of the crowd.

There were people everywhere, the first waves of those who'd escaped from the concert area running past people who had no idea what was going on, stirring them to panic. The fear was spreading as people yelled about the stabbing, or just shouted 'run!' as they passed groups of confused campers. The chaotically pitched tents and crisscrossed guy ropes were tripping people up, a camping stove or something had been kicked over and one tent was already ablaze. Everywhere I saw tents crumpling as people ran into or over them, floundering against the billowing nylon and through the clouds of acrid black smoke.

I sucked in a deep breath and ran across the campground, hoping that the others would keep up with me but not daring to look over my shoulder in case I fell. I leaped ropes and narrowly avoided stray luggage and rubbish that had been left between the tents. Snatches of conversation reached me as I went, people further from the action calling out and asking what was happening, why was everyone running? Confused and frightened girls calling for their friends, separated from sisters and boyfriends. Somewhere behind me I heard a small explosion – a gas canister? A bottle of vodka? – more screams followed.

I didn't stop, just kept going even though my lungs were burning and I felt like I was about to throw up. My side was split with a stitch and I desperately needed to stop but there was no time.

Finally, I reached the gap in the fence that I'd opened only an hour or so ago. It felt like years had passed since then. I looked behind me and saw Carla and Ari pelting along, only a short way off, slowed by a swarm of women running past. I let out a sigh of relief to see I hadn't lost them in the confusion.

Ari looked up as the women passed and spotted me. She came to a screeching halt, stumbling over her own feet. Her face contorted in panic and within a second she'd grabbed Carla's arm, bringing her up short as well.

"Jody!" Ari's cry came slicing through the mayhem, but it was too late. I felt a hand close in my hair, dragging me backwards. I flung my arms up, trying to tear the fingers from my hair, but then I felt something cold and sharp against my neck. I froze.

"Jody," Andrei said, in a strained but unnervingly light voice, right next to my ear. "I've been looking everywhere for you."

Ari and Carla were the only still things in the entire campground, frozen in fear. The crowd flowed around them, tents kicked loose of their ropes pitching and rolling in the dusty wind, rubbish sailing past in the smoky air. Still, I kept my eyes fixed on them, hoping that they wouldn't be the last thing I ever saw – already imagining the moment that their horrified, gaping faces would give way to darkness.

I felt Andrei's arm clamp around my waist, dragging me with him as he moved backwards so that we were hidden between the portaloos and the shower block. No one rushing past would see us, though everyone was so panicked my hopes of rescue were already low. Without moving the weapon from my throat he lifted his other arm and beckoned my friends closer.

My chest was heaving as I tried to get enough air, panic making my throat tight. I widened my eyes at my friends, begged them silently to run, to leave me. He wasn't going to let me go. I knew that. They wouldn't save me by obeying him – they'd just be putting themselves in danger. I wanted to scream when Ari shakily reached for Carla's hand and the pair of them came towards me and Andrei.

"Good – see, it's not so hard to do as you're told. Now why can't you be like that?" Andrei asked me, under his breath. "I thought you were a good girl but you've been nothing but a disappointment. That's not going to go well for you."

I shuddered. How had I ever thought he was kind?

That he was different? He was exactly like Nick – using my fear against me, forcing me to obey him.

Once my friends were within speaking distance, he waved at them to stop.

"That's close enough – now we can talk properly." I felt the knife, or scissors, or whatever it was, press tightly against my throat. "I'm Andrei, and you must be Ari and Carla. I've heard all about you…Jody was really eager to leave you behind, wasn't she? How about you return the favour?"

They stared at him, at me, in silent dread and I looked back at them, helpless even to say that I was sorry for bringing this man into their lives. I wondered briefly if it was worth simply trying to duck away from him. Without me as a hostage he had no power over my friends. I was going to die anyway, maybe it was worth the risk. As if sensing the direction of my thoughts, Andrei's free hand returned to my hair, practically pulling it out at the roots. I wasn't getting away from him.

"You two," he said to the others, jerking me from side to side as he looked between them, "are going to leave us. Leave the festival, the city, I don't care where you end up – just go. If I see you coming back or if I see police, security, anyone you bitches might have sent after me? I will cut her open and leave her on the dirt. Do you understand?"

Carla was openly crying – mouth wobbling, eyes streaming – but Ari was frozen stiff and pale as a statue. Her eyes met mine, as wide and helpless as those of the rat in the trap.

"Do you understand!?" Andrei yelled.

Carla jumped and Ari's head twitched in what might have been a nod.

"Say 'goodbye' Jody," Andrei said, pulling me slowly back towards the fence, clearly planning to take me through it into the backstage area. "Say, 'please don't come after me, or I'll be the next dead slut they find with the rats'."

"Jody!" Carla sobbed, as if she was calling me back to them.

"I'm sorry," I blurted, tears of pain and fear springing from my eyes. I stumbled as he dragged me, terrified that if I fell it might cause him to stab me by accident. Or annoy him enough that he did it on purpose. The words came boiling out of me as I was dragged out of view, "Please don't tell my mum!"

I wish it had just been about sparing her, but no. As much as I didn't want her to think she had pushed me into this, trying to get me to 'be a joiner' that wasn't all it was. It was some instinct, some desperate need to not have her disapproval heaped on me. Even though I'd probably be too dead to care what she said. As if getting into trouble with her would be the final straw for me now. Maybe it would be.

I could feel Andrei shaking and it took a second for me to realise he was laughing at me. Laughing as he whirled me around and shoved me through the fence, the edge of the blade warm from my skin but still digging in enough to remind me it was there.

"What do you want?" I asked, as he forced me along in front of him between the piles of rubbish and the humming generators. Even the rats had made themselves scarce, the place was abandoned. "You can't take me anywhere I…I won't go."

"I am down two girls, and if you hadn't stumbled around, ruining everything, I'd have recruited so many more. You couldn't even die right! I thought I had you and it was just some other ginger bitch," he snapped steering me with a harsh yank to my hair. "All the girls I had lined up, scattered. That's your fault, and I refuse to leave with less than I came with. I'm not leaving here without a replacement for Evie – Roisin, we'll find her. She can't go anywhere and she'll be hurting by now anyway. Surprised she hasn't come crawling back yet."

"I'll run away, like she did," I hissed. "Why not just leave me behind? I don't know anything about what's happening. I don't...I won't tell anyone." I was spiralling, bargaining and for a second I hoped it would work. Then reality slapped me in the face. He wasn't going to let me go, he was too angry to do that.

His fist tightened in my hair and I yelped, convinced I must be bleeding by now. My body was drenched in sweat, skin tight with sunburn, yet I couldn't stop shivering. Every time I stumbled Andrei twisted his fistful of my hair, using it like a dog's lead.

"You won't run. You're not like your friends, Jody – you've got no spark." We were at the far edge of the maze that was the backstage area now. I saw a rust-speckled minibus at the end of an aisle, surrounded by girls in cheap, generic clothes like the ones Evie had worn. A few had bags on their shoulders or at their feet. They must have been preparing to leave before the panic started. The women were milling around, thin and scared and clearly waiting for something. Waiting for Andrei, I realised as first one, then another caught sight of us. They grew still as rabbits gauging a threat, waiting for just one of them to break ranks and run. But not a single one of them did.

"I won't sell drugs for you," I hissed, willing myself to struggle, but too scared to do more than twitch. "I won't help you do this to anyone else."

"You'll be surprised what you'll do when your next fix is all you can think about," Andrei said. "Or when you know what'll happen to the others if you try and get away."

I looked over the cowed women with fresh understanding. They were all hostages. Just like Roisin and Evie – they were answerable for each other's actions. Andrei had made them each other's jailers.

We stopped a few feet from the girls. I felt Andrei move behind me, looking around at them. "Where's Ivan?"

A vague muttering rose up as each girl shrugged or said something too low for me to hear. Like nervous school children shrinking from blame. A couple shook their heads, several just looked at the ground as if preparing themselves for the punishment that they clearly expected to follow this question. Whoever Ivan was – Andrei's brother as he'd previously said or just his partner in crime – he wasn't here. Maybe he was still caught up in the chaos Andrei had caused, or maybe he'd fled in case the police were on their way. I had no idea. I didn't care. The only thing that mattered was the vague glimmer of hope his absence provided. Andrei was alone.

The wary eyes of the gathered girls met mine as I looked from one to the other. None of them looked ready to help me and honestly I couldn't blame them.

What would happen if one of them tried? Andrei could just slit my throat and turn on whoever stuck their neck out for me. From the looks of things they didn't trust each other to back them up either. There was careful space between most of them, as if they were strangers who all just happened to be waiting for the same bus. The few who stood together were probably friends but two or three girls against Andrei, against any of the others who might try and stop them...they didn't stand a chance. I didn't stand a chance.

But what choice did I have? I was dead either way, eventually. There was no way I was getting on that bus, not with him. I thought of the rat in the glue trap, waiting to die, feral with fear. But unlike that poor animal, no one was coming to help me. If I wanted to live, I had to fight for my life like a cornered animal.

I bent my neck and sunk my teeth into the hand at my throat.

Chapter 24

Andrei yelled in pain, ripping at my hair with his other hand. I could feel the hair being torn out at the root, practically hear the follicles ripping out of my skin. I felt it when he dropped the weapon, which hit my foot and bounced off. Whilst Andrei wrenched my head back and forth by the hair, shaking me the way a terrier shakes a rat, his injured hand was grasping for my throat. I had to get away before he could choke me out.

I gathered all my strength and rammed my elbow into his stomach as hard as I could. I was smaller than him, bony where he was muscular, but my elbow was sharper for it. He grunted in pain and crumpled to the ground, taking me with him. I landed on his leg and he yelled and cursed at me, grabbing for my hair again. The fight was on to stay out of his grasp and I wasn't going to let him get me again.

I fought as hard as I could, unable to keep myself from squeezing my eyes shut as if that would save me from his fists. My resolve wavered as fear flooded me again. But then I saw a flash of Nick in my head and felt my jaw tighten, my fingers stiffen into claws. I was strong and Andrei wouldn't break me when Nick had already tried and failed. My eyes flew open and I hit out at Andrei, catching him full in the face. He cursed, grabbing at me even though his eyes were watering so much he couldn't possibly see me. I kicked out and rolled away from him, nearly colliding with a pair of legs.

I looked up and found a girl looking down at me with wide, terrified eyes.

She was sunburned and dotted with mozzie bites, dark circles under her eyes. One of Andrei's girls, held hostage like Roisin and Evie. Coming to his rescue out of fear, or to safeguard her supply of drugs? I had no idea. Her arm moved and I saw the knife in her hand – the one Andrei must have been using. I flinched away as she extended it to me, but she wasn't trying to stab me.

She was offering it me. Handle first. Giving me a weapon.

Her fingers shifted, leaving the handle exposed, and I took it from her without hesitation. She backed away, like she was afraid of being caught, even though Andrei was still trying to rub his eyes clear, hunched on the ground.

After I staggered to my feet I turned back to Andrei, who was levering himself up off the ground, still holding his nose. Blood was pouring through his fingers from where I'd hit him, soaking into the yellow dirt immediately as it fell. He was standing with his weight on one leg, I must've fallen quite hard on his knee, injuring him. That gave me a chance. I didn't stop to think, to second guess myself, I just ran at him.

I shoved Andrei with my shoulder, using my full

281

weight and momentum to send him staggering before he could get his footing. He stumbled, tried to steady himself but tripped over his own feet and fell to the ground, face down. I heard the air rush out of him as I dropped down to my knees on the dirt, pinning him to the ground under me. He froze when I put the knife to his throat. Blood dripped out of his nose onto the ground. I could smell it, smell him and it made me sicker than the bin stench.

"Don't move," I ordered, wishing my voice wasn't shaking, though the hand holding the knife was steady – a miracle given how hard my heart was beating. "I mean it, I'll use this."

He was struggling to get his breath back, and I quickly tugged the back of his jacket down, using it to trap his arms, without them he'd have a hard time knocking me off. Still, it wasn't impossible. As I pinned his arms and wrestled with his jacket, I felt a bundle shifting around in an inside pocket and dug it out. It was a stack of passports, held together with an elastic band. Various different coloured covers, different countries. Andrei had clearly victimised girls from all over the world.

"You won't kill me," Andrei growled, apparently able to breathe again, even with me on his back. He started to struggle, but I pressed the knife against his neck and misjudged the pressure a bit. A bead of blood welled up and trickled down his throat, dripping off to join the blood from his nose in the dirt. A fly was buzzing on it already. Andrei went very still.

"You don't know me," I said, attempting to put as much threat as possible into those four words. "You don't know what I'm capable of."

"Oh please... I know so many girls like you," Andrei hissed. "Desperate for love, for someone to tell you what to do and what to think."

"No one's telling me what to do now," I said, voice shaking slightly. I tossed the stack of passports towards the girls, who backed away like it was a grenade.

"He can't stop you now. You can go," I called. "Please, just run! Get out of here!"

Andrei laughed, half choking on the dust stirred up from the ground. The fly buzzed up into his face, angry at being disturbed. He spat as it hit his lips, infuriated. "They don't have anything without me! Not enough for a taxi between them."

"We'll see about that... What else have you got on you?"

"Keep your hands off!"

He struggled when I reached into his jacket again, swearing and snarling when my hand closed around a stallholder's money belt packed with notes in dozens of different currencies. Notes and a plastic baggie stuffed with smaller bags of pills and powder, which tumbled to the dirt beside me. Those I didn't care about, they belonged in the dust.

"You're a dead woman," Andrei snapped as I threw the money belt towards the passports, still untouched by the crowd of fearful women. Slowly, they began to move forwards, I saw them glancing at each other, waiting for someone else to make the first move. To cross the line that must have felt impossible to get over. But they didn't have the luxury of time. The police were coming. I knew that by now they must have had dozens of reports about the stabbing. What they'd make of this crowd of likely undocumented addicts didn't bear thinking about. They needed to get away, to escape before they could be locked up or taken back into the custody of Andrei's friends.

"Go!" I yelled. "Just leave me Roisin's passport and get out of here. Now! Before it's too late!"

At the mention of Roisin's name, Andrei renewed his attempts to buck me off.

"Tell me where that bitch is! I knew she was still here, skulking around, too stupid to find her own way home."

He nearly managed to unseat me but I kicked the back of his knee and held his arms in place with all my weight. He fell back onto his belly and I steadied myself. I was braced, using my position and his injured knee against him. He wasn't going anywhere for the moment.

I watched as the girls scrabbled for the passports. They were finally moving, all at once as if they were a herd, stirred into action by each other. One, a woman who looked to be in her mid-twenties, picked up the money belt. She dug around in it and pulled out a set of car keys, waving them over her head as if for attention. The other women looked to her, and in that moment she became their leader.

"We'll take the minibus," she said it whilst looking at me, as if she was asking permission, or my blessing.

"Go," I said. "Good luck!"

"You do that and you're dead, you hear me? All of you, dead!" Andrei yelled, spittle frothing between his clenched teeth as he struggled to breathe and rage at the same time.

"She's right, he can't stop us," the woman with the keys said, giving Andrei a look that held both fear and hatred – with hatred winning out.

Other girls in the group nodded at their leader, looking at each other hesitantly, then heading onto the minibus. One by one, reminding me of scared mice racing around the edges of a skirting board, nose to tail. Only two passports remained on the ground – I already knew who they belonged to; Evie and Roisin. Only one of them would be needed, but still, I wanted to know.

"What happened to Evie?" I demanded, pressing the knife harder against Andrei's neck, but using the full length of the blade, to keep from piercing the skin. I was learning, I thought wildly, learning how to be forceful without being blinded by my emotions. "Did you kill her?"

"She did it to herself, stupid bitch," Andrei snarled, twisting underneath me like a snake trying to escape my grasp. "Stole from me and used too much. Like an idiot. I found her out there, covered her up to save myself some trouble. Didn't realise you'd go digging through the rubbish, looking for rotten meat."

I swallowed back my nausea, mind working frantically as the minibus reversed and turned, crawling through the dust towards the main gate. My only allies were gone. I was still on top of Andrei and if I got up he'd attack me within seconds. I was as trapped as he was. Both of us locked in a stand-off. What was I going to do with him now? Apparently Andrei had realised the same thing as me.

"Stuck now, aren't you?" he said, voice laced with

cunning, I could feel him shifting slightly, testing my grip. "I'll make you a deal – if you let me up and tell me where Roisin is…I'll let you walk out of here and back to your friends. You go your way, I go mine… Everyone wins."

As if I'd fall for that. I'd just let his girls go, with his money. I'd made him bleed and humiliated him. There was no way he would ever let me get away with any of that. But pretending to consider it bought me precious seconds to try and come up with a plan.

"Who said I know where she is?" I said. "I'm still looking for her."

"That's crap. You wanted her passport for a reason. I'm not stupid," Andrei spat into the dust.

No, but apparently I was. That was the second mistake I'd made since gaining the upper hand. I wasn't willing to risk a third, in case it was my last.

Andrei wasn't done. "You found her and she asked you to help her – poor Roisin," his voice went high and mocking, "I just want to go home to my mummy! Pathetic. Worse than you – but please, tell me what your plan is for getting out of this mess without making a deal with me? Let's see how stupid you really are."

"I could just kill you," I said sharply, playing for time. I needed to think, to formulate a plan. Maybe Ari and Carla would circle around and appear in time to help me? If they hadn't run away or tried to find help outside of the festival grounds. My chest tightened with the realisation that I couldn't rely on them coming back for me. I had to find a way out of this myself – I was the only person I could count on.

"I doubt it," he gritted out. "You barely had the nerve to kiss me."

How quiet it had gotten. I only realised it in the silence that followed those words. The crowds of people had flooded out of the festival and left behind an eerie quiet, tense and expectant. As if this wasn't a festival anymore, but a battlefield awaiting an army.

Into that silence, came the howling of sirens. The police? An ambulance? Both? Relief flickered in my chest. I wasn't alone after all. The cavalry was coming.

"Fuck!" Andrei started to struggle harder, frantic to get away. I had to fight hard to keep him pinned down and I was running out of energy after all that had happened since that morning. "Let me go, or it's the end for you! I know people – all over the world – you'll never see it coming, bitch! There's hundreds of men just like me."

"I know there are."

That decided it. I wasn't mercenary enough to kill him, or trusting enough to let him go. But I was strong enough to hurt him. I hit him, hard, in the temple with the handle of the knife. His head flopped forwards into the blood-soaked dirt, and he went limp. A fat, black fly landed on his cheek and he didn't so much as twitch. With my heart racing I checked his pulse. He was alive, thank God. I'd had only the vaguest idea of how to knock someone out, mostly from half-remembered action films Nick had made me watch. But it had worked. He was unconscious and I was free.

Once I was sure Andrei was truly unconscious and not just faking, I got off of him and quickly removed his belt and shoelaces. Was I being ridiculous? Maybe, but if he came-to I didn't want him immediately chasing after me. So I tied his hands behind his back and belted his feet together. It might buy me precious seconds if it came down to it. The bag of pills I arranged so it was clasped in his bound hands, locked into place by his bonds and easy to spot with him lying face down on the ground. I fumbled my new eyeliner from my bag and pulled the cap off. I'd leave something for the police, just in case they got to him before me.

With Roisin's passport in hand I ran towards where her tent had been, leaving Andrei in the dust. The words 'Drug Dealer' and 'Kidnapper' written in large, black letters on the back of his white shirt. The police would probably be able to put the details together if they got to him before I could explain. I just had to trust that Roisin and he shared the same overinflated idea of his own power. There were probably hundreds of men out there like Andrei. Thousands. Hundreds of thousands. But they weren't all working together. They weren't inescapable – they just counted on appearing to be.

Whatever happened now, whatever happened next, I had to believe that I could handle it. That I'd survive. I'd escaped Nick and I'd beaten Andrei. If there was ever a third bastard trying to trap and control me, well, I would deal with him when I had to. But I would, could, deal with him. I knew that now.

I looked at Andrei's unconscious body. How long would it take for the police to get here? To find him? Were they already inside the festival grounds, searching for injured attendees and the knife-wielding attacker? Or were they still setting up a cordon or whatever they had to do to try and contain this?

"...hello?"

I nearly yelped, jerking around to find two of the women from the minibus standing a few feet behind me. The dust behind them was swirling from where they'd walked over it. I'd been too lost in my own thoughts to hear them. Careless.

"What are you doing back here?" I asked, hand on my chest as if my heart might punch through my ribs. "You need to get away!"

"We wanted to help," the taller of the two, a brunette in jean shorts and an 'I love New York' t-shirt said, in a soft French accent. "To tell the police what happened. What he," she glared at Andrei, "did to us. Or he'll just do it again. Besides, we couldn't leave you alone with him...even though you seem to be OK now."

They were so brave that I felt my throat turn thick. I was so grateful to not be carrying the weight of telling this story by myself. Still, I had to make sure they knew the risks.

"Did he tell you he has friends, in the police?" I asked. "That they might try and silence you, or have you arrested on false charges?"

The taller girl and her friend, a middle-eastern girl in a pink t-shirt dress, exchanged a look. "Andrei says lots of things...but we've only ever seen him talk to Ivan and Erik. He pretends to be important, but he's just a horrible little drug dealer. Without our passports, he can't hurt us."

This time I heard the running footsteps and turned in time to see two people arrive in a cloud of dust.

"Jody!"

Ari and Carla had come running from one of the

meandering paths through the catering vans and trucks for the stage equipment and practically collided with me. With the pair of them clinging to me we nearly toppled over. I was so glad to see them that I nearly burst into tears.

Behind me, I heard the two girls talking together, in French. Maybe wondering who Ari and Carla were or discussing what to do next.

"Are you OK – what did you do to him? Did he hurt you? I can't believe you're OK! We thought you were…that…" Carla had clearly been crying, hard, and I hugged her tightly. Her face was covered in dust, sticking to the tear tracks.

"It's OK – they helped me – the other girls. They got me his knife and I made him hand over their passports and all his money."

"Jesus, Jody," Ari let out a teary laugh. "I didn't know you were going to go full Rambo…thank fuck you did. And you two…thank you!"

The girl in the pink dress looked past us, to where voices were calling out to each other. Male voices shouting in Greek, and lots of thumping footsteps, the sounds of dogs. The police were here.

"You should leave," the girl in pink said. "Find the Irish girl – Roisin, help her get home, she won't be able to cope with the police. We'll give Andrei to them, make sure they know everything he and Erik did. They'll find Ivan soon, he's probably still waiting around for Andrei to tell him what to do – he's not very clever. Just…help Roisin, we'll take care of the rest."

"I will. I'll get Roisin home. Make sure she's safe. Thank you – again."

The tall girl shrugged. "Thank you, for not giving up."

There was no more time. Ari, Carla and I ran into the side avenues between the rusting catering vans and headed for Roisin's tent. When we reached it the collapsed canopy didn't seem to have changed much or been righted. Wherever she'd decided to hide it wasn't in there.

"Roisin!" I called. "It's me – Jody. I've got your passport. It's over. He can't get you now. Come out!"

For a second there was no response and then, furtive as a fox, she slipped from between two metal storage containers and came slowly towards us. When she saw the others she flinched back, but then, apparently realising they weren't Andrei's girls, she kept walking towards us. I held the passport out and she took it with a sigh of relief, fumbling the cover open to look at the photograph. Her hand went to her mouth and her shoulders shook with sobs, clutching the leather case to her chest.

"You really got it," she whispered. "How..."

"The police are coming," I explained. "Andrei's... he's trapped, for now with two of the others watching him. The police'll get him. The rest of the girls have made a run for it already. If he has other men here still, like Ivan, they'll find them."

"And me?" Roisin asked. "What'll the police do to me once they get their hands on me?"

"I don't think the police are part of this," I said, trying to sound more certain than I felt. Really this was all conjecture, a gut feeling I had, only partially confirmed by what the other girls had told me. It was a big risk to take, for both myself and Roisin. Still, I couldn't believe that Andrei was as powerful as he'd led her to believe.

"You didn't see Andrei, he was desperate not to be caught. I think if he knew the police would help him he wouldn't have been so afraid," I said.

Roisin's frightened eyes were tracking every movement of my face, as if she was trying to interpret every twitch and crinkle as I moved. Desperate to believe me but terrified that I was lying, or wrong, or confused.

"I promise, we won't leave you," I said. "No matter what. We'll all stick together. Won't we?"

"Yeah," Carla said. "Don't worry – we'll take care of you. Girls have to stick together, right?"

"We do," Ari came to stand close by me, Carla on the other side of her. The three of us shoulder to shoulder as I held out a reassuring hand to Roisin. And she took it.

Epilogue

All the way up from the front door of the building I told myself that I'd faced worse. It was true, I knew that. But the truth doesn't always feel like the truth. It didn't at that moment. I was half trapped in the past, back before I knew how strong I really was, deep down. I had my doubts but I didn't let the weight of them keep me from climbing the stairs, one after the other. That was the important thing. I was allowed to be afraid. I just couldn't let that fear stop me, not any more.

I could have taken the lift but I wanted to take my time, and make sure I was prepared. I wanted to give myself the space to be scared. I had so many memories of taking those echoing, vinyl covered stairs, delaying my inevitable return to Nick and his control. Even the sound of my own footsteps on the metal stair runners made my skin prickle with unease. I swallowed down my panic and felt it burn inside me, fuelling my resolve.

At the top of the stairs I went down the hallway, my muscles remembering how many times I'd come this way, day after day. I felt my chest tighten as I smelled its familiar combination of bland fried food and the sudden punch of smoky burned bacon that hung around at the end of the hall almost constantly, the odour of cats from three doors down from Nick's flat and the overpowering reek of rose air freshener from the flat opposite – like there was a war going on for the very air between the two doors. Finally, after stepping over the brown stain from a long ago dropped cup of coffee, I stopped at the front door to the flat and knocked.

Nick answered it in his joggers and no shirt, fresh from the shower. His face changed from bland curiosity to surprise and finally landed on smug confidence. He leaned on the open door and smirked openly at me.

"Jody! What a surprise – do you have my money?"

I took a moment, just a second, to look him in the eye and let the silence stretch between us. I'd always rushed to fill these silences with words, with apologies and flattery and endless, pointless chatter. My nerves getting the best of me and letting my mouth run riot.

This time he was the first to look away. It was only for a moment and then he was glaring back at me, but I knew I had him then. More importantly, I knew he didn't have me.

I took a step into the flat, then another and another, until I was across the living room and by the flat screen. My flat screen. On the way I noticed the mess of takeaway containers on the coffee table, the discarded gym clothes in a heap where he'd dumped out his bag. There were bits of fluff and crumbs all over the carpet and dust on the TV. He'd always scolded me for failing to tidy up, but obviously his standards were looser when he was the only one around to pick up after himself.

"Earth to Jody? The money you owe me for the rent? Where is it?" Nick was saying, following me across the room. I turned just as he reached me and looked him in the eye. He stopped short, a confused smirk hanging on his lips like a crooked picture on the wall.

"I didn't bring you any money. I'm here for my stuff," I said. "My TV and the coffee machine, my computer...all of it."

Nick let out a surprised little laugh. "Really?"

"Yes, really. I want my stuff back and I'm taking it with me – now," I said, evenly.

His expression clouded. "You owe me—"

"I don't owe you a fucking thing."

My words hung between us and I saw him react to them the way anyone else would a buzzing insect – a sudden jerk of his head that he quickly tried to style out. Too late though. I'd seen the flash of surprise and uncertainty in his face and I would never let myself forget that I had been the one to put it there.

"You don't get to come in here and take my shit," Nick said, taking a half-step towards me. Once I would have stepped back, unconsciously allowing him to manoeuvre me into a corner where he could stand over me and talk – just endlessly talk down to me. This time I didn't move, though it took everything I had to crush the impulse, the instinct to be herded by him.

"Are you going to call the police?" I asked, keeping my voice pleasant and level, not letting it creep up into a higher octave the way I always did when confronted by an angry man. As if I could make myself enough of a girl, enough of a child, to keep myself safe. As if that wasn't exactly what he wanted.

"I don't need to." Nick folded his arms across his chest and sneered at me. "But if you try and take any of my stuff out of that door you're going to need an ambulance."

"OK," I said, and walked away from the TV, across the living room and towards the front door. I heard Nick laugh under his breath, then swear as I picked up my Nintendo Switch from the charging dock, slipping it into my bag. By the time he reached me I'd disconnected the dock itself and was wrapping the wire around it. Nick grabbed for my wrist but I slapped his hand away with my free one. He flinched, momentarily surprised, and then filled the doorway, glaring down at me.

"Put it back, now," he demanded. "Or…"

"Or what?"

At the sound of Carla's voice he twisted around, looking over his shoulder. She and Ari stood together in the hallway, having come up in the lift. Ari had her arms folded but Carla had her phone out, recording him. He gaped between her and the camera lens, eyes darting up and down the corridor.

"Don't be shy, Nick Pearson, from CMR Electrical," Carla said pleasantly. "You can tell us – all," she checked the count in the corner of the screen, "twelve hundred of us, just what you want to do to Jody, if she takes her stuff back."

"That's twelve hundred, and counting, by the way," Ari put in. "Say hi, you're live."

Nick turned back to me and said, in a voice noticeably quieter than before, "What the fuck do you think you're playing at? You can't just take my stuff."

"I think we already settled that it's my stuff," I said. "And I'm taking it with me."

I took a step backwards and he followed me, allowing

Ari to slip into the flat. Carla followed her, pivoting to keep Nick in shot as Ari went to my TV and started to unplug it.

"Hey!" Nick moved in her direction but came up short when Carla followed him, phone held up and trained on his every movement. Nick's face ran the gauntlet from fury to calculation to loathing.

"Fine! Get your shit out of my flat. Like I care," he snapped, and stormed off into the bedroom, slamming the door behind him.

Carla flipped him off and crossed the room so she could keep the door in shot and make sure he didn't come storming back out without warning. She winked at me on her way and I felt pride rush through me.

"Little help?" Ari called, snapping me out of it.

"Got it." I went to the front door and brought in the wheeled trolley we'd rented to get my stuff into the lift and out to the hired van. Together, Ari and I loaded up the TV, coffee machine, folding treadmill and everything else that I'd carefully listed to make sure we didn't have to come back.

From the bedroom I heard the sound of Nick kicking the shit out of the walls. A few months ago, actually, a few weeks ago, that would have sent me scurrying for cover. I still wasn't sure if I wouldn't be doing so now if my friends weren't with me. But that was the thing, they were with me. I didn't have to do this on my own. Even if Ari and Carla hadn't agreed to come with me, even if I'd never met them, I knew now that there were at least twelve hundred people (and counting) rooting for me, believing in me. Twelve hundred people who could see what Nick was like and who knew that I wasn't crazy.

"That everything? Sure there's nothing in the bedroom?" Ari asked.

"No, that's everything," I said, checking the last thing off my list. "Let's go."

We had the trolley out the door with Ari and Carla on either side when I heard the bedroom door slam open. Nick, red-faced and now wearing a crumpled t-shirt came hurtling across the room, then ground to a halt right in the front doorway. As if he was a reverse-vampire and had to be invited out of his little world.

"Bitch!" he yelled, once he saw that Carla was too far down the hallway to get his face on camera. As if that made a difference. He was done for and we both knew it. His name was out there, his job – twelve hundred people, and it just needed one or two of them to leave a review, to write an email. He wouldn't lose everything, but he'd lose something. That was enough for me.

"You fucking bitch!" he yelled again.

"Yeah, I'm a bitch," I shouted back. "You're so right, Nick. Well done! I'm the worst! But I'm still your *ex*. So...never contact me again, OK?"

I walked to the lift, even though there was a part of me that wanted to run. Carla and Ari stepped in on either side of me, like body guards. They waved as the doors slid closed. The moment they did I sagged against the back wall and shut my eyes.

"You were amazing," Carla said, wrapping an arm around me. "And thank you everyone, for watching along, link to his employer's Facebook is in my bio," she waved to the camera and ended the live.

"Fantastic," Ari said, hugging me from the other side.

"Thank you, both of you. For doing this with me," I said.

"Roisin was on there," Carla said. "She followed you and I tagged your account, anyway, she left a comment. 'Kick his arse from me!'"

My heart ached – that Roisin had wanted to encourage me, after everything she'd been through. I was so grateful. The last time we'd spoken it was just by text, telling me she'd moved back in with her parents and was being spoiled rotten. She'd also sent me a link to the news that Andrei and 'other men arrested in connection with his operation' had been denied bail following their arrest. The trial wouldn't be for a while yet, but there were so many women prepared to speak against them – the minibus group might have left the festival, but they were coming forward, as were others. Girls who'd managed to get away or been left to wait for Andrei to return from Lethe. The article itself mentioned forty-eight, but the online support group Roisin had joined contained more than double that. Erik had been in the game a long time, before recruiting Andrei. He'd hurt a lot of women and they were finding their voices now that they knew they weren't alone in speaking out.

"She's amazing," I said, and meant it from my very core. Roisin was dealing with more than me, and doing so brilliantly as far as I could tell.

"Girl power, right?" Carla said, throwing up an ironic peace sign. "Now, let's get your stuff home so we can go for brunch. I'm thinking pancakes and a ludicrously expensive smoothie. My treat."

"Our treat," Ari corrected. "For the first brunch of the rest of your life."

"Least we can do since you're seeing your mum later," Carla said, pulling a face.

I rolled my eyes. "But at least by tonight it'll all be over with. Nick's out of my life, I've got my stuff back…"

"We've got a new flat to move into – and a big fuck off telly to put in it," Carla grinned.

"And you're about to read your mother the riot act, on a stomach full of pancakes," Ari finished.

I wasn't so sure about 'riot act', but I was definitely going to share a few truths with her. I'd written out everything I'd wanted to say to her for years and gone over it for the past few nights. Nothing to do now but take that speech to her and see what she made of it.

I knew she was probably going to be annoyed, hurt, scathing and dismissive. Her full range, essentially. But I still needed to say it. I needed her to hear it. I was going to tell her every, single, detail about what Nick had done to me. What it had taken for me to get away from him, and that despite everything I still wasn't going to give up on my course or my goals. Even if she thought I was being ridiculous or ungrateful or childish. Even if she said that to my face, I still needed to tell her. I needed her to know that I was done living my life based on her worries and her fears. I was my own person and I wanted different things for myself than she did. If and when I made mistakes, they were mine to make and I wouldn't be cajoled or manipulated into believing I was a failure every time I screwed up. My future might not look like what she'd planned, but it was mine. Not hers.

I'd learned how to stand up for myself, in spite of her. I wasn't about to be ground down again. Not by anyone. Not anymore.

300

Author's Note

Trigger Warning Notes:

A large portion of the climax to the novel takes place during a mass panic event at a music festival, which some readers may find triggering given recent real-world events. During this event, there is a stabbing, and several other characters are held at knife point.

Part of the novel details an abusive relationship which features elements such as coercive control, gaslighting, the threat of violence, moderate intimate partner violence (grabbing, shaking and pushing) and an attempt to pressure the main character into a sexual act which they are not comfortable with.

This novel features characters who have been trafficked into a drug dealing operation and forcibly addicted to drugs, there are allusions to sexual and physical violence. There are multiple references to drug addiction and overdose throughout.

Acknowledgements

I'd like to thank my family for supporting me during the absolute madness of this year. So many ups and downs; books coming out, books being written and edited and books piling up on the doormat. I feel like there were days when I didn't see you, but I heard you moving around downstairs and you made me enough tea to keep me going, so thank you!

An extra shout out goes to my brother Jack, for learning how to say 'My sister is famous' in Japanese, you little kiss-ass. I'm not buying you a new console, but it was a brave effort.

Thank you to my longest serving editor, Rachel Hart. Rachel it has been such a pleasure working with you, as ever. This one was a struggle at times but you never stopped giving it your all and I'm especially grateful for your help in reaching the '100 thousand books sold' milestone with Avon. Thanks go to everyone else working with you as well, to bring these manuscripts to life as the novels they become, from cover art to copy editing.

Enormous thanks are due to Laura Williams, my incredible agent at Greene and Heaton. It's been a busy year and I probably would have lost my mind and wandered off into the wilderness with nothing but a penknife and a compass if you weren't around to offer support, advice and good news. Thank you so much for all your hard work.

Further thanks are due to Kate Rizzo, also at Greene and Heaton, for her continued efforts on the international front. It's always exciting to see new editions of my books popping up across Europe. Even if my shelves are getting worryingly full.

Lastly, thank you to everyone who has read and reviewed my previous books. It really helps the book to reach a wider audience and I try and read as many as I can, because I want to make each book better than the last. I hope you enjoyed reading The Festival just as much as I did writing it, and that you're just as excited as I am for the next one.

As always, to everyone reading this, stay safe and look out for yourself and your friends. The world is a scary place sometimes.

Loved *The Island*?

Read on for an exclusive short story
from Sarah Goodwin…

"Liv! Livy! Take my picture!"

I glance away from the street vendor filling my cinnamon coated trdelnik with ice-cream and spot Sophia posing on the bandstand. Around us, Letná Park is packed with other tourists also working their way down a list of 'Top 10 Things to do in Prague' and she's attracting a lot of attention. It's sort of her default state – my oldest friend is something of a head turner.

Part of the reason she stands out is what she's wearing. Where I'm dressed in chino shorts, a Breton striped t-shirt and walking boots for touring the city, Sophia has pulled out all the stops. She's fully made up and wearing a rainbow striped tea-dress, purple tights and glittery jelly sandals with six inch heels. Which have already caused some issues for her on the way here, through the cobbled streets. I already know she'll be blistered and moody later. Thankfully I have plasters in my bag for just such an eventuality.

"Hang on!" I pay for my delicious ice-cream filled doughnut cone and head over her way, taking my phone from the cross body pouch I bought just for this trip to hold it and my guidebook. It's meant to be completely pickpocket proof, and has a secret compartment for my cash.

I snap a few pictures one handed while Sophia poses and preens. The stares of other tourists and a few business looking types who must be locals is making the back of my neck hot with embarrassment. But Sophia must be used to it by now. It's her job after all, to take pictures and show off for her social media audience. Apparently she's already got two sponsorships out of this trip – mascara and a coffee cup she's taking everywhere with us, even though it's massive and she keeps accidently leaving it on the floor at restaurants.

The photoshoot is interrupted when a notification goes off on my phone. I wave Sophia over to a wrought iron bench nearby, under the shade of the trees. Every other bench is already occupied with families and couples, this being the height of holiday season. A Segway tour rolls past us, clearly a stag-do with all the men in matching t-shirts, some holding beers as they ride through the leafy green park. Across from us a group of girls are going through their shopping bags, excitedly showing off silk scarves and garnet jewellery.

"What is it?" Sophia asks, as I scroll my phone and attempt to head my melting ice-cream off before it drips over my hand. "Not work is it? You're on holiday – tell them to get stuffed."

I snort. It's true that I've had several messages from work while we've been away. It's ironic but not unexpected for the HR department to be the worst offenders at overstepping boundaries. As soon as we reached out rented flat in a gorgeous red-brick tenement I'd connected to the Wi-Fi and been bombarded with emails as well. My manager didn't seem to understand the meaning of 'annual leave'. So far she'd asked me everything from 'where is the spare toner cartridge?' to 'what is the temp's name??'. As if I knew when I'd never even met my temporary replacement. I'd stuck to short replies and stuck my phone on airplane mode when I was trying to listen to audiobooks at night.

"It's not them, it's just someone on Marketplace, wanting to buy a few bags of my old clothes. I fancied a sit down, that's all." I quickly fire off a message to them saying where to pick up from and that I'll be back from my holiday on Monday and put my phone away.

"Same, my feet are killing me already," Sophia complains. "What are we doing today? The castle and...?"

"Charles Bridge and the Old Town Square," I say, feeling quite smug in my comfy boots with their extra supportive insoles. "With a stop for lunch somewhere – obviously got to have some goulash and bread dumplings."

Sophia pulls a face. "Think I might stick to a steak or something with salad."

I shrug, no skin off my nose if she wants to pass up some local food. She has her thing and I have mine. Which means today we're doing all the historical stuff I want and tomorrow we're visiting Sephora and a bunch of other shops so Sophia can put together a haul video for later. The day after, it's my turn again and I'll be taking us on a foodie tour of the city. Compromise, it's what makes our friendship work so well. Besides it's fun to do things I'd never think to try on my own, like getting a makeover at a luxury beauty counter or trying on the best of Prague's fashion houses.

"Come on then, let's go check out the pavilion, then we're off to the castle," I say, and we head of through the park, arm in arm. Only pausing when Sophia decides she wants a trdelnik of her own. While she pays I take out my guidebook and re-read the safety tips for female travellers. It's pretty standard stuff, Prague isn't really any more dangerous than other big cities but it makes me glad I remembered to bring everything that was suggested to me; the portable deadbolt, drink cover and secure bag.

You can never be too careful.

A week later, with our bags weighed down with artisanal chocolate, gingerbread and dark beer (me) as well as hand-painted silk scarves, jewellery and cosmetics (Sophia) we arrive back at Heathrow. It's already gone nine at night by the time we get outside and I hug Sophia goodbye. She's on her way back to central London and I'm getting the coach to Stevenage. I won't be seeing my bed before midnight.

"See you soooon!" Sophia bugles from the tube station entrance.

"Bye!" I yell back, waving madly. "Get home safe!"

As I reach the coach station I feel my shoulders relax a little. As much as I love Sophia I also like my own space and being with her every moment of the day for a week has been stressful. I'm glad to have a bit of a break to grab a latte from Costa (I'm already missing the cute coffee houses of Prague) and spending some time on my Kindle.

On the coach the lights are dimmed and the five other people on board are all either asleep or trying to be. Headphones in and coats pulled over them as makeshift blankets. It's not glamorous or fast but it's cheap. I settle down in my seat with my headphones in and check my phone for messages. My manager has apparently taken the hint, on the last day of my holiday, that I'm not actually working for her right now. There's nothing from Marketplace either. Just a couple of eBay bid notifications and chatter in the group thread from my co-workers. Apparently there's a big investigation going on because one of the company's drivers threw a hot coffee through someone's car window at a red light, because they cut him up. Lovely. Just what I want to be dealing with when I get back to work.

I settle in and take a nap, lulled to sleep by the thrum of the coach engine and the rumble of its wheels. I'm only awoken when we reach the battered roads of rural Hertfordshire and the jolting makes me bang my head on the back of the seat in front of me. Squinting out of the window I recognise a pub sign. We're just outside Hitchin, arriving at my stop in the next ten minutes. A quick check of my phone tells me it's now quarter to midnight. And I still have to walk home.

As much as I enjoy travelling, nothing brings me back down to earth harder than getting home. The various stages of glamorous sparkling clean airports to slightly grim coach station, down and down to the empty regional bus station I end up in, watching

McDonalds containers blow past in the wake of the coach's exhaust.

The town centre is completely deserted save for a huddle of teens doing BMX tricks near the boarded up back. I hurry towards home and my jeans and t-shirt, perfect for the balmy afternoon weather in Prague, have me shivering before I reach the end of the road. But getting my coat on would require stopping to unzip my bag. Dragging my wheelie case through reeking underpasses and over cracked pavements, I find myself comparing them to the gorgeous park walks and pristine subway system I've just left behind in Prague.

I'm on the home stretch when I reach the really long underpass near the massive ASDA. It stretches on in front of me, half the lights broken and the breeze spiralling down it, turning it into a wind tunnel. I drag my bag onwards. So close to getting home. I can't wait to get into bed and warm up. Some proper sleep will chase the post-holiday blues away and tomorrow I'll be glad of waking up in my own bed.

Halfway down the underpass I hear echoing footsteps behind me. More than one pair. Like most women my age I've perfected the 'quick over the shoulder' glance and check my periphery. My heart sinks. It's two men, older than me, shabby and clearly reeling. I don't want any trouble so I put my head down and march onwards. Internally begging them not to notice me.

A beery "Alright Darlin'!" Hits me between the shoulder blades, followed by throaty laughter. Normally I'd have no problem outpacing two drunk fifty-somethings but I'm lumbered with my case and it's slowing me down.

I ignore them both. Engaging, out here on my own, is not a good idea. I know that. If I can just get to the twenty-four hour ASDA at least I won't be all by myself. Unfortunately I've still got to get out of the underpass and them up the steps beyond.

"Hey! I was talkin' to you!" one of the men shouts as I put on a burst of speed.

I reach the steps. There's a ramp which goes back and forth up the steep embankment. But I take the direct route, picking up my suitcase as much as I can given its weight and dragging it up the too steep steps.

"Stuck up bitch!" the first one calls after me.

"Snotty cow," his friend slurs in agreement.

They're not coming after me but that doesn't mean I want to hang around outside. Besides I'm freezing cold and getting into the warm for a few minutes is too strong a lure to resist.

I make it to the sliding doors and into ASDA, where a few staff members are around, restocking. I spot one other customer, a woman with a baby in a sling buying bananas. After letting out a sigh of relief I decide to wait for a while and make sure those men are gone, just in case they're out there hanging around. The last thing I want is the pair of them following me home. Besides, I need to buy milk and some bread. My fridge at home is empty and at least then I won't have to go out tomorrow. I can just recover from the long trip home and do my post-holiday laundry.

Shopping with my suitcase isn't ideal but after another half hour I'm leaving ASDA with a bag of essentials on top of my wheelie bag. There's no sign of anyone outside and I move at a pace, desperate to get home and into bed. My house is only ten minutes away but I walk so fast that I'm there in under six. Key in the door, bag in, door locked behind me, locked. I lean back against it. Thank God that's over.

I leave my suitcase in the hallway and flick lights on through the living room to the kitchen. The back door and all the windows are of course locked and the air has that stale, unlived in quality that always greets you after time away. There's a fine layer of dust, barely there, on my kitchen surfaces. I put the shopping away, supressing a yawn as I check my phone.

Sophie has texted me, 'home safe! Hope your journey didn't suck!' I huff and text back that I've just gotten in and I'm heading to bed. The rest of it I'll tell her over the phone tomorrow, when I have it in me to be funny about the whole thing. Right now I just feel tired and jumpy.

Upstairs I unplug the timer lamp in the bedroom and shut my curtains all the way. I was careful to not leave them shut but being open all the time was just as bad. I decided half open, half closed, was the best option to make the house look 'lived it'.

I'm happy to remember that I changed my sheets before I went away. A nice clean bed is waiting for me. I change into my pyjamas and climb in, humming with relief to be lying down and cosy, my eyes burning with the need to sleep. I groan as I remember that my phone charger is still downstairs in my bag. I'm not going back to get it. I just toss my phone onto the bedside table and turn the lamp off. Sleep first, everything else later.

Exhaustion claims me and I snuggled deeper into the duvet, inhaling the familiar scent of my laundry liquid.

312

There really is nothing like your own bed. That's the last thought I have as I drift off to sleep.

I wake up with a body on top of me and immediately panic.

A horrified scream strangles me, as there's a hand clamped over my mouth to hold it in. Crushing my lips against my teeth. I try to move, to thrash and slap my way free, but his legs are pinning mine down. My arms are trapped and his weight is suffocating me. My nose is full of the smell of sweat and unfamiliar soaps. I know it's a man – even if the most obvious clue wasn't digging into me, I can feel it in the bulk of his body and smell it on him. I scream into his hand again, furious and terrified. Tears rolling across my cheeks.

"Shut up," he hisses, hand pressing down on my face so hard that my head is sunk deep into my pillow, my neck protesting the pressure. "Shut up, or I'll fucking strangle you."

My throat closes up around a whimper. The pressure on my lips decreases but he doesn't take his hand off my mouth as his other palm slides downwards, pulling at my pyjamas.

I start to struggle again, and his hand slips on my spittle covered face. His finger hits my teeth and I don't think. I just bite down hard and shake my head like a dog. My mouth floods with blood and I hear him roar in pain, before he backhands me and my ears ring with the shock of it.

My heart is punching at the inside of my ribs and I grapple blindly for the edge of the bed, using the leverage to drag myself out from under him. He's still cursing and hitting at me, legs on mine. Still, I manage to wriggle out of my pyjama bottoms and slither to the floor.

Before he can make a dive for me, I'm up and running. I blunder into the wall, tripping over my own feet, but I reach the door and stumble onto the landing.

My house feels unfamiliar and frightening in the dark, with him thudding after me. I trip over the leg of a little table on the landing, sending a monstera plant crashing to the floor in a shower of soil. It nearly takes me down too, but I stagger on, shin bursting with pain.

My only thought is getting a door between me and the man. I ignore the stairs completely, knowing I'll never get the front door open in time. Down the hall is my craft room and the main bathroom, which doesn't have a window. I make my choice in a split second.

I duck into the craft room and slam the door shut, fumbling with the button lock in the handle. Seconds later my attacker blunders into the door and starts rattling the handle. I back away towards the window. I'm under no illusions that an internal door lock will keep him out for long.

"Go away!" I half scream, half sob, bloody drool running down my chin. "I don't know who you are just – go!"

In response he starts to kick at the door, which bulges under the assault. He'll break it down in minutes. I dive for the window and practically rip the venetian blinds down in my struggle to get them out of the way. The handle is stiff and uncooperative but I wrench at it until it opens, letting in the cold early morning air.

"Help!" I scream so loudly that the back of my

314

throat feels like it's being snapped by an elastic band. "Help me!!"

Aside from sending a few pigeons fluttering in alarm, my yelling goes unanswered. I look down and see the concrete paving slabs of my front garden, far below. I'm on the second floor and one wrong move in trying to get out of here will see my skull meeting those slabs, hard.

Behind me, I hear a crack and then a splintering sound.

I turn just in time to see the man's foot being pulled back through the door, lining up for another kick. I cast about in the shadows further from the window for something to defend myself with. There's a paint-spattered mug pull of craft knives on the desk and I grab the longest one, pulling off the plastic cover.

Having widened the hole, the man shoves his arm through, reaching for the handle.

He yells when I swipe him with the blade, opening a shallow bloody slash several inches long. He doesn't stop trying to fumble the lock open though. He only seems more determined to get at me.

"Bitch!"

I slash him again, again, sobbing and losing control as desperation takes hold. My ears are full of his cursing and the pounding of my own blood. So I don't notice the sirens until they're right outside, screaming and wailing into the morning stillness.

The man vanishes like mist. I hear his footsteps hammering the stairs as he flees. Then comes the sound of my front door being smashed off its hinges – security chain and all – and multiple voices shouting for him to stop and get on the floor.

My legs give out and I crash to the floor, the bloody craft knife still clutched in my hand. My chest hurts from screaming and I'm sawing air in and out of my aching lungs. Every breath tastes like his blood. It all happened so quickly and now I can't stop myself from sobbing. Added to that, I'm shaking too much to wipe my eyes properly.

"Hello sweetheart, can you put that down for me?"

I look up and find a woman's face at the shattered hole in the door. A police officer. She nods her head to my hand and I let go, the craft knife falls out of my grip.

"Can you open the door? It's alright now, my colleagues are taking him out to the van."

I can hear muffled thuds and swearing from below, but I crawl over the carpet and unlock the door. It swings open drunkenly, and the woman scoops her arms around me and gets me to my feet.

"There's an ambulance coming just to check you over. Is that his blood?"

I nod.

"OK then, love. I'll let them know. Are you hurt anywhere else?"

I shake my head and she half carries me back towards my bedroom, but I dig my feet in and refuse to go further.

"Did he attack you in there?" she asks, and I nod.

"Right, let's go downstairs."

She takes me to the living room and through the gauzy curtains I can see a couple of male officers and another woman loading my attacker into the van outside.

"Do you know how he got inside?" the officer beside me asks.

"I was asleep," I manage to get out between hiccupping sobs. "I just – got back from h-holiday."

She makes a sympathetic noise and her radio crackles, which she ignores. "Ambulance will be here soon, don't worry."

It's a blur, really. The ambulance comes and they check me over but aside from some bruises and a cut on my face where he hit me, I'm unscathed. Their biggest worry appears to be the fact that I bit him. They tell me all sorts of things about blood tests and that I'm going to be OK and that the hospital will give me PEP, in case I've been exposed to HIV. I hadn't even thought about that.

While this is going on, the police are in and out, talking to each other and making sure the house is empty and secure. I hear them in the kitchen, talking about the back door and how the lock's been damaged. As I'm being taken to hospital for tests even more police officers arrive, and I'm almost glad to be shut in the sterile ambulance, away from all the fuss.

By the time they come to get my statement I've been swabbed for evidence, allowed to take a shower and given some joggers and a t-shirt to wear. My pyjama shirt was taken away in a bag. I've seen CSI, I know they're probably going to get hair and skin off of it. Not that they'll need much, they caught the man trying to get to me, saw the mess he'd made of my door.

I don't have my phone and I want to ring Sophia, just to hear her voice.

It's the female officer from before who turns up to speak to me. Still gentle and careful, but with a firmness underneath. A purposeful way of speaking which oddly

317

puts me at ease more than straight sympathy would. I feel like she knows what she's doing and she's going to make sure I'm OK.

"Glad to see you looking a bit better," she says. "I just need to ask you a bit about the man we arrested at your house this morning, is that OK?" she asks and I nod. "Have you ever seen him before?"

"No," I say, throat sore enough from screaming to make me wince. "Never."

Even in the dark I'd known he was a stranger. I barely knew any men. All my colleagues were women and my friends, barring a few of their boyfriends. But I'd known them for years and would recognise their voices. This was a stranger.

"Does the name 'Graham Jones' sound familiar at all? Someone you've spoken to on the phone or emailed with for work?"

"No, but I work for a pretty big company, in HR. There's thousands of employees but...that name isn't familiar."

She nods and writes something in her notebook. "And...Daphne Morgan?"

"No...actually, wait that does sound...where have I seen that?" I ask myself.

She takes her phone out and shows me a picture on it of another phone, with a screenshot of the Facebook app on there. I squint at the twice removed image and recognise the green plastic sacks. They're the clothes I was giving away.

"She messaged me on Facebook, she wanted the clothes I was selling..." realisation hits me and I start to tear up. "Oh my God...I'm so stupid! I told her...

told him, where to pick them up from. I told him I was away!"

The police woman holds out a hand, gesturing for me to calm down. "You weren't to know, it looks like he's used this identity a few times now. We're checking but a few of the other names he's contacted rang a bell. He's been mass messaging people, looking for empty homes to burgle. On this occasion it looks as if he managed to gain entry to your property and had been waiting for you to come home for most of the day."

"Oh my God," I murmur, thinking of how empty the house had seemed when I got in. How wrong I'd been to assume it was just as I'd left it. Where had he been hiding? In the cupboard under the stairs? Under my bed? I shiver, suddenly aware of how many places a man could hide away inside my home – the wardrobe, the airing cupboard, the loft...

"Is there anywhere you can stay, while things are sorted out at your house?" she asks. "A friend or..."

"Yes, I have people I can phone, um, I'll sort something out. I just need my phone.""

"OK," she relaxes a little and pats my hand. "I'll let them finish checking you over here and then escort you to the house to pack a bag and get your phone, things like that."

I nod and she leaves me to go and tell the nurses that I'm ready for them to come back and take blood samples for testing. Looking down at my lightly tanned arms, I laugh humourlessly. My bag's still packed from my holiday. I'd been so ready to take care of myself while I was away, had researched sketchy areas to avoid and kept my money carefully hidden. I'd dressed to blend in and not gone out late, despite Sophia's urging. All that effort, to come home and be attacked in my own bed. How could I expect to ever feel comfortable travelling again, if something like this could happen to me at home?

"Hey."

I look up and find the police officer has come back, holding a cup of tea out to me.

"I know right now you feel dreadful and you're blaming yourself...but you're here because you fought and you got away. If you hadn't your neighbours wouldn't have heard you or he'd have gotten to you before we arrived. One mistake doesn't mean you didn't do really well tonight. So don't beat yourself up about it. You did really well."

She leaves me with the tea and I watch the steam spiralling from the hole in the lid. She's right, I tell myself. Even if it was a stupid mistake, telling someone that I wasn't home, and giving out my address. I still managed to get away from him, when it counted most.

I shut my eyes and I'm back under the sun dappled leaves in Letná Park, cinnamon sugar on my fingers and the spires of Prague castle in the distance. That's not worth giving up on, for anything or anyone. No matter what my blood tests say or how scared I'd been.

I still want to see the world.

He didn't get to take that from me.

You'll want to stay. Until you can't leave . . .

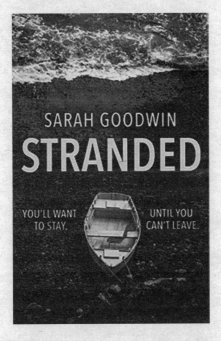

A group of strangers arrive on a beautiful but remote island, ready for the challenge of a lifetime: to live there for one year, without contact with the outside world.

But twelve months later, on the day when the boat is due to return for them, no one arrives.

**Eight people stepped foot on the island.
How many will make it off alive?**

A gripping, twisty page-turner about secrets, lies and survival at all costs. Perfect for fans of *The Castaways, The Sanatorium* and *One by One.*

'Because he chose you. Out of thirteen girls. You were the one. The last one.'

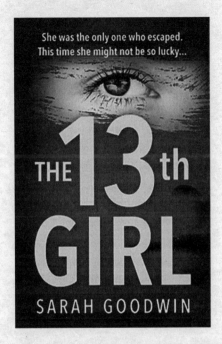

She was the only one who escaped.
This time she might not be so lucky...

THE **13**th GIRL

SARAH GOODWIN

Lucy Townsend lives a normal life. She has a husband she loves, in-laws she can't stand and she's just found out she's going to be a mother.

But Lucy has a dark and dangerous secret.

She is not who she says she is.

Lucy is not even her real name.

A totally gripping, edge-of-your-seat thriller with twists and turns you just won't see coming. Perfect for fans of *Girl A* and *The Family Upstairs*.

It was a safe haven . . . until it became a trap.

Mila and her husband **Ethan** are on their way to her sister's wedding at a luxurious ski resort, when the car engine suddenly stops and won't start again.

Stranded, with night closing in, they make their way on foot back to where they saw a sign for some cabins. They find the windows boarded up and the buildings in disrepair. They have the eerie sense they shouldn't be there.

With snow falling more heavily, they have no choice but to break into one to spend the night.

In the morning when Mila wakes, Ethan is gone.
Now she is all alone.
Or is she?

A totally gripping and spine-tingling psychological thriller. Perfect for fans of *The Hunting Party* and *The Castaways*.

You can't outrun the past...
...for what's done in the dark will come to light...
...and someone wants revenge.

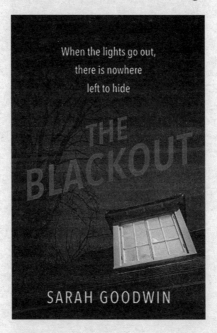

When the lights go out,
there is nowhere
left to hide

THE
BLACKOUT

SARAH GOODWIN

Summer, 2022. When Meg and Cat are forced to take a dangerous shortcut home one night, they notice two men silently following them. Suddenly running for their lives, they scramble into an abandoned building to hide and wait for help.

One year later. Attempting to escape the horrors of that fateful night, Meg barricades herself into a safehouse at the edge of a crumbling sea cliff. As a storm rages outside, a blackout plunges the house into darkness. But Meg's not alone.

Don't miss the new, totally addictive psychological thriller from Sarah Goodwin, with bombshell twists that will leave you stunned. Fans of *The Sanatorium, The Paris Apartment* and *One of the Girls* will be hooked from the very first page.

**When the truth surfaces,
who will sink and who will swim?...**

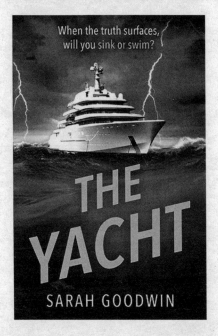

New Year's Eve, 2023. When Hannah and her friends rent a
luxury yacht in an Italian marina, they party in style
under the stars until they pass out.

The next morning, they are horrified to find they have been cut
adrift into the open ocean, with no sight of land and no fuel in
the engine. And that's when the first person goes missing...

The Yacht is a twisty locked-room thriller that
will have fans of *The White Lotus*, Lucy Foley and
Amy McCulloch addicted from the very first page!